Summer
at the
Cornish
Beach
Café

BOOKS BY DONNA ASHCROFT

Summer at the Castle Cafe

The Little Guesthouse of New Beginnings

The Little Village of New Starts

Summer in the Scottish Highlands

The Little Cornish House

The Little Christmas Teashop of Second Chances

The Christmas Countdown

If Every Day Was Christmas

Christmas in the Scottish Highlands

Snowflakes and Secrets in the Scottish Highlands

Donna Ashcroft

Summer
at the
Cornish
Beach
Café

bookouture

Published by Bookouture in 2023

An imprint of Storyfire Ltd.
Carmelite House
50 Victoria Embankment
London EC4Y 0DZ

www.bookouture.com

ISBN: 978-1-83790-227-9
eBook ISBN: 978-1-83790-226-2

To Hester Thorpe
For following your dreams

1

JULY, FOURTEEN YEARS AGO

Jessie Levine sprinted out of the cosy cottage she was holidaying in with her beloved grandparents, straight onto the sandy beach at Indigo Cove. It was late and the moon was halfway up the sky with a cluster of clouds beside it riding the wind, suggesting it was going to rain soon. Warm air still lingered from the hot July day, so she didn't have to worry about getting cold – and she had enough temper fizzing through her veins to keep her internal furnace stoked for a few hours. She puffed out a breath and sped up, stroking away a tear from her cheek as she rehashed the phone call that she'd just had with her stepmother Maria, gulping down the barbs of annoyance and hurt. She was seventeen – in just over a year she'd be at university, and she'd barely need to see or speak to the woman again.

Jessie clenched her hands into fists, wondering how many more times Maria Levine was going to comment on her size nine feet, or the outrageous cost of finding shoes for them. She already felt like enough of a freak next to Maria's tiny frame, and didn't need their differences being pointed out constantly. It wasn't just Jessie's looks either. Her straightforward nature was equally at fault because apparently being blunt was 'tactless and gauche'.

If only her father were still alive, but an unexpected heart attack had taken him from them three years before, leaving Jessie the victim of a will that insisted she remain living with a stepmother who seemed to loathe her. Was it down to jealousy because Jessie and her father had been so close? She'd never worked it out.

As Jessie approached the shoreline, her pace slowed. She could hear the quiet hiss of the waves as they caressed the beach, then a whistle and the high-pitched bark of a dog in the far distance. The sound was followed by a scatter of footsteps, then a tiny ball of fur with legs bounced out of the darkness and shook itself, spraying her with droplets of icy seawater. Jessie laughed and bent to give the tiny dachshund puppy a quick brush on the head as it yelped in delight and nipped at her fingertips. The dog had a dark chocolate coat and huge brown eyes, and she wished she could scoop it up and take it home to Oxford so she'd have something to love her – not that Maria would ever allow it. The puppy yelped again and wiggled its bottom and tail before peeing on the sand, obviously overcome with excitement. As she rose, Jessie heard the crunch of heavy footsteps.

'Do you always have that effect on the opposite sex?' A bone-melting voice asked, making Jessie's insides pitch forward. The boy moved closer just as the clouds caught up with the moon, shadowing the finer details of his face, but she could tell he was a similar age. Jessie could see hints of his features too: the angular jaw; dark, defined eyebrows; and a full mouth that was curved down at the edges, suggesting life might have given him a battering too. Despite his frown, he was gorgeous – mother nature had definitely dealt him a full house. Plus, at almost half a head taller than her, it was impossible not to be struck by his height. Jessie was almost six feet, so it was refreshing to meet someone with equally freakish genes and found herself warming to him.

'According to my stepmother, the only effect I'm ever likely to have on a man involves him running in the opposite direction.' Jessie sighed, pouting before shaking herself. 'Ignore me, I came for a walk to work off my bad mood... it's not a pity party for one.' She jutted her chin and gave him one of her winning smiles, hoping to emphasise the mouth she knew was her best feature – attractive, if you could see past her long nose and wonky eyes.

'Parents,' he huffed, turning away and shoving his hands into his pockets, looking towards the horizon as the little dog wagged its tail and began to run rings around them. 'Should be a law against them.' He grinned, and Jessie saw the flash of perfect, straight teeth. 'So you're on holiday with yours?' He twisted back and stepped closer, and Jessie felt herself leaning into him. Like something was arcing between them, tugging at her.

'No. My mum died when I was a baby and dad passed away three years ago,' she said quickly.

'I'm sorry.' The look of sympathy on his face seemed genuine.

'I live with my stepmother, but I'm here with my grandparents now,' she added before he could ask more. 'They honeymooned in Indigo Cove in the 1960s. It's an important place for them, and they wanted to show it to me.' Jessie shoved her hands into her pockets, feeling awkward under his intense gaze. 'Are you from around here?'

'Yep.' The boy jerked his chin. 'You can't live with them instead?' His tone was relaxed despite the personal questions.

Jessie shook her head. 'My grandma's got bad arthritis; it wouldn't be fair to ask. I try to spend as much time as I can with them during weekends and holidays, though. Besides, it won't be for much longer and I can handle Maria.' She straightened her shoulders as if having good posture might help.

'Even though she's wicked?' he teased.

'She's just mean.' Jessie dipped her chin and picked at her T-shirt, suddenly feeling embarrassed.

'I understand mean,' he said seriously. 'My parents both have PhDs in it.'

'I'm sorry,' she said, as a thin thread of emotion lassoed her heart. 'How do you...' She puffed out a breath. 'How do you live with it?' she asked earnestly, wishing she didn't sound so desperate. She was glad it was dark because he couldn't see her face, couldn't see how much she needed to know. Jessie had to learn how to shut the power of her stepmother's words out, how to stop them from breaking her.

The boy shrugged. 'That's easy. I don't let it matter; that way, things can't hurt. I have a baby sister, and I worry about how they'll treat her when she's older – that does matter.' He frowned. 'Why does your stepmother dislike you?' he asked, taking a step forward.

'You ask a lot of questions for someone I've just met,' Jessie said, trying out some of her bluntness for size, wondering if Maria was right and if it would annoy him.

'You keep answering them,' he observed, just as bluntly. 'Maybe you should be asking yourself why.' His gaze was intense.

'I've no idea.' Jessie pulled at her T-shirt again, trying to cover herself because sharing with him was making her feel exposed. 'Mostly I don't talk about it. Maybe I just like your dog.' She sighed. Telling him wouldn't matter. She wasn't going to talk to anyone else. Her grandparents would be horrified if she told them about Maria's unkind words and would probably invite her to live with them, which wouldn't be fair. 'I think Maria hates me because I'm a misfit. She's stunning, dad was really handsome too... I look more like my mum and grandparents. I think she believes I somehow chose to take after them, like I had a choice. She's a model and only understands beauty. It's like anything that's not gorgeous doesn't deserve to exist.' Her shoulders sank under the memory of a thousand unkind words.

'You don't think you're beautiful? Because you know there are all kinds.' The boy took another step towards her as if he were trying to see her face, but the clouds were still shadowing the moon's light, and Jessie knew her looks were mostly obscured. But the intensity of his stare still got to her, his attention stirring feelings: excitement, anticipation, embarrassment – some kind of sexual awakening. *She didn't even know his name...*

'I'm not beautiful, but I don't mind,' Jessie said gruffly. 'I'd rather be me, even if that means...'

'What?'

'That no one will ever want to kiss me.' The dig her stepmother had made months before when she'd overheard Jessie and her friend discussing making out with boys slid over her tongue like bile and she sucked in a breath. She hadn't meant to share that with him. Jessie took a jerky step backwards as the puppy stopped running, as if it were taking on the weight of her words. 'Sorry.' She swallowed. 'I need to...' She pointed back up the beach, her cheeks burning.

'We don't become other people's opinions,' he said gently. 'If someone says something mean, it doesn't make it true.' She should have left then, taken the chance to run. She wasn't ready for this, wasn't ready for the way he was making her feel. 'We have to decide who we are. No one gets to do it but us.'

Jessie swallowed. 'You're right.' Her mouth winged up as she digested his words and something inside her unfurled. She'd needed to hear that. He'd just said exactly the right thing. How was that possible?

'Shall we sit?' the boy asked, pointing to the sand. 'Watch the waves for a while?'

'I suppose,' Jessie said, as he sank to the ground and stretched his long legs in front of him. She hesitated for a moment before nodding and lowering herself, too, until they were sitting side by side. They gazed at the waves in silence, and Jessie thought she could hear his breathing, the slow rise and fall of his chest. The sound relaxed her, and she leaned backwards so she was resting on her palms and their shoulders bumped, but she didn't move. After a few moments of silence, the boy shifted his left hand closer to hers until the edges of their little fingers touched. Jessie's breath caught in her throat, but she left hers there, enjoying the warm brush of his skin, the flood of tingles it evoked.

'How old are you?' he asked finally, still staring forward.

'Seventeen,' Jessie answered without thinking, although the question had come from nowhere. 'How old are you?'

'Almost nineteen, so not too old,' the boy said thoughtfully.

'For what?' She frowned, turning and trying to make out his features again, but it was getting darker, and she couldn't see much.

'To kiss you. Can I?' he asked.

'Why?' Jessie squeaked. They'd only just met – she didn't even know his name. He'd never asked for hers. Was that strange? If it was, why did she want to say yes?

There was just enough light for her to see the edge of his mouth twist. 'Maybe I've had a really bad day and kissing you will make it better. Help me to forget it. Or perhaps I don't like the sound of Maria, and I'd like to help you prove her wrong. Us misfits need to stick together.'

Jessie didn't respond and he didn't move. She liked that, liked that he was letting her choose. So many of her choices had disappeared over the last few years. 'Okay,' she whispered, swallowing before slowly climbing to her feet. 'If you want. But you should know I'm really good at kissing.' She almost choked on the lie. 'So you'd better know what you're doing.'

'I can hold my own.' The boy chuckled, getting up too. The puppy barked before starting to run around them again, like wind circling the eye of a storm.

'Wait,' Jessie said, waving a finger between them as he started to edge closer. 'I don't know your name. If I'm going to share my lips with you, I think I should.'

He hooted out a delighted laugh and shook his head. 'I don't know why it matters, but it's Ashton.'

'Mine's Jessie,' she said, even though he didn't seem remotely interested.

Ashton moved again until their shoes were touching. Jessie looked up but could see nothing but shadows and the silhouette of his head. He brought a hand up to cup her face, and she could feel his warm palm – it was large and for the first time ever she felt delicate, even small. He bent and brushed his lips over hers. Jessie had been expecting a quick peck, the kind of thing you saw in movies on the Disney Channel. She'd barely kissed anyone in her seventeen years. There'd been that one boy at the school disco, but she'd been almost a foot taller and bending to meet his mouth had been uncomfortable and nothing like she'd anticipated. There'd been no zing, no pounding of blood in her veins – instead, she'd got a crick in her neck. And even worse, some of the girls in her class had pointed at them and laughed. But now, Ashton obviously knew what he was doing. He tipped her face up and stroked his lips over hers, traced his tongue across the seam of her mouth, setting off a swirl in the pit of her stomach as she eagerly opened for him, practically inhaling him in her need to connect. Within seconds, the kiss had grown hot and wet, and Jessie moved up to her tiptoes and pushed her fingers into his hair. It was thick with a wave on top that made it easier to grab. Ashton made a moaning sound, and she wondered if he was hurt, but then his hand slid down to her bum and he pulled her towards him, pressed himself into her hips. She widened her eyes at the contact and hard swell of his body but didn't pull back. This felt incredible, like every one of her fantasies had come true at the same time. Maria was wrong, and now her heart was bursting. She'd suspected it all along, but nothing had prepared her for how it would feel to have someone kiss her like they couldn't get enough.

Jessie wound her arms around Ashton's neck just as the cloud moved away from the moon and a shaft of bright light slid across her eyelids. Then he was pulling away, looking surprised as he gazed down into her face which was now illuminated. She felt gorgeous, amazing, and she beamed up at him, waiting for him to kiss her again. It had been everything she'd imagined, and he'd made her feel beautiful and perfect. But instead of bending and capturing her lips once more, a crease burrowed its way across Ashton's forehead and his arms dropped to his sides. He began to shake his head, looking shocked before turning and sprinting away from her down the beach with the little dog following, yapping at his heels. As she watched, Jessie's eyes filled and something inside her broke. Because for the first time ever, she understood that Maria *was* right.

2

PRESENT DAY

Jessie steered her grandfather's mint-green Ford Anglia along the windy Cornish coastal road as George Levine angled the huge map he was holding onto its side and slid his gold-rimmed spectacles over the long nose Jessie had inherited.

Phoebe, her grandad's young golden retriever, barked as she pressed her nose against the window in the rear of the car.

'She's spotted a butterfly and wants to make friends,' George explained, rustling the map as he reached into the back seat to pat Phoebe. 'Down, girl,' he ordered, and she immediately sank onto the seat with a doggy sigh.

Jessie wound her window down and took in a breath, inhaling the sweet aroma of the pink summer flowers which lined the edges of the narrow track, realising they were exactly the same shade as the ones she'd chosen for her bridal bouquet. Jessie blinked back a wave of annoyance – she couldn't let herself think about that, or that she should be Mrs Brendon Jackson by now. Would be, if she hadn't found out her boyfriend of six years had been cheating and so had pulled out of their wedding less than a fortnight before it.

'I predict there's a seventy-eight per cent chance that we're heading in the right direction,' her grandfather said, twisting the map again and pointing to a red cross he'd scrawled across the centre of it. As an ex-maths professor, he liked to sum up life in a series of numerical calculations – some of which he occasionally got right.

'We could check the satnav on my phone?' Jessie asked hopefully, as she reached the top of the hill just before she spotted a pretty, hand-painted board declaring they were about to drive into Indigo Cove.

'We don't need it.' George pointed to the sign as he carefully refolded the map. 'I told you Dorothy and I would get us here.' He lovingly patted the pristine walnut dashboard.

He'd bought and named the car five years ago, soon after Jessie's grandmother, Dorothy Levine, had passed away to ensure his wife was with him wherever he went. This was the longest journey he'd taken with it.

'I can't believe I've made it back to Indigo Cove.' George reached out to pat Jessie's hand. 'Thank you for agreeing to accompany me.'

Her grandfather had booked the holiday to Indigo Cove months ago to celebrate his and her grandmother's fiftieth wedding anniversary, but he'd unexpectedly had a hernia operation just one week before and couldn't drive. It would have been impossible for him to come, and Jessie couldn't bear the thought of him missing the trip.

'I should be thanking you.' Jessie sighed, thinking about the saucy emails she'd found on Brendon's laptop fifteen days earlier when she'd been checking the booking for their wedding venue. They worked for the same insurance company – at least they *had*, now Jessie wasn't sure what the future held. She could still remember the look in her fiancé's eyes when she told him what she'd found.

'I'm sorry, Jess, I've been trying to find a way to tell you,' Brendon had said, his gorgeous face contorting as he'd tried to wind his arm around her shoulders. 'In truth, it was one of those instant attraction things – the chemistry is off the charts and the sex...' He'd puffed his cheeks into mini globes. 'I honestly couldn't help myself. I think she and I are meant to be together... now I realise you and I, we were never the right fit. We were more friends. There was just...' He'd clicked his fingers. '... no spark. I used to think that was okay, but now I know how it should be. I hope once you've had time to get over what's happened, we can all have a drink and talk...'

'Talk,' Jessie now growled, clearing her throat, as she pushed the memory out of her mind. She'd spent so many years feeling like second best that she'd wanted to marry someone who really loved her. Despite all the things her stepmother used to tell her, she'd hoped there would be someone in the world who could adore her despite her faults. Now, she wasn't so sure...

Jessie had cancelled the wedding and their honeymoon and resigned from her job, using the holiday time she'd already booked as her notice period. It was time to make a change – she couldn't bear the idea of working alongside her ex, or enduring the pitying looks she'd get from their colleagues and friends. Almost immediately her grandad had received a call about his hernia operation and had asked Jessie to join him on his trip to Indigo Cove, so she'd jumped at the chance.

'I'm sorry you had to call your wedding off, but I'm going to say, the pudding-head didn't deserve you. I always thought he had a high opinion of himself – and what kind of person cheats on a gorgeous woman like you?' Her grandfather sniffed and shook his head.

'I'm just glad the affair came out in time,' Jessie said.

'Me too.' George nodded. 'Dorothy never took to Brendon, and she was always such a good judge of character.'

Jessie shrugged. 'She said he didn't photograph well,' she remembered.

'Always a bad sign according to your grandmother,' George

grumbled, taking a closer look at the map again. 'The Look Out Hotel where Dorothy and I stayed on our honeymoon is the next right – if you don't mind, I'd like to swing by and stop for a bit. There's no rush to get to The Beach Café to pick up the keys to our accommodation, is there?'

'Of course we can,' Jessie agreed. 'I remember that place from your honeymoon album.'

'We stayed for the whole fortnight.' Her grandfather sighed. 'Dorothy took so many wonderful shots there... She was such a talented photographer.' His smile warmed.

'I haven't looked in that album for years,' Jessie said, remembering the gorgeous photobook her grandmother had created, filled with hundreds of colourful memories from the honeymoon, including many from the hotel they'd stayed in. Dorothy had been a professional photographer once, years ahead of her time. Jessie had spent many hours poring over her pictures, imagining how it might feel to step into each one. She'd studied photography at university for three years and had hoped to follow in her grandmother's footsteps once. But none of her photos had ever come close to her grandmother's.

'Oh Jess, the album went missing when I moved into my flat,' her grandad said. 'I've been so upset. I looked and looked, but it's definitely gone.'

'What? Why didn't you tell me?' Jessie asked, jerking her head to glance at him.

'I didn't want to worry you, love. Besides, I kept hoping it would turn up. I think the removal firm I used lost one of the boxes because some ornaments and puzzles disappeared too.' As if commiserating, Phoebe let out a low whine from the back of the car.

'Oh Grandad...' Jessie whispered.

'It's one of the reasons I booked this holiday,' he admitted quietly. 'I packed Dorothy's favourite Nikon F2, and I thought I'd try to recreate as many of the pictures as I could.' He swallowed, crinkling the map he was still holding in his hands. 'But now I can't walk as far after the op, I don't know how many I'll be able to take by myself. It's not as if I can easily get to half the places now...'

'I can help take any you can't,' Jessie offered tentatively. 'I mean the pictures won't be as good as Gran's but...' Jessie had got a job working in a small studio after university and loved it but had struggled to make ends meet. Then, when she'd met Brendon, they'd wanted to move into together, so she'd started to work at the same insurance company as him so she could earn more. The job was supposed to be temporary, but, over time, she'd realised she just didn't have the talent to make a proper living as a photographer. Over the last six years, she'd used her camera less and less and hadn't taken a proper picture in ages. Jessie grimaced, almost regretting her offer when her grandfather cheered.

'I was hoping you'd say that, but I was only fifty per cent convinced you would. I think you'll be surprised at what you're capable of with a little encouragement, Jess,' he said softly. 'We're only a few minutes from the hotel now,' he added, pointing back at the road.

'I'm looking forward to seeing it for real,' Jessie said. 'We didn't make it when I holidayed in Indigo Cove with you.'

'Yes, it was closed for renovations back then,' George explained. 'When I booked this break, I was hoping I'd be able to picnic there in the gardens overlooking the cliffs. Just like Dorothy and I did on our honeymoon. She took some pretty photos of the views. I tried to call ahead to book in to stay for a night. I got the number from an old article I found online about the hotel, but I called and called, and no one answered.'

'Well, this is the perfect opportunity to check it out now,' Jessie reassured.

Her grandfather grinned. 'Take the next right and follow the cliffs round, I'm sure it's only a few minutes down the road.

If we're lucky, we might be able to squeeze in a quick bite to eat while we're there.' He licked his lips. 'I remember the cook did the best sausage rolls, and cheese and pineapple on sticks. Maybe she'll be able to whip us up a snack?'

Jessie nodded. The cook would most likely be long gone after fifty years, but it was so lovely hearing her grandad get excited about being here. She smiled and took the right following the road until she saw the tall building in the distance.

She recognised the hotel immediately from the photographs she'd seen in the album. Even from this distance, she could see the building was stunning. An eclectic architectural mix of modern and traditional with flowing lines, pretty wooden containers brimming with flowers underneath large windows angled in every possible direction. No doubt offering mind-blowing views of the surrounding cliffs and wild meadows. Jessie drew the car to a stop just outside, and frowned at the large oak gate which was blocking access to the driveway and the matching six-foot fence circling the grounds.

'This is definitely the hotel,' her grandfather said, pulling out the map again so he could double-check. 'It's exactly where I remember it was. Right by the cliffs, just a few miles out of the village. When your grandmother and I honeymooned here, you could drive up to the front door.' He let out a wistful sigh.

Jessie sighed out a breath and opened the car, carefully unfurling her long legs as she eased her way out of the driver's seat before she opened the back door to let Phoebe out to sniff the grass. They'd left Oxford early in the morning and been travelling for five hours straight, aside from a couple of pit stops at service stations. Everything ached and she could murder a cold drink. As she breathed in the fresh sea air, it instantly put her in a lighter mood. She peered through the slats in the gate and caught a glimpse of the glittering sea at the edge of the horizon. 'It looks like it might be someone's house now.'

'It has been almost fifty years...' her grandfather said,

sounding disappointed. 'I should have expected things would have changed. I guess that article was older than I thought. I really wanted to see the place again and get some photos.'

'Perhaps the owner will let us take a look around?' Jessie gazed at the house.

'It's worth asking, I suppose...'

A Cornish slate plaque set into the fence to the right of the gate read *Look Out House* and there was a small camera and buzzer secured below it, which Jessie pressed. She waited, making sure her face was visible just in case someone wanted to check she wasn't an axe murderer.

A dog yapped in the distance, perhaps sensing Phoebe was outside, and she glanced through the narrow wooden slats to where a chocolate-brown dachshund darted to the front of the building, closely followed by an overweight golden retriever who lumbered along a few paces behind. Phoebe trotted up so she could press her nose into the small gap to stare at them.

'There are a couple of dogs wandering around, so someone's bound to be in there somewhere,' Jessie said, turning to her grandfather, as one of the dogs by the house began to bark – although neither seemed inclined to make their way any further down the driveway.

Jessie frowned at the camera. 'Perhaps it's broken?' She pressed the buzzer again, holding it down. She heard a crackle as if someone had picked up the receiver, but no one spoke. 'This is weird,' she murmured, just as she spotted a silhouette at one of the bottom windows of the building. She was too far away to make much out but guessed it was a man because the figure looked tall and athletic.

'Hello!' she shouted. 'Someone's coming,' she told her grandfather, stepping away from the intercom as the front door slowly swung open. Then she heard a low whistle and watched both dogs scamper inside before the door slammed shut. 'Well...' Jessie's jaw dropped. 'That was rude.'

'Maybe the owner didn't hear you call out? I'm almost ninety-five per cent convinced there's a simple explanation. Perhaps if we head into town, we can see if anyone knows who lives here?'

Jessie drew in a long breath, confused. Whoever was in the house had clearly known they were here, but why they'd chosen to ignore the buzzer was anyone's guess. Perhaps they didn't like strangers? An introduction from someone they knew might make all the difference. Then they'd be able to visit Look Out House to take some photos, and her grandfather would be able to enjoy his trip down memory lane.

'You're probably right. I suppose we can come back another time.' She opened the car door and called Phoebe, then folded herself back into the car before starting the engine.

3

Jessie followed the narrow road down towards Indigo Cove, passing a railway station on her left with overflowing baskets of pink, purple and blue flowers positioned at intervals around the small car park. She turned sharply at a sign pointing her towards the harbour, then let out a quiet gasp as the vibrant greens and blues of the sea appeared as they started to descend. Light from the sun bounced off ripples in the waves, creating glistening arcs.

A bubble of excitement rose in her throat, overshadowing the raw feelings of humiliation and hurt that had been hounding her for days. Jessie found herself smiling as they continued their journey down the road while her grandfather pointed out a row of quaint cottages painted in pastel pinks, yellows and blues, eagerly identifying the species of multi-coloured flowers in the baskets and pots strewn around their windows and doors.

Indigo Cove looked almost exactly as it had when George and Dorothy had brought Jessie here years before. It had been a wonderful holiday, aside from one awful night. Her stomach roiled at the memory of the boy who'd kissed her and ran. She shook her head, blocking it out, but it lingered like a black shadow at the edges of her mind, merging with the pain caused in the past by Maria and now Brendon.

They reached the bottom of the hill where the road curved around a harbour filled with boats of varying sizes. The beach was a blanket of smooth, white sand, with holidaymakers dotted across it, walking, swimming and sunbathing on towels. Couples, families and a few stray people wandered along the pavement, staring in shop windows, chatting or simply admiring the pretty views.

'Pull up over there!' George suddenly pointed to a parking space. 'The Beach Café's in the other direction, but I don't think we can stop outside.'

Jessie parked and switched off the engine before helping her grandad out of the car. George was recovering well from the hernia operation, but he got tired if he tried to walk too far so was trying not to push things. She let Phoebe down from the back seat, clipped on her lead, and walked beside her grandfather trying not to hover too much. They passed The Pasty Place, its delicious aromas mixing with the warm sea air making her stomach rumble. She'd barely eaten on the journey here because her insides had been such a jumble of emotions, but she was starving now.

Her grandad stopped momentarily beside a quaint corner shop with a window filled with large shells and beach souvenirs. 'I remember this place,' he shouted before turning and flashing Jessie a quick grin, pointing to The Beach Café next door. 'And that's barely changed at all!' he declared, shaking his head. 'Your grandmother and I used to come here most days for coffee and cake. I think we brought you a few times when you holidayed with us too?'

Jessie shrugged. 'I remember going to a few cafés, I don't recall this one specifically.' She'd probably been too caught up in her heartache about the boy to pay attention.

George clasped his hands in front of his chest as he gazed ahead, clearly caught up in his memories. Phoebe sniffed the ground beside his feet and then pulled ahead, encouraging them to follow.

The café was a pretty, white-fronted building with metal chairs and tables set on a blue-grey square patio outside. Interspersed between the tables were colourful parasols offering welcome shade from the sun and in the corner sat a large sandpit cluttered with buckets and spades, which had probably been left out to entertain holidaymaker's children. The café had a striking leaded glass window, and the front door had been propped open to let in a breeze. There was a sign to the right of the doorway declaring dogs were welcome inside.

Jessie followed her grandfather up the few steps and in through the entrance, then she paused to look around.

'Oh I remember all this,' her grandfather gushed. 'It's changed quite a lot, but the feel of it is so familiar.'

The walls had been painted a bright sunshine yellow and there were white wooden tables and chairs throughout. Some of the tables were covered in blue-and-white chequered tablecloths; some had puzzle boxes piled up on top, and a few had half-finished jigsaws scattered across their surfaces.

A couple of tables positioned at the back of the room were occupied: a family of four tucked into sandwiches and cakes, and a couple were making googly eyes at each other. In the far corner, a woman with pink hair that reminded Jessie of candyfloss and a feather poking from it sat bent over a small table. As Jessie drew closer to the main counter, she realised the woman was sliding puzzle pieces into a colourful photo of a big wheel. She wore glasses perched on the tip of her nose and clutched a brown feathery handbag under one arm.

'I'm ninety-eight per cent sure she's cuddling a cockerel,' her grandad whispered, as they passed the woman and approached the main counter. Jessie did a double take.

'I'm one hundred per cent sure you're right,' the woman said loudly, looking up and studying George with her bright blue eyes before winking and gazing at Jessie. 'Aren't you a beauty?' she declared, giving Jessie a thorough up and down, making her stomach pitch forward.

Jessie hated being the centre of attention. Who knew what the older woman really thought? Was the compliment genuine, or was there criticism hiding somewhere under the surface? Jessie pulled at the bottom of her T-shirt so it covered her hips. 'I always wanted to be tall, but alas mother nature had smaller ideas.' The woman shrugged before looking back at her puzzle.

'I see you've met our resident jigsaw queen, Elsie Green.' A woman with long dark hair tied up in a ponytail said from behind the counter as she turned away from the coffee machine she'd been grappling with. The woman was beautiful with pale skin and bright red lips. She wore a long floaty skirt and a dark blue shirt with a frilly white apron and reminded Jessie of Snow White. 'I'm Ella Santo. This is my café. Are you here on holiday?' Her smile was warm.

George nodded. 'We've come to stay in Indigo Cove for a while.'

'Wonderful. I hope we'll see you again, we're open most days.' She waved a hand towards the tables. 'We run a puzzle club here every day which my regulars and the holidaymakers can join in with too – Elsie's the chairman if you're interested?'

'Peaches here is on my team,' Elsie said, nodding at the cockerel who was in fact very real and not a handbag. The bird was now openly staring at them with a beady brown eye. 'He's got a knack with puzzles, always seems to find the pieces I can't. Must be those small eyes.'

'Odd name for a he,' George remarked, looking curious.

'I named him after his favourite fruit,' Elsie explained, as the bird pecked at a puzzle piece on the table and she picked it up and slotted it into place. 'Best jigsaw partner I've ever had.

And he never argues or tries to take credit when I finish first.' She picked up a mug from the table and sipped before swiping a foam moustache from her top lip.

'Is he okay being inside?' Jessie's grandfather asked, trying to get a better look at the bird.

'Oh yes, he's very tame and completely house-trained!' Elsie said, grinning. 'That's why Ella allows him in the café.'

'It's true. Would you like something to eat or drink?' Ella asked, pointing to the array of cakes, sandwiches and plump scones laid out in the fridge in front of them. 'There's jam, honey or clotted cream if you fancy a Cornish cream tea?' Jessie's stomach grumbled. 'It's one of the specialities of The Beach Café.' Ella beamed.

'We've been travelling since early this morning,' George said. 'I'm definitely ready for something. A cream tea sounds grand.'

'That would be lovely, thanks,' Jessie agreed.

'I think I've rented Sea Glass Cottage from you,' her grandad said, stepping further forward. 'We exchanged emails a few weeks ago.' He offered Ella his hand. 'This is my grand-daughter, Jessie. She's joining me on my holiday to help out and walk Phoebe. She was supposed to be getting married last week-end, but I'm afraid her groom is...' He pulled a face. 'A buffoon.'

'I'm sorry to hear that.' Ella's eyes shifted to Jessie, and she gave her a sad smile. 'The world is full of them, I'm afraid. My husband ran off with my best friend a couple of years back, cleared out my business accounts before he went, so you're in good company. Of course I remember you, Mr Levine. I'm happy to have you. Sea Glass Cottage is all made up. There are two bedrooms, so there's plenty of room for you both.' She eyed him thoughtfully. 'I should warn you, though; the steps down to the cottage from the car park are very steep.'

'I'll be okay. I'll take it slowly,' George soothed.

'Well, please be careful.' Ella looked concerned. 'You've had a long drive, why don't you sit? I'll get a bowl of water for your dog.' She smiled at Phoebe. 'I'll make your Cornish cream teas and get the directions and your keys. Feel free to start on one of the puzzles while you're waiting. We never clear them away once they've been started. I want my customers to know their puzzle will be waiting for them like an old friend whenever they return.' She waved a hand at one of the tables closest to Elsie, and George walked over and pulled out a chair. Phoebe followed and curled up in a ball under his feet. There were a few jigsaw boxes piled on the top of one of the tables. George shifted through the pile of jigsaw boxes on the table next to them and chose one that featured a close up of Elvis Presley. He opened it and scattered the pieces as Jessie joined him.

'We had a bag of gorgeous vintage puzzles donated to us recently by someone who'd heard about the club. I haven't made many of them up, but that's one of the new boxes. I'd love to see it completed!' Elsie said, as Peaches eyed the pieces and bobbed his beak.

'My wife used to love Elvis. When we were in Indigo Cove on our honeymoon, we went to an Elvis evening in a club close to the beach and boogied to his songs for most of the night. Oh those were the best days...' George sighed as he started to organise the pieces into different heaps – one for edges and then smaller piles of similar colours and shades.

'Have you lived here long?' Jessie asked, leaning back and stretching her legs. She still felt bent out of shape after the long drive and her back hurt. She'd do some stretches once they got to Sea Glass Cottage to work out the kinks. This was one of the many perils of being so tall.

'I've been here all my life. I've outlived four husbands, but I've never wanted to live anywhere else. My family are from around Indigo Cove and go back five generations, it's a beautiful area – plenty to see and do. I remember that dance hall, I used to go a lot with husband number two.' Elsie stroked a hand through her pink hair, fluffing the sides and the white feather as if she were a peacock preening.

'So you will know of the Look Out Hotel?' her grandfather asked, as he started to piece the top edge of the Elvis puzzle together. He was focused and his nimble fingers worked quickly, slotting the pieces in one after the other. Jessie hadn't seen him so absorbed in anything in a long while.

'Of course, I worked there as a cook for two decades and it was the venue for wedding number one.' Elsie tapped her pointy chin with a fingertip. 'Or was it number three? I always get those two confused because James and Jim both had green eyes and their names were so similar.' Her forehead creased, but her face was filled with humour, suggesting they were being teased. 'It was a beautiful hotel, and the gardens were quite breathtaking. I remember feeling quite perturbed because our guests kept looking at the view instead of my dress.'

George chuckled, making Jessie glance over at him in surprise. It had been a long time since she'd heard that light tinkling sound, and she was suddenly extra glad she'd agreed to join him on his holiday. Being away from Oxford, Brendon and what had happened would give her some thinking time too. Time to figure out what she wanted to do with her life. She had a clean slate now. No job or fiancé, nowhere to live – she needed to work out what she wanted. What she needed in her life to be happy.

'We stopped by the hotel today,' she said. 'Grandad wanted to ask the owner if we could look around and take some photos. He and my grandmother stayed there on their honeymoon, and they used to have cocktails and picnics by the cliffs. We wondered if they'd let us see the grounds.'

'I'm happy to pay a fee for any inconvenience,' her grandfather added.

'But whoever was home wouldn't answer the door.' Jessie frowned, still put out by the way they'd been ignored. It felt like

one more rejection after so many others that were already
weighing her down. Such a silly thing, why did it matter so
much?

'Ah.' Elsie's mouth lifted at the corner. 'I know the owner
very well. He's like a son to me. I had a flood in my bathroom
recently, and while the damage is being repaired, I'm staying
there with him. Look Out House is a private residence now.'

'I thought it might be.' George nodded.

'It was converted about four years ago,' Elsie continued.
'My friend's not that keen on visitors, although he's not
normally rude, so he can't have realised you were calling for
him.' She tugged the cockerel closer to her chest when he
started to peck at the tablecloth. 'I can speak to him if you like? I
can't imagine he'll mind you looking around, taking photos or
having a picnic there. His family used to live next door to me
when I was married to husband number four, and he came
round for tea at least five times a week back then.' Her forehead
crinkled. 'He was always such a kind boy. Still is, despite
everything...'

Her eyes flashed and she looked behind them towards the
entrance. 'I had to give my car up a year ago because of dizzy
spells and even when I'm not staying with him, he drives me to
the café each day, picks me up from my house and then drops in
again to take me home.' She checked her watch. 'I'm expecting
him any minute actually, so if you're still here when he arrives, I
could introduce you?'

'That would be great,' George gushed, deftly finishing the
top edge of the Elvis puzzle before starting work on one of the
corners.

'You're a natural.' Elsie's lips stretched as she watched him.
'How long are you staying in Indigo Cove?'

'Jessie and I are here for four weeks.' George answered
without looking up. 'Why?'

'We're hosting a Jigsaw Championship here in three weeks,

and I'm looking to add to the teams. Perhaps you could think about joining in?'

George nodded, glancing up and gleaming at her.

'The Puzzle Club and Jigsaw Championship were both Elsie's idea.' Ella walked up to the table with a huge tray. She carefully placed the pot of tea, two cups and saucers and a cake stand beside Jessie, taking care not to put them over any jigsaw pieces. Then she laid out plates, napkins and knives, and George immediately began to dig in.

The older woman shrugged. 'I was lonely after my fourth husband Jeff died. He always loved puzzles, and I popped into the café about nine months ago with Peaches when I was having a particularly low day and spotted some jigsaws lying around. I started to make one up because it reminded me of him, and Ella and I got talking.'

The café owner nodded. 'When my husband left me, I buried myself in work. It was a bad time and I felt isolated,' Ella took over. 'It's easy to stop interacting with people when something bad happens. But I loved puzzles as a child and they're such great connectors. You can be around people, share something you love without having to talk if you don't want to.'

'It's all those pieces waiting to find their perfect spot. They're just like people really,' Elsie joked, sliding another bit into her puzzle.

Ella smiled. 'We have a lot of regulars now – they pop in and out. But there are still a lot of lonely people out there, and I think we could reach more of them if we hosted a Jigsaw Championship.'

'How will it work?' George asked, biting into his scone. Jessie thought he looked so at ease with the puzzle – there really was something quite brilliant about Elsie's idea.

'Multiple teams of two will compete to finish a puzzle as quickly as they can. There will be hot drinks and cakes – even the local press are coming,' Ella explained. 'It's just a community project, but I'm hoping the championships will help us to reach more people who would benefit from company.'

'And cake.' Elsie laughed. 'Don't forget the cake. Everyone feels better after a slice of one of Ella's treats.'

The café owner's eyes twinkled. 'Once you're both ready, I've put the keys and directions for you in a pack. I live close to Sea Glass Cottage, so I'll visit in the next few days to make sure everything's okay and you haven't had too much trouble with the steps. I've included my number in the envelope, so call if you need anything.' She turned away and walked back to the counter as the family wandered towards the till to pay.

Jessie busied herself pouring their tea.

'Ah speak of the devil,' Elsie gasped, grinning towards the door and waving a hand just as Jessie was considering reaching for a scone.

Jessie twisted around to see, and her stomach flipped over before dropping to the floor like a stone. She was frozen, as if every molecule of her body had decided to lay down tools and go on strike. She opened her mouth and closed it, opened it again but couldn't form words. The man at the door was tall, about half a head taller than her, with long limbs and a broad muscular chest. He had an angular jaw, dark, defined eyebrows, and a full mouth which curved down at the edges. Jessie knew that face – it had haunted her dreams for years, and she'd never forgotten it, suspected she never would. She swallowed a rush of bile.

'Let me introduce you to Ashton Reynolds, my hero, adopted son and the owner of Look Out House,' Elsie continued gleefully, as the boy who'd kissed Jessie and then run fourteen years ago – the man who'd shattered her fragile heart – gazed at her with unreadable eyes.

4

Ashton Reynolds stared at the woman who'd haunted his dreams since he was eighteen and cursed. He'd thought he'd recognised her face earlier when she'd gazed into the camera at Look Out House. That long regal nose, the large, faintly slanted eyes and the mouth that had made him feel like he'd fallen into a maelstrom when he'd kissed it. Reluctant to see her – to have all those inconvenient feelings stirred up – he'd called the dogs inside, but had decided after a few minutes that he must have been mistaken about recognising her. But by the time he checked, she'd already driven away. He'd put the whole thing down to too many hours staring at his laptop screen with his cyber security head on, as he'd hacked his way through a customer's computer firewall, proving it was about as effective as a chocolate teapot.

Jessie – he still remembered her name – stared at him, her face pale. His eyes swept over her, and he saw the moment when her frozen mind obviously rebooted itself because her mouth settled into a grim line. Elsie continued to gaily chatter introductions in the background, but Ashton could barely hear her now. The girl he'd kissed had changed, grown into her unique looks. She looked less vulnerable now, less like she might break in two if he said the wrong thing. He swallowed. She'd terrified him fourteen years ago, the way she'd made him feel. That one kiss had turned him inside out, made him want things he'd decided even at his young age to never seek. All that need, all that want pumping through his blood. A disaster waiting to happen, a lifetime of pain and regret. He knew exactly where feelings like that would lead, and he wanted no part in them.

'Pleased to meet you,' he said carefully, as he stepped forward. He held out a hand and waited to see what Jessie would do next.

'Oh, I think we've already met,' she said, her voice filled with disgust, ignoring his hand and calling his bluff, making something inside him unfurl. Reluctant respect for her honesty and desire to call him on his bullshit flooded through his veins, along with yet more memories. She'd been blunt back then, he remembered that – and funny.

'You have?' Elsie looked delighted, and the elderly grey-haired man sitting at the table beside Jessie perked up.

'Ashton here was the first boy I ever really kissed,' Jessie said, her voice as cold as winter snow in the Arctic.

'You were?' Elsie gave him the eye, and Ashton guessed she'd be grilling him all the way back to Look Out House in the car.

He sighed. 'I was seventeen.' Jessie shrugged a shoulder. 'A late developer, but I made up for it in the end.' Her gaze stabbed at him, and he wondered if she was imagining just how it might feel to run him through with a spear. 'He gave me the best kiss of my life and then ran off.' She cocked her head. 'I always wondered what had scared him so much.'

'Dear God, another nitwit, it's like a disease,' the old man muttered just loud enough for them all to hear. Ashton wondered if the volume was deliberate but couldn't help liking the protective heckles. He was glad Jessie had someone to fight her corner now.

'So, what was so terrifying?' Jessie asked, still appraising him, her expression cool. 'A ghost? Giant mouse? Mist from the sea intent on devouring all hope?' She continued to stare, waiting for a response. She had the bluest eyes – he hadn't been able to make out the colour in the moonlight all those years before, but he'd often wondered. They glittered like ice, but he guessed they'd change colour if she laughed or got turned on. Suddenly, he wished he knew...

He shook himself and took a small step back so he was situated in the doorway of the café, with a clear escape route. 'I don't remember exactly,' he lied. 'Perhaps it was just getting late?'

The corner of Jessie's lip curled, and she nodded, making Ashton experience a wave of shame. He usually faced his problems head on, said exactly what he thought. Honesty meant everything – he'd learned that lesson from his parents, so why had he just lied? He opened his mouth, but no words came. He could hardly tell Jessie she'd affected him so much he'd been too terrified to stick around. Too afraid he'd never be able to leave, or stop kissing her. He'd been *eighteen* for feck's sake, a bundle of confused hormones with a heart just as vulnerable as hers. At least he could control his feelings now.

'Jessie and her grandad George called by Look Out House earlier,' Elsie continued, rising from the chair and tugging Peaches closer to her hip as she slowly moved away from the table, slotting a couple more pieces into place on her puzzle for good measure before joining him.

'Did they?' Ashton asked in his most guileless tone.

Elsie narrowed her eyes – she'd always been able to see into the heart of him. 'They want to visit, take some photos and look around, perhaps have a picnic in the gardens beside the cliffs.

For sentimental reasons they'll explain to you, I imagine. I said I was sure you wouldn't mind?'

'I... um...' Ashton paused, as the older woman stared into his eyes. She'd been more of a mother, father and everything in between to him than any other living person. She could read him like a book and probably knew there was something strange happening here. Something he wasn't prepared to share. 'Sure, fine,' he said, casting a quick look at Jessie whose forehead was now marred with parallel lines. 'Why don't you drop in on Monday and I'll show you around?'

'You'll open the gate this time?' Jessie asked, frowning.

'Yes,' Ashton promised, as Elsie's eyes bored into the side of his head. 'We should probably go now.' He reached down to take the older woman by the elbow. She'd tripped a few weeks ago when she'd been alone in his house, and he wasn't about to risk his friend getting hurt. 'Isn't it almost time for Peaches' afternoon tea?'

Elsie patted his hand and gave him a look that said she knew exactly what he was doing. Although her expression was tinged with enough surprise that he guessed she'd be quizzing him once they were safely inside his Land Rover. 'Whatever you say, dear,' she said mildly, before turning back to Jessie and the older man. 'Meet me here on Monday morning so you can join in with the Puzzle Club, and we can organise a time. I'll come up with you to Look Out House. It'll save Ashton a journey and I have a key – that way if he doesn't hear the buzzer again, I'll be able to let you in myself.'

She walked out of the door tugging his arm, and Ashton allowed himself to be led, wondering exactly what had happened to his nice and ordered life – and precisely how many storms Jessie might blow his way before she left Indigo Cove...

. . .

'So, what was all that about?' Elsie asked, when they finally made it to Ashton's car after a quick detour to the souvenir shop, tucking her seatbelt around her waist before twisting into position so she could hold on tightly to Peaches. Ashton had given up asking her to put the bird on the back seat of the car – a woman and her cockerel were impossible to separate it seemed.

He let out a long sigh. 'Nothing – a teen romance. I had a few, so it's not a surprise that I can't remember every girl I kissed.' He winced as he started the car and backed out of the parking spot just as Jessie and her grandad wandered across the road heading for the Ford Anglia parked in the space beside them. She was tall, just as he remembered, her limbs elegant and long. He swallowed and looked back in his wing mirror, keeping his attention firmly fixed on the road in case Elsie clocked the real focus of his thoughts.

'You forget. I know when you're lying. I've known since you tried to steal food from my fridge for you and your dog,' Elsie said dryly. 'How old were you?'

'Fifteen,' he grumbled. He'd been starving – it was the only excuse he had. He'd never coveted a life of crime, but his parents had been fighting, this time because his mother was pregnant. It had been one of those cyclical sparring matches that could last for days. There'd been no food in the house and he – and the old Labrador he'd adopted – had been ravenous. He'd seen the back door of Elsie's house was open, and Ashton had simply been desperate, too hungry to see sense.

'You took me under your wing,' he said, knowing if he didn't fill in the blanks, tell the story of their friendship, Elsie would be upset.

'I just made sure you had enough to eat.' She sniffed as he took a right, steering the car up the hill that would take them out of Indigo Cove's main high street. 'I made you go to school and do your homework, encouraged you to take those college

courses and sign up to the open university while you were struggling to keep that roof over all your heads...'

'Because no one else would,' Ashton agreed quietly. 'You
were there when my sister was born, and when my parents
upped and disappeared.' He swallowed the wave of pain which
always hit him somewhere mid-chest when he thought about his
parents leaving and how they'd taken his younger sister without
a word and never come back for him. He'd been out that night
working in a bar, and the house had been so quiet when he'd
returned. He hadn't cared about them, but losing Merrin had
cut him to the bone. 'You stepped up for me, I'll never forget it.'

Elsie turned to stare at him. 'I did what I wanted to, and
you're not in my debt. You're as much of a son to me as my own
would have been, if I'd been blessed with children. That's why
your happiness matters. Why I know that girl we just met
means something to you. I've never seen you react to anyone
like that.' Elsie narrowed her eyes, but Ashton knew she
couldn't fully read his mind despite trying enough times.

'No.' He shook his head as he took another right, steeling
himself for the journey which would take them past Elsie's
house.

She lived in the same place as she had when he'd lived next
door, about half a mile along the cliffs from Look Out House.
He still felt an odd jerk in his chest whenever he passed the
cottage, saw the long chalet-style building next door with the
neat envelope of grass at the front. The place he'd grown up in,
the place his parents had left, ripping his younger sister from his
life.

'I only met Jessie for a few minutes,' he said, as he followed
the road past the short row of houses. He wouldn't stop now –
he'd popped in to see the builders earlier to make sure the work
on Elsie's house was coming along okay and would visit again
tomorrow when he had more time.

She let out a long sigh. 'I know I've had more husbands than most, but I loved them all. So much so that I'm reluctant to risk the grief of losing one again. But you're still young and you've never really let yourself feel—'

'It suits me,' he said, as he drew up outside the gates for Look Out House, then waited until the camera recognised the car and the gates swung open. Then he drove along the driveway and parked, shutting off the engine and unhooking his seatbelt, hoping Elsie wasn't going to say more.

'Love doesn't have to be scary, Ashton,' Elsie said, stroking a hand over the cockerel's back. 'It doesn't have to twist you up and turn you inside out. You've only ever seen the darkness of it – you never allowed yourself to see the light.'

He opened his mouth to tell her she'd said all this before, but she held up a finger.

'You're all about firewalls and impenetrable passwords, locked networks and vaults, making things nice and secure and shutting everything scary out. You've made a living out of it.' She flashed her straight teeth. 'An extremely good living – you're great at what you do. But what's the worst that could happen if you eased up a little, let something in?'

'A virus or hacker or cyber-terrorist,' he listed dryly. 'Armageddon might not be too far behind.'

She shut her eyes and Ashton could feel the cockerel's beady eye on him, giving him its death stare. 'Now you're being obtuse. Just think about it. Allow your mind to open to the possibilities. Jessie is only here for a few weeks. Again, I ask, what's the worst that could happen?' She turned to open the car door, and Ashton hopped out, jogging around to the other side of the Land Rover so he could guide Elsie to the front door.

He knew what could happen – he knew the dangers as well as he knew the positions of the letters on his qwerty keyboard. He'd promised himself years before that he'd never unlock his heart, and he wasn't about to change his mind now, even if a small part of him wished he could.

5

'That's a long way down,' Jessie's grandfather gasped, as he, Phoebe and Jessie stood at the top of the long wooden staircase that led down from the small car park to Sea Glass Cottage. 'I'm going to need to take this slowly.' His eyes darted to the dog. 'I'm glad you're here to help me, Jessie.'

'Didn't Ella mention all the stairs when you booked?' Jessie asked, gathering their bags from the back of the car and putting them down at the top of the stairs.

'Probably.' He shrugged, frowning as he gazed down. 'But I reserved it before the hernia and knowing I'd have to have the operation. It'll be fine if I take it slowly. You go ahead with Phoebe.' He wafted his hand downwards. 'I'll join you in my own time.'

'I'll take the largest luggage first and come back to help. Please wait there,' Jessie begged, carrying the heavy cases down the seventy-three steps and leaving them at the bottom before skipping back up to meet her grandad. He hadn't waited and was already five steps down, carrying his small bag which Jessie immediately commandeered. It took ten slow minutes for them to get to the bottom, and they had to rest a few times. George didn't complain, but Jessie could see the journey was taking its toll because his cheeks took on a chalky quality.

'I'm not sure we're going to be able to stay here for the whole month,' she said, as they reached the bottom and followed Phoebe round the side of the building with her grandad hobbling beside her.

'I'll be fine,' he rasped. 'This place is only one storey, so there are no other stairs to worry about, and there are lots of places for me to put my feet up if things get too much. Phoebe here will keep me company. Besides, I'm expecting to feel like my old self in a week or two.' He scratched the dog's ears and grinned as they rounded the wide American-style deck that wrapped all the way around the cottage's right side and reached the back where a covered hot tub sat in the far corner, opposite a pretty white table and chairs.

'This is gorgeous,' Jessie purred, as she stood taking it all in. A wooden awning had been pulled out to protect the furniture from the elements, and Ella had left out soft baby-blue blankets and squashy cushions along with large silver lanterns filled with tall, cream-coloured candles. It was beautiful, comfortable and romantic, everything Jessie had dreamed of for her own honeymoon.

Ignoring the squeeze of pain in her chest, she fixed a smile on her face as she helped her grandad inside before transferring their luggage into the kitchen. It had bright white cabinets and baby-blue walls. A long, grey granite counter separated the kitchen area from a square dining table which had already been laid. Floaty sheer curtains offered privacy without blocking the views of the sea which rolled in over the beach just a few metres away. A set of steps led down to the sand from the decking.

'I'll take the bedroom at the back,' George said, after wandering through the cottage. 'The bed's lower than the other one, which I prefer and there's a bathroom next door.'

'Take the big bedroom,' Jessie implored, as she surveyed the room beside it. It had a four-poster bed piled with white linen and crisp cushions, and stunning views of the beach visible through the floor-to-ceiling sliding doors. It was obviously supposed to be a honeymoon suite. 'It's got an en suite with a huge claw-footed bath and a walk-in shower too,' she told her grandfather, hoping that might persuade him.

'Nope,' he said, his jaw tight. 'That's yours. You're supposed to be on your honeymoon in the Maldives with the nincompoop, but instead, you're here looking after me. It's only right you get the best room.' He didn't wait for Jessie to agree. Instead, he walked back towards the kitchen and picked up his light holdall before heading towards the smaller bedroom, waving away her offers of help.

Jessie sighed and picked up both of the suitcases before wandering slowly to the honeymoon suite. She didn't look around as she dropped hers onto the huge bed, although her eye caught on a bottle of champagne that had been left chilling in a silver cooler on the sideboard, next to chocolates, a bowl of strawberries and two long-stemmed glasses.

'Perfect. I suppose the people who stay are usually enjoying a romantic getaway of some kind, so it's all part of the service,' she said dryly, gathering up the tray so she could take it back into the kitchen. 'Looks like our evening is sorted.'

She placed the bottle into the fridge and spotted an oval plate laid with slabs of cheese, meats, olives and a crisp salad. Ella had done everything she could to make her grandad's stay in Sea Glass Cottage special.

Brendon would have loved holidaying in a place like this. He'd have pulled out the plate of food, kicked off his shoes and draped himself over the sofa so he could eat and enjoy the views. But her ex wouldn't have reached for her, wouldn't have pulled her into his arms. Their relationship had never been like that, had never been particularly sexual. The lack of chemistry had disappointed Jessie at first, but not everyone got that with their other half – and she knew acceptance and companionship were the things that really mattered. Although obviously Brendon hadn't felt the same, which is why he'd gone looking elsewhere for sex. Was it because she wasn't capable of inspiring those kinds of feelings? Or because her ex had been wrong for her all along?

Jessie's mind drifted to Ashton, to the hum in her veins when she'd seen him in the doorway of The Beach Café. To the explosive kiss she'd never forgotten. How could one person have such a huge effect? Especially someone who was obviously repulsed by her.

She frowned and took her grandad's suitcase to his room, finding him sitting on the double bed with his holdall unzipped beside him. He'd started to unpack his clothes, but had obviously been distracted because he held a small photo in his hand.

'What's that?' she asked.

'One of the few photos I have left of our honeymoon,' he replied softly, smiling at Jessie. 'Dorothy put all her favourites in the album, but I found this. It's us at one of our picnics. Someone took it for us, which is why it's a little crooked.'

He handed Jessie the photo. It was crinkled in the corners, suggesting it had been handled a lot. Her grandmother was dressed in a red gauzy shift dress and matching clogs. She held a glass of champagne up towards Jessie's grandfather, who was grinning so much he glowed. George wore bell-bottom jeans and a stripey shirt and his glossy, dark hair was wavy and long. Jessie could see hints of her own face in her grandmother's – she was around the same height and their colouring was almost an exact match. Jessie had only inherited George's long nose, but he was tall too, so her freakish genes came from them both.

'You look so much like her,' George sighed. 'Just as beautiful. I fell for Dorothy the moment I met her at our school dance. One kiss and I didn't look at another woman for the rest of my life.' He shook his head.

Jessie slumped beside him on the bed. 'You were lucky,' she said, gazing at the photo, feeling a twinge of grief coupled with those familiar stabs of inadequacy. 'Where was this taken?'

George pulled a face. 'The Look Out Hotel I think, in the gardens. Dorothy took dozens more, but they were all in the album.' He reached into the holdall and pulled out a Nikon F2. 'But the photos we take will be a reminder, a memento of all the wonderful times we had. Something for me to look at when I'm back in Oxford.'

Jessie grimaced. 'I haven't taken any photos for such a long time. I'll do my best, but I'm not sure I'll be able to do your memories justice.'

Her grandfather gave her a long hard stare. 'You're capable of far more than you realise, Jessie – I think somewhere along the way you've forgotten that. Take the camera now.' Jessie took it, felt the weight of it in her hands. 'Maybe things will look different if you view them through a new lens.'

Jessie peered through the narrow optic at her grandfather. He looked tired, but there was a light in him she hadn't seen since Dorothy had passed away. Perhaps he was right?

'I'm hoping to get some snaps of the views from Look Out Hotel on Monday. There's this one place in the garden where you can see the sea and it goes on for miles.' His eyes misted. 'There's a huge rock at the edge of the cliffs that looks just like a rocket.' He made a triangular shape with his hands. 'We had a wonderful view of that rock from our honeymoon suite.'

He picked up another picture from the bed and handed it to Jessie. 'That's the only one I have of the inside.' The photo showed a huge four-poster bed with large cabinets on either side. Jessie could just make out a set of veranda windows to the left of the room where her grandmother stood between billowing white curtains gazing outside. 'I took that one, but we had loads more of the bedroom and grounds. Which is why I'm really looking forward to going to the hotel again.'

'When we pack our picnic, I'll bring extra in case Elsie wants to join us,' Jessie said. 'Maybe we could take some pictures of us having lunch just like you and Grandma did?'

Her grandfather beamed. 'Can we have sausage rolls, and cheese and pineapple sticks?'

'Of course,' Jessie said, hoping Ashton would be out. She wasn't sure she wanted the man who'd fractured her heart watching while they picnicked in the sun. It was as if he'd spoil it somehow because he wouldn't understand its significance – maybe he'd laugh at them?

She handed her grandad back the photos. He kissed them and placed them between the pages of the crime novel he'd brought to read before putting it down on the bedside cabinet.

'Ready for some food?' Jessie asked, rising as Phoebe shot up at the sound of the last word. 'There's cheese, meats and olives. We could sit outside and watch the sea and take photos? Maybe we could go and collect seashells later, just like you and Grandma used to do. Do you remember, we looked for shells a few times when I was on holiday here with you too?'

'I do, love,' George said wistfully. 'Give me a few minutes to unpack and I'll help you prepare the meal. But I'm not sure I'm up to a walk on the beach tonight, I'm exhausted after all the travelling and those stairs. I don't want to run the risk of feeling sore tomorrow. Perhaps we could do it another day?'

Jessie nodded and rose before making her way to the kitchen.

'So, what's it like?' Rose Briggs, Jessie's best friend and the office manager at her old job in Oxford, asked eagerly when Jessie picked up her mobile a couple of hours later. She'd been laying on the bed in the honeymoon suite after eating dinner, trying to make herself feel at home while her grandad rested.

'It's beautiful,' she said truthfully. 'Although I'm not sure

how practical it is for Grandad. There are far too many steps.'
And no way of avoiding them. She put the mobile on speaker so
she could get up and arrange some of the downy cushions from
the bed into the shape of a body in the exact spot where
Brendon usually slept. It didn't look right so she thumped the
pile a few times, then picked up her sunglasses from the bedside
cabinet and positioned them where her ex's head would have
been. She hadn't slept properly in two weeks and hoped having
something beside her would help.

'How are you feeling?' Rose asked.

Jessie blew out a breath. 'I don't know. I don't really miss
Brendon, which is weird considering we were together so long.
But I'm glad to be away from all the reminders. Grandad wants
us to take photos of the places he and Grandma went on his
honeymoon, so it's going to be a busy month. He's not healed
enough to get around on his own, so I'll need to stay with him
wherever he goes – which means less time for me to think about
what a mess my life's become.' Jessie regarded the lumpy pillow
and frowned, then she threw a blanket over it. With any luck,
she wouldn't be able to tell the difference in the dark.

'Brendon was never good enough for you,' Rose said,
sounding annoyed. 'He made you leave the photography job
you loved—'

'—because I wasn't good enough to make it in the business,'
Jessie interrupted. 'I made so much more money working in
insurance. I was wasting my time...'

'Oh, Jess...' Rose sighed. 'You weren't good enough at
anything according to Brendon. He always behaved as if he was
doing you a favour by being in a relationship with you at all,
which he clearly wasn't because he's a total knobhead.'

'I don't know...' Jessie muttered, thinking about her ex. He
was handsome, with one of those chiselled jaws you read about
in books, and he was clever too. She'd often wondered why he'd
picked her out of all the women he could have had.

'Seriously, Jess, you should look at yourself in the mirror sometime. I don't want to speak ill of the dead, but after all the crap your stepmother used to spout, you have no idea how lovely you are. Maria's been gone for over seven years, and you still believe all the awful things she used to say about you – which means you set the bar for men far too low. I wish I'd said all this before, but I couldn't when you were seeing Brendon. You deserve someone who adores you, someone who makes you feel like you matter and like you can do anything you want.'

The words were such an echo of the conversation Jessie had just had with her grandfather, it took her a few seconds to respond. 'I'm not going to hold my breath, but I'm not giving up entirely,' she said eventually. 'I'd like to meet someone who cares for me. I hope he's out there somewhere…'

'I'm glad Maria didn't knock your optimism out of you entirely, despite how hard she tried,' Rose said. 'I know you'll find someone who deserves you. But you have to stop settling for second best. You deserve fireworks and the kind of tingles that rock you to your toes – in and out of bed.'

Jessie swallowed, thinking about Ashton. No one had ever made her feel the way he had when he'd kissed her all those years ago, and look how that had turned out. 'How's your love life?' she asked, desperate to change the subject.

'Oh you know, so many men, so little time,' Rose teased. 'I just want to have fun and there's plenty of that to be had here. Have you met anyone interesting in Indigo Cove since you arrived?' She redirected the interrogation back to Jessie. 'What about that boy you told me about?' she asked, her voice low and sexy. 'The one you kissed…'

Jessie absorbed the wave of embarrassment. She'd told Rose about her encounter with Ashton one evening after too many glasses of wine. She was hazy on exactly which details she'd shared, but Rose had never forgotten the story and their conversations would often wind their way back to the beach. 'I've only been here for a few hours.' Jessie thought quickly, desperate to put her friend off the scent. 'I did bump into an old lady who runs a puzzle club and takes a cockerel everywhere with her, and I met the lovely owner of a café. Do they count?'

'Sounds interesting, but not very promising,' her friend sounded disappointed. 'Hopefully, someone gorgeous will turn up soon. I'm counting on you to have a holiday romance, something to take your mind off Brendon and make you feel good about yourself. Why don't you take a walk on that beach where you met your mystery man? Who knows, perhaps fate will throw him in your path again. Promise me you'll at least consider the possibility?'

'I promise,' Jessie lied, because romance – and having anything to do with Ashton Reynolds – was the last thing on her mind.

The beach was quiet when Jessie and Phoebe made their way onto it later that evening. Jessie had her grandmother's camera dangling from her neck. Her grandfather had decided to turn in early after taking his painkillers. Hopefully, he'd be better by Monday – he was so excited about visiting Look Out House.

She shrugged off her sandals as she got to the bottom of the decking and reached the sand, letting the warm silky grains slide between her toes as the golden retriever bounced off into the distance. Hopefully, a quick walk to the shore would help put them both in the mood for sleep. It would be difficult for Jessie to settle in the bed, even with her pillow boyfriend. She was still deeply rattled by everything that had happened with Brendon, not to mention thoroughly confused about where her life was now going. Added to that, she'd just seen Ashton for the first time in fourteen years, and a lot of uncomfortable feelings she'd buried had begun to resurface. *Why had he run – what was so awful about her? Had Maria been right, or was there another explanation? Would Ashton ever confess – or was he too embarrassed to admit how repelled he'd been?*

Jessie heard a dog bark in the distance, but it wasn't Phoebe, who then stopped and pricked her ears up before making her way to where the waves were frothing at the shore.

Jessie shoved her hands into her pockets, fighting a torrent of emotion because this was exactly the type of moonlight walk she'd imagined taking with Brendon on their honeymoon. She stared towards the horizon, making herself think about her holiday with her grandfather and Dorothy instead.

'What would you do, Grandma?' she asked, grabbing her camera and looking through the lens. 'You'd take pictures,' she murmured. 'You always did when you wanted to think. You told me it helped you focus.'

Jessie tried to frame the perfect shot as her finger hovered, ready to take the picture. But there was something missing, everything looked wrong. It was either too dark, the image too boring or she was just too talentless to see it. It had been so long since she'd photographed anything. She'd lost confidence in her ability to capture a scene and was almost afraid to try. What if her photos were awful? Maria had often accused her of lacking imagination, and since she'd worked in insurance, she'd had no reason to pick up a camera. When she had, nothing had looked right, and over the years she'd begun to accept that photography wasn't for her.

A dog barked again, and Jessie peered into the half-light and spotted a figure far in the distance beside two dogs – one was tiny and the one lumbering beside it was huge. She watched Phoebe take a few tentative steps in their direction. The moon was glowing in the sky and the cliffs jutted upwards behind the figures, creating an arresting composition. Actually, it was quite breathtaking.

Heart thundering in her throat, Jessie took in a breath and quickly snapped a photo, feeling a rare tingle of pleasure. Then she wandered further up the beach and took another snap as the walker drew closer. The figure suddenly waved, and Jessie waited as they approached, worried they might be unhappy she'd been taking pictures of them without their permission. When they were about ten metres away, she recognised the broad shoulders and her body stiffened.

'Are you following me?' she grumbled, as Ashton emerged from the shadows and the same little dog she suspected she'd met fourteen years ago scampered up to greet Phoebe, while the larger dog lumbered across the sand, wagging his tail. What were the chances of them all bumping into each other like this? Then again, perhaps Ashton would finally give her the answers she craved?

'*You're* the one taking the photos, I thought I recognised you,' he said dryly, nodding at the Nikon. 'I walk the beach with the dogs most evenings – this is part of my route.'

'It's a huge coincidence,' Jessie said, although it was unlikely Ashton would deliberately seek her out. He hadn't been able to get away fast enough when they'd been in The Beach Café earlier. A fact that both irritated her and made her feel sad.

'Indigo Cove isn't that big – we're not that far from where we met the first time,' Ashton explained.

'Oh, so you do remember?' Jessie narrowed her eyes.

Ashton flushed. 'The odd thing has started to come back.'

'Like the reason why you ran?' she snapped, wishing she hadn't when his expression shuttered and he shook his head. Jessie should be able to let the whole thing go. It had been long ago, but the wound inside her, the one that had clearly never fully healed, had opened since she'd arrived in Indigo Cove. It joined the searing welt of pain that had emerged since her split with Brendon – and she wanted to heal it with the truth so she could feel whole again. She knew why her ex-fiancé didn't want her, but what had happened with Ashton was still a mystery. One she wanted solved.

'It was a long time ago. I think some things are best left in the past,' he said, looking unhappy. 'What are you doing out here on your own?'

Jessie paused wondering if she should push for an answer. She glanced around. It was late and she was getting tired and didn't particularly want to spend any more time around this man. 'Our accommodation's not far from here, and I was walking Phoebe and taking pictures for Grandad.'

'And of me?' he asked.

'Of the beach,' Jessie said dryly. 'I'll crop you out later.'

Ashton nodded, but the edge of his mouth twitched. 'Do you want me to take any of you?'

Jessie shook her head vigorously. 'I don't like seeing myself in pictures.' She clutched the camera close to her chest. 'I need to get back.' She glanced down the beach in the direction of Sea Glass Cottage. She'd walked further than she'd realised, and it was time to go to bed.

'I guess I'll see you on Monday,' he said, his eyebrows drawing together as if he were seeing her properly for the first time.

'So long as you or Elsie open the gates,' she muttered, but secretly she wondered if it would be a whole lot easier for them both if they stayed shut.

6

Ashton pulled his Land Rover up outside Elsie's house on Monday morning. He'd dropped her at The Beach Café with Peaches but decided not to go in for his usual coffee. He didn't want to see Jessie yet and was still coming to terms with having her visit Look Out House. She stirred up too many feelings, too many memories he was more comfortable blocking out. Even their brief encounter on the beach had left him tossing and turning in bed. But he could do one afternoon – he'd do anything for Elsie. Besides, after today, he probably wouldn't need to see Jessie ever again.

He hopped out of the Land Rover and watched Murphy climb down from the front seat. Bear had stayed behind at Look Out House, too tired after their morning run to summon any energy to move. The dog was impossible – getting him to do anything aside from gobbling down piles of food was like pulling teeth. Their walk two nights before had taken almost an hour and a half, and he'd had to bribe the retriever with treats to encourage him back to the house. The only thing the dog had been interested in was the little retriever Phoebe – it had been a battle to stop him from following her to where Jessie and her grandad were staying and neither of them would have wanted that.

The door of Elsie's house suddenly swung open, and Tristan Harvey staggered out carrying an old porcelain sink. The builder's face was flushed and covered in dust and his filthy grey overalls suggested he'd spent the last hour knocking out the old bathroom and ripping up tiles.

'Morning, mate,' Tristan said, grinning at Ashton, as he heaved the sink into the back of the truck he'd parked at the end of the driveway. Murphy paused on the path to sniff the lawn – Ashton had popped in two days before to mow it and to water Elsie's flowers which were now dancing prettily in the sunshine. 'Didn't expect to see you so early. Fancy a cup of tea?'

'Where are the others?' Ashton asked, searching for the rest of the building crew.

'It's only me this morning, the other lads are up at Roskilly Brewery. They're putting the finishing touches onto the new warehouse today, and it's all hands on deck.' The brewery was located a few miles out of the village, and the owner, Gabe Roskilly, and his new partner and Head Brewer, Jago Thomas, had been expanding the premises over the last year, ensuring the business had plenty of room to grow. Elsie made sure she kept Ashton up to date with all the local gossip, so he knew exactly what was going on.

'I'll have a coffee, please,' Ashton said, following the younger man into Elsie's house. He didn't usually find time to chat, but he'd been feeling a pull in his chest recently, an uncomfortable sense that he'd been shutting himself out. Seeing Jessie again hadn't helped – there had been a tug, a visceral ache, a need he didn't want to examine. Then after hearing Elsie say in the car that he was holding himself back, he'd decided it was time to make more of an effort to socialise.

Ashton took a moment to pause as he walked into the bright yellow hallway. Tristan and his team had covered a lot of the doors downstairs with clear plastic sheets to stop dust from spoiling the paintwork and furniture. Elsie thought they were just fixing up the bathroom after the flood, but Ashton had hired them to recarpet and repaint the whole house, ensuring they stuck to all the older woman's favourite colours. He'd also chosen a new kitchen in the same style as the one in Look Out House. He knew she loved it because she'd helped him choose the design, spending hours ogling the different options until she'd settled on the perfect one. He suspected Elsie would be a little cross at him for spending his money on her, but he hated the idea of her living with tired cabinets and paintwork when he was surrounded by new.

Tristan marched ahead and Ashton took his time walking along the narrow hallway. There were so many memories woven into the fabric of this house. He paused just outside the kitchen, taking in the old grey counters and back door which had been propped open to let in a breeze. He'd crept in through that same door when he was fifteen, starving hungry and so desperate for food he'd been prepared to steal it. He'd watched Elsie and her husband working in their garden a thousand times and had listened to his father sneer at all their hard work. The postage stamp-sized lawn at the back of the bungalow his family rented was always overgrown, and his parents were too busy arguing to worry about cutting the grass.

He'd been so mixed up – his mind polluted with all the wrong things, and he'd decided the couple had so much in their lives it was only right they shared it. Besides they were asking for it, weren't they, leaving their back door open like that? So he'd crept in with his dog and searched the kitchen for food while Elsie and her husband Jeff chatted and laughed in the front room with the TV buzzing in the background. They'd been watching a game show, he still remembered that. He also remembered wishing he could just go in and join them. He'd often wondered where he'd be now if Elsie hadn't somehow heard him open the fridge and start to pluck slices of chicken, bits of salad and hunks of cheese.

'You look skinny, boy, do you fancy a sandwich? I've got jelly and ice cream for afters. There's leftover roast chicken and water for the dog too.' The kind voice had almost made him jump out of his skin and he'd leaped back, expecting the woman to scream and then call the police. But he'd stayed where he was because he knew he deserved it – he'd been caught, hadn't he?

'Take a seat.' The woman had pointed to a yellow Formica table in the corner of the kitchen, framed by four high-backed chairs. She'd kept her voice low, like she was dealing with a skittish animal. 'We've eaten already, so you'll have to make do, but if you come back tomorrow, I'll make you a hot dinner and you can eat with us. I'm a cook at The Look Out Hotel, so I promise I won't poison you.'

She hadn't waited for him to agree; instead, she'd pulled out a glass and filled it with milk, grabbed a plate and started to pile it up with bread, salad and cheese. He'd been so hungry his stomach had started to rumble, and he'd pressed a hand over it, feeling embarrassed.

'What do you want for it?' he'd shot back, riddled with suspicion. No one did anything for nothing, his mother and father had taught him that.

Elsie had twisted round then, and her gaze had been assessing but kind. 'Bring your homework – you'll do that in return for your meal.'

'I've already done it all,' he'd lied, still suspicious.

'Then you can show it to me while you're eating. History and science were always my favourite subjects, you can tell me all about what you're learning. My husband Jeff loves maths and English too.' She'd grinned then, and he'd felt the warmth of it right through to his bones.

After that, they'd settled into a routine with Elsie feeding him and the dog most nights in return for the insight into his studies. She and Jeff had been so interested in what he was learning, they'd bombarded him with questions, really made him think. Learning had stopped being an embarrassing chore and had started to be fun. It was then he'd begun to work hard at school – realised it was okay to be interested, that he was bright and lightning-fast at picking things up. He still thought of those days as the true beginning of his life.

Tristan finished making the drinks and turned around, jerking Ashton back to the present as he handed him a black coffee before leaning against the kitchen counter. 'So the bathroom suite is arriving tomorrow along with the kitchen, it should be a simple in and out aside from the new floors. I've booked a tiler and various fitters to do it all quickly. I know you were keen for Elsie to be able to move back in as soon as possible. We've finished most of the repainting in the rest of the rooms and the new carpets are ready to go in as soon as the tiling's done. At a push, she should be able to move in the week after next.'

'That soon?' Ashton asked, feeling a sharp throb in his chest.

'You did say you wanted a fast job?' Tristan's forehead pinched.

'Of course, that's great, thanks,' Ashton replied quickly. Elsie had been staying with him for over three weeks now. He hadn't expected to enjoy having her in the house, so now he wasn't sure he was ready to go back to living alone. The place would feel so quiet. Where he'd once enjoyed the peace, now he wondered if it would seem empty and cold. He shook his head. He was being ridiculous. He'd never coveted company in the house – he'd get used to being alone once Elsie had moved out.

'Oh, I've got some kitchen splashback options in the van I

wanted to show you. I know you chose a style similar to what was here before, but I saw something at the builder's yard I thought Elsie would get a kick out of.' Tristan put down his mug and jogged into the hallway, looking excited.

Ashton wandered to the back door so he could look out into the garden. Murphy scampered ahead, making his way into the lush grass, so Ashton followed the dog outside. From here, he could see right over the low fence into the small back garden of the bungalow next door, could see the patio doors which had always been shut when he'd lived there with his parents, and the window to the bedroom where he'd slept. He knew a family were living in the bungalow now and saw a bright pink slide and swing, suggesting they had a small child. He swallowed as his mind suddenly filled with thoughts of his baby sister and a heavy weight settled in his chest.

Ashton had been sixteen when Merrin Grace Reynolds was born, nineteen when his family had upped and disappeared just a few months after he'd kissed Jessie. His parents had ripped his little sister from him with no prior warning or word. Leaving him feeling like he'd been broken in two. He'd looked for them, but he hadn't had the skills or contacts to actually track them down, and after three years, he'd stopped trying at all. It was the only way he could handle losing her.

Ashton drew his wallet from his back pocket and pulled out a tiny picture of him and his sister together. He'd been swinging Merrin around outside, and Elsie had taken a photo over the fence. His sister had just turned two, she'd been giggling, her pigtails waving behind her like wings. She'd be seventeen now. He hadn't thought about her for ages, but as her birthday had approached, he'd found it harder and harder to block her out. But he knew he had to, or he'd go mad.

He shook his head and swallowed, annoyed by the rare indulgence into his feelings. He pressed the photo back into his wallet when he heard footsteps from the kitchen.

'Here they are!' Tristan shouted from the doorway, and Ashton turned to walk inside.

He wasn't going to think about his sister, she was no longer in his life. He had a successful business, the dogs and Elsie. He didn't need or want anything more.

7

Jessie, Elsie and George pulled up outside Look Out House later that day. The gates slowly swung open, and Jessie drove the Ford Anglia inside and swallowed a flurry of unease.

'I said he'd be watching out for you this time!' Elsie sang from the back of the car, pointing at Ashton who was waiting at the end of the driveway with the two dogs. She practically bounced on the back seat while clutching tightly onto Peaches.

They'd met Elsie in The Beach Café an hour before and had enjoyed poached eggs and toasted fresh bread for breakfast. Jessie's grandfather had spent a few quiet moments completing the Elvis puzzle he'd started when they'd first arrived in the village. He'd been disappointed to discover two of the pieces were missing, which meant the king of rock and roll was missing his right eye. None of the other villagers had been around, but Elsie had promised to introduce them to the rest of The Puzzle Club the following day.

Ashton waited while the gates shut and then slowly walked down the driveway towards them.

'Thanks for being here to greet us,' Elsie said, as they climbed out of the car.

Ashton took a long look at Jessie, making her stomach dip, but didn't say a word. Instead, he led them to the front door, past two brilliant red Japanese Maple trees which were positioned in large pots on either side of the porch. Then he pushed the door and waited for the three dogs to go in ahead.

'It's not healthy to let a pet get so overweight,' her grandfather complained, watching the rotund golden retriever pant heavily as he struggled to keep up with the smaller dogs. George stepped to one side so Elsie and Peaches could follow them into a wide hallway.

A black-and-white tiled floor led to a stunning sweeping staircase with oak balusters and a cream carpet. The high walls had been painted a soft white colour and there was a sparkling chandelier hanging from the ceiling on the second floor, where Jessie could see the top of the landing. It still looked like a grand entrance to a sumptuous hotel.

'I once had a neighbour who wouldn't stop feeding her guinea pig, the poor thing could hardly walk by the end...' her grandfather continued, seemingly oblivious to their magnificent surroundings.

'Bear isn't Ashton's dog. He's mine...' Elsie said, sounding embarrassed. 'My last husband Jeff got him a few months before he died.' She frowned. 'The dog hates walking and loves his food a little too much, but I haven't had the heart to take him in hand. Then I hurt my ankle when he tripped me in my hallway at home and couldn't walk him for a while. Now he'd rather lie in the sun than stretch his legs.' She winced.

'Ashton took him on just before I had a flood in my bathroom and had to move in here. He put Bear on a diet and is taking him for regular walks and runs.' She shook her head. 'But the dog's always finding ways to sneak food. I think he still misses Jeff. I suppose we both do,' she said wistfully, patting the dog on the head. 'I need to put Peaches in the garden so he can exercise, please excuse me for a moment.' She walked slowly down the hallway with the cockerel balanced under one arm.

Ashton watched the older woman go, tracking her movements. His obvious affection for Elsie was disarming, and Jessie wondered if she should give the man the benefit of the doubt. Perhaps he had a heart, after all? But she couldn't risk letting her guard down – she was a terrible judge of character.

'Good of you to take on Elsie's dog.' Her grandfather's voice held a hint of respect, suggesting the older man might be coming around.

Ashton looked uncomfortable. 'Bear keeps Murphy company.' His eyes drifted to Jessie. 'I got Murphy when I was eighteen after my old Labrador passed. But the house has always felt like it needed another dog in it – especially now Murphy's getting older. Bear helps to keep Murphy young now that he's part of the family, even if he is a little lazy.'

Jessie guessed Murphy must be the dachshund puppy she'd met on the beach fourteen years ago, the one who'd been bouncing around them while they'd kissed. Her lips tingled and she ran a fingertip over them, surprised. Then the retriever let out a sudden low groan and wilted onto the wooden floor before gazing at Ashton, his huge brown eyes filled with reproach.

'It's not time for lunch and you are definitely *not* starving, so there's no point in trying those dramatics on me,' he said, as Phoebe wandered over to give Bear a playful nudge, which resulted in the other retriever hopping to his feet again.

'The garden is this way,' Ashton said, walking through the long hallway and taking a left into a huge sitting room surrounded by floor-to-ceiling windows.

A phone started to ring somewhere in the house, but he ignored it. Jessie took a moment to look around the space. Four squashy leather sofas sat facing the stunning views, and a fireplace in the far corner told her that even in winter this was the place Ashton relaxed. There was a walnut coffee table set in front of one of the sofas and Jessie's grandfather strode over to take a look. It showcased a marble chess set with pieces dotted around the board, suggesting someone was halfway through a game. Jessie wondered who Ashton played, who might sit on the sofa beside him in the evenings, before she pushed the thought away. She wandered towards the tall French doors so she could stare out.

'I remember this room,' her grandfather said, wandering over to join her. 'It was the main sitting room. There was a bar over there – I used to have a photo of it in my album.' He pointed to the far wall where a large computer screen and laptop had been set up on a long desk. 'One of the waiters used to make these old fashioneds – they were Dorothy's favourites. She was always partial to anything with whisky in, didn't seem to matter what it was.' He smiled.

Ashton shoved his hands into the pockets of his black jeans, and Jessie tried not to watch the way the muscles underneath his T-shirt bunched. He was tall, with a runner's body, but had broad shoulders, which meant he didn't make her feel big. 'I changed a lot of the rooms when I bought the house. I don't get a lot of visitors, so I took the bar out. This is my office now. The kitchen and bedrooms are all as they were, though, and the gardens are the same too.' Ashton added gruffly. 'I employ the same gardening company that the owners of the hotel did, so I'm sure you'll recognise everything outside.'

'Is it okay if we have a picnic while we're here?' Jessie asked, unhooking the backpack she'd slung over her shoulder just as Elsie came to join them from the hallway. 'There's enough food and drink for everyone, courtesy of Ella.' She'd asked the café owner to put something together and had packed some white wine along with a bundle of plastic glasses she'd found in one of the cupboards in Sea Glass Cottage.

Ashton nodded. 'I put a tablecloth on the table outside and cushions on the chairs to make you comfortable while you eat.'

'Thank you,' Jessie said. The gesture was thoughtful and unexpected. Then again, Ashton was probably hoping to keep them as far away from the house as he could.

Elsie reached up a hand and patted him gently on the cheek. 'You're a good lad,' she murmured.

'I need to get back to work,' he said, his wide shoulders stiffening. 'Everything's been set up on the grass at the back end of the garden.' Ashton didn't look at them – he was clearly uncomfortable with having guests around, but Jessie suspected he didn't want to upset Elsie, which might have been the only thing stopping him from insisting they leave.

'It's the best place to see the sea and there are some incredible views. If you sit outside for long enough, you'll be in the right place to watch the sunset. There are blankets in a basket by the chairs if you decide you want to stay late. I believe that's the spot where the hotel used to put guests if they wanted a late evening drink.'

George stared out of the window. 'I remember it.' He tugged the old photo he'd shown Jessie a few evenings before from his pocket. 'My wife and I used to sit there in the evenings.' He squinted. 'There's the cherry tree on the right of the garden.' He pointed to a beautiful tree in the background of the picture, which had a bed of bright magnolia, delphinium and rhododendrons underneath. Then he took a tentative step onto the patio, and stood for a few seconds gazing at the view.

Jessie went to link arms with him as a phone in the house began to ring again. Ashton hesitated and glanced back at the sitting room towards his desk.

'You going to get that?' Elsie asked.

'It's the landline. I should just unplug it.' Ashton sounded annoyed. 'I've stopped picking up. Every time I do someone's either trying to book a room in the hotel or sell me something. I should never have kept the old number, I only did it for sentimental reasons.'

'Don't you have an answerphone?' Jessie asked, when it rang off and started again.

'That would just encourage people to leave a message.' He shook his head as Elsie wandered onto the patio too. Ashton took hold of her elbow, and Jessie walked with her grandfather to the grass.

George was still trying to hold the photo up as if he were divining where to go next. 'I remember there were rocks to the left of the tree which had pretty purple flowers growing all over them.' He patted a finger on the picture and held it higher so Ashton could see. 'Here, just to the right of Dorothy's ear.'

'Everything's almost exactly as it was aside from a few of the flowers.' Elsie sighed. 'I used to sit by that rockery and have lunch when I was working at the hotel. Those were such good days...' She sighed and moved closer as sunlight picked out the white feather and pink highlights in her powdery hair.

'It's like I've stepped back fifty years.' Jessie's grandfather gazed around before staring back at the house. 'Dorothy and I stayed in that room for a full two weeks. I used to have so many pictures of the view.' He pointed towards the house to a pretty veranda on the ground floor with tall glass doors. They were open, and sheer white curtains billowed in the breeze. It was exactly like the photo George had shown Jessie a few nights before.

Elsie nodded. 'That was the honeymoon suite. Gorgeous room. Sadly, no one uses it now, but I've been opening the windows every day to air it while I've been staying. My bedroom's on the same floor. I'm a bit further towards the front of the house so I don't get woken by Peaches in the morning. Ashton says he's like a sergeant major on speed.' She giggled.

'Dorothy was an early riser, but I like to sleep in too.' Jessie's grandad smiled, still looking towards the room. 'I can't believe I'm here.' He studied the photo. 'You have no idea how much it means.'

Elsie scratched a hand across her chin. 'This might sound a little odd, but why don't you come back one night for a sleepover?' Jessie glanced at Ashton who was staring at the older woman, his eyes huge. 'You could stay in the same room,' she continued. 'I know it might be bittersweet, but being here reminds me of so many good times.'

Jessie was about to refuse, but her grandfather's eyes glistened and he gazed longingly back towards the house. 'I'd love that.' He sighed. 'Just for one night. I could sit out here and watch the sun set. Jessie, we could use that time to retake all the photos I lost so we don't have to rush today.'

'And I could cook us a meal, just like I did when I worked here.' Elsie jiggled on her feet. 'This will be so wonderful.' She clapped her hands. 'We can talk about everything we remember. It's been such a long time since I've had more than Ashton to cook for. You must promise to stay too.' She turned towards Jessie. 'There's plenty of space upstairs. All of the rooms have been redecorated, but it's essentially the same – soft beds, en suites with gorgeous views.' She waved her arms enthusiastically. 'That's okay, isn't it?' She turned and winked at Ashton who sighed, then shrugged.

'It's a big house.' He frowned. 'I'll probably be working anyway.'

'Stay on Friday!' Elsie said excitedly. 'That'll give me time to get everything together for a meal and we can meet at The Puzzle Club that morning so I can introduce you to some of its members. Ashton will drive me back here so I can prepare for your visit and then you can come around five o'clock?'

Jessie shook her head. 'I really don't need to stay. I could drop Grandad here and pick him up the following morning, drive you both to The Beach Café?' She couldn't imagine anything worse than hanging about for even longer with Ashton, and from the expression on his face, she guessed he felt the same.

'Oh no, you must!' George said, shaking his head. 'If you don't, Jessie, I won't either. I'm not leaving you on your own. If you're uncomfortable with the idea, that's understandable and I'm sure we can get all the pictures we need today...'

Jessie knew her grandfather would give up on the sleepover if she didn't do it too, and it was obvious he was desperate to spend more time at Look Out House.

'It's okay.' She tipped a shoulder. 'I appreciate the offer – as long as we're not going to be in the way.'

'We'd love the company, wouldn't we, Ashton?' Elsie said gaily with a hint of mischief in her eyes. 'This house is meant to be filled with people. It would be wonderful to have you both overnight.'

'Wonderful...' Ashton echoed, his tone dull.

George began to walk further into the garden. 'This is so exciting; I can see a sea stack now and I'm one hundred per cent sure it's the one Dorothy had in her photos. Jessie, we must capture it while we're here.'

He drew closer to the picnic table at the edge of the lawn and pointed past the flowerbeds towards the horizon, where jagged cliffs climbed upwards from the waves and a big rocket-shaped stone soared skywards. Then he pointed back at the photo. 'See, it's all still here. I remember it never got hidden by the water, even at high tide.' He gave Jessie a sad smile. 'I'd forgotten that until now.' He tapped a finger against his fore-head. 'It's why I need my photos.'

Jessie moved so she could look at the picture too. She glanced towards Ashton and found him watching her. As soon as he realised she'd seen him, he glanced away. What had he been looking at? She quickly checked her shirt for stains and just stopped herself from picking at the collar.

'Isn't it weird how you can remember things so vividly but forget so much,' her grandfather said suddenly. 'There are prob-ably a million other places Dorothy and I went to on our honeymoon, but I only remember a few.' He shrugged. 'Shall we open that bottle of wine now and take a moment to enjoy the wonderful views?' He watched Jessie draw the glasses and chilled bottle out of the backpack.

Ashton was hovering at the corner of the table as if he wasn't sure what to do next. It was almost like the man didn't want to join in but didn't want to leave either. She nodded at one of the glasses, but he shook his head.

'I should get back to work,' he said gruffly, even though his expression suggested he'd really rather stay.

So why didn't he? Was it something to do with her? The dogs, who'd just wandered up to join them, circled Ashton's legs. Jessie watched as he turned and made his way back towards the house with all three of them following at his heels.

'Are you going to pour?' her grandfather asked, watching her thoughtfully.

'Of course,' Jessie said. She removed the cork and slowly transferred the liquid into the three glasses before handing one to Elsie and another to her grandfather.

'A toast to replacing the photos Dorothy took on our honeymoon, and to you Elsie for your wonderful hospitality.' George clinked his plastic glass against Elsie's before doing the same to Jessie. 'And to you my dearest granddaughter – let's hope this trip rekindles your love of photography and finally brings some good things into your life.'

'I'll drink to that.' Elsie raised an eyebrow at George. Then she turned her head so she could watch Ashton make his way back up the steps towards Look Out House.

8

The Beach Café was busy, and Jessie and her grandfather stood by the entrance, searching for Elsie. They'd spent the last few days at Sea Glass Cottage relaxing, avoiding the stairs and anything that might wear George out, but the journey up to the car park this morning had taken over twenty minutes and Jessie could see it had taken its toll.

'There she is!' Her grandfather suddenly waved towards the far corner where Elsie was sitting with Peaches. As they made their way towards Elsie, Jessie's stomach grumbled as she inhaled the gorgeous scent of fresh baking.

'Make yourselves comfortable and I'll bring you over some drinks,' Ella suddenly shouted from behind the counter, her red lips stretching into a wide grin. 'I made a lemon cake this morning, I'll cut you both a slice.'

'Grand,' her grandfather said, rubbing his hands together as he walked to the table closest to Elsie, pulled out a chair, and then slowly sat down. Phoebe took a moment to look around the space and then settled onto the floor underneath George's feet.

'I trust you're both packed and ready for tonight? I've got a wonderful menu planned. I chose all my favourites from when I worked at the hotel. I'm planning on cooking all afternoon after Ashton picks me up,' Elsie sang, as she placed a jigsaw piece into the carnival wheel she was working on, the cockerel bobbing its head as if congratulating her.

'Our things are all in the car ready for when we drive up later. Jessie helped me prepare last night, I can't wait,' George replied. They planned to take a walk along the waterfront this afternoon, both to reminisce about their trip with Dorothy to Indigo Cove fourteen years ago, and also to capture some photos of the views.

There were a few Jessie could remember from the honeymoon album. She was nervous about the stay and wanted to keep busy to stop her nerves from getting the better of her. She still couldn't believe she was going to spend the evening around Ashton, or sleep in his house. *It's no wonder he ran when he saw your face!*, a voice inside her head snapped, sounding remarkably like Maria's, but she brushed it aside. She was too old to let the woman's words hurt now, but being cheated on by Brendon had brought all her old insecurities bubbling to the surface again.

Elsie handed her grandfather a pile of jigsaw boxes. 'I thought you might like to make one of these up next. They're all quite complicated and good practice if you're planning on entering the Jigsaw Championships.'

'Tell me a bit more about how that works?' Jessie asked, as her grandfather began to shuffle the boxes about, considering each picture in turn.

'We work in pairs and there's enough room at The Beach Café for twenty teams.' Elsie waved a hand around the space, pointing to the busy tables and then to the patio outside. 'At the start of the event, everyone will be given a thousand-piece jigsaw and we'll all have up to five hours to complete our puzzles. The winners will be the ones who finish first. Ella's planned a wonderful spread of food and drink for all the contestants, and we've got the local press booked to take photos.' She smiled, her silver-grey eyes sparkling.

'Have you got enough teams?' Jessie asked, looking around.

Elsie screwed up her nose. 'We've got plenty of our regulars signed up, but the idea was to attract new people. Ashton put something on Instagram and Facebook, but we've not attracted a lot of interest from that. I don't think people like to admit that they're lonely...'

'I'd definitely like to enter the competition. Coming here in the mornings to do puzzles is the perfect start to the day. Dorothy and I used to pop in for cake after breakfast at the hotel, and when Jessie holidayed with us, we all came a few times,' George affectionately patted Jessie's hand. He put the boxes into a neat pile before tipping out the pieces of his chosen jigsaw, then he started to turn the bits the right way up.

'That's brilliant news,' Elsie replied.

'Who are you entering with?' Jessie asked her.

Her mouth pinched. 'I work with Peaches – but I contacted the World Jigsaw Puzzle Federation to find out if working with a cockerel is against the rules. I want to make the competition as professional as I can, that way if we get enough people, we can turn it into an annual event. If it's not okay to team up with my bird, I'll have to find a human partner, but so far I've not found anyone quick enough for me.' Her eyes slid to Jessie's grandfather as he studied his jigsaw box.

'Okay, so I'm eight-seven per cent sure I've been here.' George tapped a fingertip onto the picture on the lid. 'It's a lighthouse. I remember it, Dorothy took a photo from the top of a nearby hill.'

'I think we went somewhere close to there too.' Jessie cast her mind back to their holiday.

'I know that place. The lighthouse is still there, but it's an art gallery now,' Elsie said. 'I can show you where it is on a map. There are some amazing walks around the area. Lots of cliffs.'

She pulled a face at George. 'Although they might be tough for you to walk since you're still supposed to be taking it easy.'

'We could visit and if I can't walk to the right place, Jessie can take the pictures for me.' Her grandad's face brightened, and he began to gather the edges of his puzzle just as a woman's voice rang out from the entrance.

'Elsie, pet, you're here!'

When Jessie turned, she saw an older woman standing by the door, her grey hair tied up in a bun with a set of wooden tools poking from it. The woman strode towards them, her olive smock and bright green Dr. Martens glowing in the light that was shining through the front window. Her companion, a tall man with salt-and-pepper hair, wandered towards the counter and started to chat with Ella.

'Lila Penhaligon,' the woman announced as soon she reached them, thrusting out a hand so they could shake. 'You must be George and Jessie Levine – Elsie rang and told me all about you last night, although I knew Ella was expecting guests.' She squeezed Jessie's shoulder. 'I'm sorry to hear about your ex, but these things often have a funny way of working out.'

Jessie felt her cheeks burn, mortified that news of her heartbreak had travelled.

'So long as my granddaughter doesn't get together with another twerp,' her grandfather said, making Lila laugh out loud.

'Oh I like you.' She gave Jessie a sympathetic smile. 'I run the local neighbourhood watch, so I like to keep abreast of any longer-term arrivals, which is why I know all about your troubles.'

'Right.' Jessie cleared her throat, still feeling uncomfortable, although there was no malice in the older woman's eyes. She looked genuinely concerned.

Lila pulled up a chair at a small square table positioned close by. 'I also run The Pottery Project just outside of the village. If you fancy a spin on a pottery wheel while you're staying in Indigo Cove, I offer regular lessons. All levels of experience are welcome – we tailor the classes to our students. My granddaughter, Ruby, is running a course there this week and we're open most days. I try to sneak down to the café at least once every other morning if I can.'

The man who'd been speaking with Ella trooped across the café and pulled out the other chair on Lila's table and began to rifle though the pile of colourful puzzle boxes without introducing himself.

'This is Gryffyn Lowe, he works at The Pottery Project too – he's my partner and lover.' She winked when he made an irritated clucking sound, but he still didn't look up from the boxes. 'He's also a genius potter but needs to work a little harder on his people skills. He's my bad cop at the Pottery Project – you've probably guessed I'm the good one.'

Jessie smiled. 'I may have picked that up.'

'My people skills are fine,' the older man snapped. 'Small talk is boring, so I avoid it if I can. I'm here to do puzzles, not jabber.' He chose a jigsaw and turned the box upside down so all the parts clattered onto the table, then began to sort them into piles. 'I hope this one has all the pieces,' he huffed.

Elsie nodded. 'We've had a few with bits missing recently – all from the vintage puzzles that were donated. But I'm hoping it's just going to be the odd one. It would be a shame to throw such beautiful puzzles away, they were obviously important to someone once...' Ella brought a tray over to the table and began to lay out all the hot drinks and slabs of lemon cake, doling them out to the group.

'Do you have plans for how you'll pass the time while you're here?' Lila continued, smiling at George.

'Jessie and I want to visit the places I went to on my honeymoon. I lost the photo album from our trip, and we're going to replace the pictures I lost. Although I need to rest because I've just had a hernia operation – so if I'm not with Jessie or in Sea Glass Cottage, I'll probably spend the rest of my time here.' He looked around. 'It's nice to have company without having to make the effort to talk.'

'Exactly.' Gryffyn nodded as he organised his puzzle pieces.

'What about you?' Lila glanced at Jessie. 'What will you do while your grandad's here?'

'I'll probably explore the area by myself,' Jessie said.

'Perhaps you could take Dorothy's camera so you can see what kinds of photos you could take?' her grandfather suggested.

Lila grinned and squeezed Jessie's arm. 'What a good idea. You'll probably find out all sorts of things about yourself. Whenever I get on the pottery wheel, I never quite know where I'll end up. It's like a voyage of self-discovery.' She leaned forward. 'If you want any advice on where to go while you're in Indigo Cove, you let me know.'

Lila suddenly glanced towards the entrance and her face lit up. 'Darren Dean!' she boomed, as a lanky boy with jet-black hair sauntered into the café with his hands in the pockets of his jeans. As soon as he spotted Lila, his cheeks flushed bright pink. 'Come.' The older woman waved him over, waiting while the teenager studied them without moving.

'What are you waiting for, boy – Halloween?' Gryffyn barked. 'We've missed you at The Pottery Project. You haven't been for the last three weeks.' His forehead pinched.

'Gryffyn, Lila and a couple of others run a Youth Club for teenagers at The Pottery Project on Thursday afternoons,' Elsie explained. 'The kids around here have really taken to it. Darren was one of the founding members, he did a course with Lila last year. He's very talented, apparently.' She sighed.

The young boy wandered slowly towards them, keeping his hands in his pockets. 'My dad wants me to spend more time working on my maths over the summer. He wants me to study statistics at university.' He frowned. 'You know he thinks art is a waste of time.'

'Ah.' Gryffyn looked up, his blue eyes piercing. 'But what do you think?'

'I'm not sure what I think matters...' The teen shrugged, studying the picture Gryffyn was assembling.

Gryffyn sighed. 'Sometimes, you have to take a stand, be your own person.' His voice was kind. 'Only you're going to know what fits you best.'

'Dunno if taking a stand would help, I think Dad just wants a clone of himself.' Darren cleared his throat. 'Can I do that with you?' He pointed to the puzzle and pulled up a chair from one of the tables, taking a seat. 'I used to love jigsaws when I was younger,' he confided. 'Even Dad enjoys them. He says they expand the mind – unlike art.'

He plonked his elbows onto the table so he could examine the pieces, then rested his chin in his palms. If Jessie had to guess she'd have aged Darren at around seventeen. She recognised the expression – he was still young enough to be vulnerable, but old enough to want to hide the fact.

'You know you're welcome to come to the pottery club again whenever you get the time,' Lila soothed, reaching out to squeeze the young boy's arm.

He grunted his agreement and gulped without looking up. 'I don't know at the moment, I'm really not that good at maths, so I probably should spend my spare time working on it.'

'I used to teach it at Oxford University a long time ago,' Jessie's grandad said, raising an eyebrow at the boy who stared at him with wide eyes. 'If you want to bring any of your work to the café, I can look over it for you, or if you need anything explaining, I'm ninety-nine per cent sure I can help. We're hoping to be here most mornings for the next few weeks, assuming I can handle the stairs up from our accommodation.'

The young man pursed his lips, but Jessie detected a spark

of interest in his eyes. 'I am a bit stuck on geometry,' he admitted.

'Ah!' Her grandfather clapped his hands. 'That just happens to be one of my favourite subjects. I'm one hundred per cent sure I can help you with that!'

Elsie grinned at George. 'You remind me of my late husband Jeff, he loved numbers. He always used to help Ashton when he got stuck. Not that the boy did that often – except with his English homework. He never was that good at expressing himself. He was a genius, though, even then.' She puffed out her chest. 'Took us a while to discover it – then again, most things worth knowing take time.' Beside her, Lila nodded.

Jessie reached under the table to scratch Phoebe's ears and leaned back in her chair listening to the various exchanges. The café was busy with people eating, talking and doing puzzles, and Jessie felt instantly comfortable here. No one cared about her huge feet, crooked nose, or that her ex had cheated on her – aside from offering sympathy – and for the first time in a long time she let herself relax.

9

———————

Elsie had obviously been eagerly waiting for them to arrive at Look Out House because when Jessie drove up to the gates, they swept open as soon as the Ford Anglia approached.

'Gosh, I've been so excited about you coming. Once you left The Beach Café, Ashton picked me up and I've been cooking ever since,' she enthused, as Jessie pulled the car up in front of the building beside where Elsie was standing.

The tiny dachshund Murphy immediately jumped up to welcome her and Phoebe, while Bear held back, clearly too exhausted to relocate from his warm spot on the porch. His tail wagged when the younger retriever went to sniff his nose.

'Ashton's in a meeting at the moment, but your rooms are all made up. Grab your bags and I'll take you to them. I've got such an exciting evening planned!'

'I've been looking forward to it,' Jessie's grandfather said.

Jessie held her breath. After they'd left The Beach Café and the day had gone on, she'd started feeling increasingly nervous about seeing Ashton again. She had planned to do everything she could to stay out of his way – and hoped to shut herself away in her bedroom. But she could already tell her grandfather and Elsie wouldn't allow that. This was going to feel like a long visit. Her only hope was Ashton would be too busy to join them.

She picked up her overnight bag from the back seat and tried to take her grandad's too, but he tugged it away and carried it himself. They followed Elsie as she marched ahead into the beautiful hallway of Look Out House, then through a large white door which led into a long corridor with occasional tables set on either side. Huge vases displayed bouquets of pink summer flowers, which perfumed the air with a myriad of fragrances.

'Beautiful flowers,' Jessie remarked.

'I've been putting them out while I've been staying here. There's something so wonderful about the smell, isn't there?' Elsie asked and continued walking, so she didn't see Jessie nod. It didn't surprise her that Ashton wasn't responsible for the displays – he didn't strike her as the type of person who'd invest energy in making things look nice.

'My room's that way,' Elsie said, pointing back towards the front of the house. 'The honeymoon suite is in the opposite direction.' She headed left and strode past two glossy white doors which were both shut. The shiny silver door plaques on them read *High Tide* and *Sea View*. 'Those are both double rooms, but no one's staying in them at the moment – Ashton doesn't normally have guests,' she explained.

'Colour me surprised,' Jessie muttered under her breath, but an amused look from Elsie made her wonder if the retiree had heard.

'This one is your room.' Elsie grinned at George, throwing open the door to a suite titled *The Honeymooner* to reveal an enormous bedroom with a six-foot-wide four-poster bed dominating the centre. It was flanked by two silver bedside cabinets, and a redwood antique wardrobe which took up most of the far wall. To their left, huge windows had been propped open leading to a small veranda with two chairs, while floaty white curtains flapped in the barely-there breeze.

Phoebe immediately started to explore, sniffing the floors and rugs, perhaps searching for evidence of the other two dogs.

'It's hardly changed,' George said, his voice reverent, as he slowly made his way towards the open doors and set his overnight bag onto the floor, carefully twisting around so he could take in the whole space. He reached into the pocket of his trousers and pulled out the picture of Dorothy standing by the window, then propped it onto one of the bedside cabinets. 'We'll need to take some photos here later, Jess,' he said, his voice filled with emotion.

Elsie studied him and nodded. 'Why don't I show you your room, Jessie, and George can get himself settled? I'm guessing he might want some time to be alone with his thoughts. Phoebe will be here to keep him company,' she said quietly.

Jessie noticed her grandad swallow – she suspected he was finding it difficult to talk.

'I do respect a man who's in touch with his feelings,' Elsie said gaily, as she led Jessie back through the hallway and up the wide staircase. 'I know it's more common these days, but the only man who ever showed me how he felt was Jeff. I still miss that openness...'

Jessie followed Elsie onto a wide landing, which overlooked the hallway and front door.

'Ashton's bedroom is down there,' Elsie said, pointing towards a doorway further along the landing. 'Your room is above your grandad's.' Elsie swept her along the corridor until they were a further three doorways along. 'I gave you my favourite one,' she confided, opening a white panelled door. 'It's called "The Retreat". If it wasn't for my bad knees, I'd be sleeping in here myself. Though this one overlooks the back garden, so you'll hear Peaches in the morning... he has been known to wake up at 5 a.m.' She grimaced. 'I've got earplugs if you need some?'

'I'll be fine, thanks. I'm an early riser,' Jessie replied, watching Murphy as he suddenly appeared at the top of the stairs and flew into the bedroom ahead of them, his long ears flapping as he made his way towards the window, sniffing everything in his path.

The room was beautiful with polished oak floors scattered with soft white rugs. She spun around, taking in the flowers on the dressing table, various toiletries and the romance novel that sat on the bedside table beside an elegant lamp. All homely touches that she guessed Elsie was responsible for.

'Take off your shoes and sink your toes into the rugs,' Elsie demanded, kicking off her slippers and wriggling her feet into the soft wool. 'I found these for Ashton in a craft shop in Talwynn – that's our nearest large town,' she explained.

Jessie pushed her sandals off and snuggled her toes into the material, almost groaning with pleasure. 'I might just stay here all evening,' she joked.

She put her bag onto the large bed and moved so she could study the intricately carved headboard. Some of it was hidden by a swathe of squashy coral pillows and cushions. Then she walked to the floor-to-ceiling window opposite the bed and the stunning view showcasing the lush green lawn which was flanked by neat borders of vibrant rhododendrons, hydrangeas, foxgloves and sweet William interspersed between leafy shrubs. In the distance, she could see the horizon: white crests of waves frolicked on the surface of the sea. The sun was still high and tiny clouds drifted across the sky.

Jessie tore her gaze away from the view, spotting a high-backed armchair set to the right of the window where she hoped she'd be able to spend time reading later this evening – if her grandad and Elsie would let her escape.

'The bathroom is through there.' Elsie swept a hand to the

opposite side of the room. 'There's a bath and walk-in shower. You'll find towels and almost every type of toiletry you could want. It's the best bathtub in the house – don't tell George,' she whispered, grinning.

'Thank you,' Jessie said. 'You've gone to so much trouble.'

Elsie shrugged. 'I'm excited to have you staying.' Her expression dimmed. 'Look Out House is a special place. I worked at the hotel for almost twenty years. When Ashton was younger, he'd often visit in the afternoons so he could do his homework while I was working. When the hotel came on the market four years ago, I was afraid someone would buy it and knock the whole thing down.' Her chest heaved. 'There are so many memories in these walls, I'd hate to lose any of them. I'm just lucky Ashton decided to buy it. I'm pretty sure he did it for me.' She paused. 'He's a good man.'

Jessie fixed her lips together because she wasn't going to argue. Whatever she thought about Ashton Reynolds, he was clearly kind to Elsie, which made her feelings about him more confused.

'I'll leave you to settle in,' the older woman continued. 'If you can meet me at six in the garden, we'll be having old fashioned cocktails and the nibbles I used to make for guests.' She smiled. 'We'll move into the main dining room for the rest of our meal. I've gone full on retro for your grandad: prawn cocktail, followed by chicken à la king and rum baba.' She wriggled her fingers. 'All made by my own fair hands.'

'Sounds wonderful. Can I do anything to help?' Jessie asked.

Elsie shook her head. 'I haven't entertained in years, having you here is such a treat. I love this place, but it can feel a little empty sometimes...' She looked around.

'Is there a dress code?' Jessie asked. She'd packed a silver maxi dress and sandals – which Rose had helped her to pick out for her honeymoon months before – just in case Elsie wanted them to be glamorous. She hadn't intended to wear it when she'd packed for the trip. Usually, she wore trousers and a blouse on an evening out – she preferred clothes that helped her to fade into the background. But after everything that had happened with Brendon, after seeing Ashton again, something inside her was telling her to go all out. She'd even packed her make-up and she rarely bothered with that.

'Smart-casual,' Elsie said. 'I like to dress up, so I've ironed a special frock. The dogs are wearing bow ties and I've told Ashton to wear a shirt.' Her eyes glittered. 'The boy's a knock-out when he tries, but he doesn't do it often enough.'

She nodded to the bathroom. 'Take a bath and relax. I want you to enjoy your visit – it's been a long time since I got to make a fuss of guests.' She turned and practically skipped out of the room with Murphy, shutting the door and leaving Jessie alone.

Jessie made her way back to the window, then looked down into the gardens. This time she spotted Ashton standing at the corner of the grass. He was gazing at the sea. What was he thinking?

Jessie shook her head and stepped back from the window in case he spotted her, before heading into the bathroom. Pausing at the doorway, she took in the huge claw-foot bath and fluffy white towels. Elsie had left out a basket of toiletries, including a stack of fragrant bath bombs. She turned on the taps and popped a lavender one into the water and undressed before sinking into the warmth. It felt good not to be in Sea Glass Cottage – to be away from all those feelings of rejection that had been haunting her since she'd moved into the honeymoon suite.

She could do one night here for her grandad, dress up and play nice. Ashton would probably spend the evening trying to avoid her. Perhaps he'd go to bed early, paving the way for her to leave her grandad and Elsie alone to reminisce? She nodded to

herself, feeling more relaxed, and then leaned back and shut her
eyes.

Ashton and Elsie were waiting with the two dogs at the table by
the cliffs when Jessie made her way to the gardens at six o'clock.
She was followed by George and Phoebe, and the retriever
immediately scampered towards Bear. The sun was still high,
but there was enough shade on the lawn that they wouldn't get
too hot.

Her heart beat a little faster as she approached – she could
see Ashton had dressed up in a dark blue shirt and black
trousers, which fitted him perfectly. He watched as they drew
closer and everything inside her began to spark. She wore the
silky silver dress that skimmed her ankles and a pair of flat
sandals because she was always so conscious of her height.

'Oh look at you both!' Elsie gushed, rising as they
approached. She was wearing a floaty pink dress which
matched her candyfloss hair. Elsie swept an arm towards the
table, which was covered in a starched linen cloth, with a large
jug, five lowball glasses and silver platters of food. 'I taught
Ashton how to make an old fashioned earlier. He was always a
quick study.' She beamed at him. 'Please help yourselves to
olives, cheese and pineapple sticks – there are cocktail onions
too.'

'I'll have all of them,' George said, immediately digging in as
the younger man rose and started to pour from the jug.

'There's a glass for Dorothy,' Elsie said, beaming. 'I thought
we could toast her first.'

Jessie's grandad nodded and swallowed. 'That's thoughtful
of you. I'm a hundred per cent sure she's looking down on us
now.' He looked up into the sky and waved.

'I'm sure she is too,' Jessie agreed, enjoying the glow in her
grandad's eyes. He'd definitely been more chatty and happier

since arriving in Indigo Cove, but there was a marked difference in him since they'd arrived at Look Out House. Hopefully, if they replaced the pictures in his honeymoon album, he'd be able to take the new lightness home. She waited while Ashton handed out the glasses.

'To Dorothy.' George tipped his drink towards a small white cloud just as it drifted over them.

'To Dorothy.' Elsie and Jessie did the same. Jessie could see Ashton watching them from the corner of her eye and saw him lift his glass and toast too. For a crazy moment, she wished she'd brought the camera and captured it.

'That cocktail is surprisingly good for someone who'd rather have a desk in his sitting room than a bar,' her grandad said after taking a small sip.

'When Ashton puts his mind to something, he usually excels at it,' Elsie said, her chest puffing out.

Ashton didn't say anything, but Jessie saw the tips of his cheeks turn pink and couldn't help being charmed by his embarrassment – it made him more approachable somehow.

'Oh!' Elsie frowned as she took in the table. 'I forgot the mini sausages.' She looked flustered. 'I'll have to go and get them.'

'I'll go,' Ashton offered, rising from his chair a little too quickly, but Elsie shook her head.

'I'll do it. George, why don't you join me?' Elsie waggled her eyebrows, making Jessie's stomach lurch.

'I can go,' she offered, but Elsie frowned.

'Your grandad will be fine with me,' Elsie insisted, her eyes shifting between Jessie and Ashton.

Jessie knew her cheeks had started to burn when her grandad stood and the pair tracked towards the house with the three dogs following.

'I think Elsie's trying to set us up,' she confided, feeling awkward in case Ashton thought she had anything to do with it.

'Wouldn't be the first time.' Ashton turned to look at the view, sipping his cocktail before resting it back on the table. The air grew oddly charged. Jessie could feel a question creeping up the inside of her throat and tried to supress it. She took a large sip of her cocktail, and reached for an onion and popped it into her mouth.

Ashton turned and watched as she chewed and wrinkled her nose. She met his eyes as she swallowed. 'Insurance. In case you decide you want to lock lips with me again,' she said, aiming to clear the air with a joke.

Ashton chuckled loudly and shook his head, the corners of his eyes creasing. 'I remember you were funny.' He pulled his sunglasses off so Jessie could see his eyes. She couldn't tell what he was thinking, but his pupils had swelled, cloaking his irises.

'Do you remember why you ran too?' she asked, feeling her stomach knot.

'It had nothing to do with you,' he said gruffly.

She narrowed her eyes. 'Except you sprinted away seconds after you saw my face. What was it that scared you?' She traced a finger from the top of her nose to the tip. Once, when she'd been learning how to apply make-up, she'd tried to disguise it until she realised there wasn't enough foundation or contour powder in the world for it.

Ashton's eyes widened. 'It had nothing to do with how you looked,' he spluttered, shaking his head. 'You thought it was something to do with your nose?'

'What was I supposed to think?' Jessie asked, leaning forward, keeping her voice low. She shouldn't have started this, but being close to Ashton had brought it all back and she wanted him to admit it. To admit he hadn't liked what he'd seen. Perhaps because then she'd finally have the answer to why he'd run? She wasn't sure why she needed to know, perhaps she was just so used to being eviscerated?

Brendon might have stamped all over her heart, but there

was clearly enough life left in it for Ashton to finish it off. Maybe then she'd stop having all these... feelings for him.

Jessie could hear the chatter of Elsie's voice in the background and knew the two would be returning from the kitchen and joining them soon, knew she couldn't continue the conversation once they had.

'You were kissing me,' she said, her eyes boring into his. 'You pulled away, took one look at my face in the moonlight and ran. I'm not sure how else I was supposed to interpret it?' She could feel her cheeks burning as emotion heated inside her. It had been a defining moment in her life, a punctuation point in her belief that Maria had been right. Jessie could hardly believe she was talking about it now. She should have put it behind her long ago, but she had to have the conversation, had to know so she finally could draw a line under it at last.

Ashton shook his head slowly. 'That's crazy. I thought you were beautiful.'

Jessie angled an eyebrow. 'Of course you did.'

His cheeks pinked. 'I thought... think you're very attractive.' He picked up his drink and sunk the whole thing, still shaking his head. 'You told me you felt like a misfit and we connected. I wanted to kiss you, it was as simple as that. There are all kinds of beautiful, you know...'

Jessie flushed because the words affected her, and she didn't want them to. 'I don't want your compliments. I'm old enough to know what I am and to have learned to accept it. I just...' She exhaled loudly and looked towards the house to where George and Elsie were now heading down the stone steps, then stepping onto the grass with Murphy, Bear and Phoebe. 'It doesn't matter.' When she turned back, she saw something in Ashton's face she couldn't read.

'I...' He suddenly seemed to lose his puff. It was like he was seeing the situation properly for the first time.

'Here we are!' Elsie cooed, plonking a plate of cocktail

sausages with toothpicks poking from them onto the table. 'Dig in – but don't eat too much, there's a lot more to come.'

'There is,' her grandfather gushed, rubbing his stomach. 'Elsie gave me a preview of our meal in the kitchen.' He exhaled happily. 'Let's just say we won't be needing breakfast – and if you've brought an extra stomach, it might be worth unpacking it now.' He put the photo of Dorothy onto the table and placed the extra cocktail Ashton had poured on top. 'Time for another toast, I think. Here's to love.' His eyes shifted from Jessie to Ashton. 'And to the finding of it.' He finished raising his glass and toasting Dorothy, Elsie, Jessie and then Ashton.

'I'll drink to that!' Elsie said, chuckling and drinking her cocktail in one, humming with pleasure as her eyes slid from Ashton to Jessie then back. 'This is so good – I've not had one of those in years and now I don't know why not. My second husband used to adore them, but he never put enough whisky in.'

She grinned and patted George on the shoulder, leaning towards him and almost tipping her chair. 'I'm so glad you're here. I can't tell you how wonderful it is to have company of my own age. Ashton is a dear.' She gave him an indulgent smile. 'But try talking to the boy about anything before Tamagotchis, hip hop music and Harry Potter books and he doesn't have a clue. Then again, I'm sure he feels the same...' She shook her head as the man in question choked on his drink. 'George wants to visit the lighthouse that was pictured on his puzzle. We can go to the gallery in the morning,' she said to Ashton with mischief in her eyes.

He nodded, looking confused. 'And?'

'I thought we could head there before Jessie and George move back to Sea Glass Cottage. It's a Saturday, so we could all drive up in your car – I presume you don't have to work? Why don't we pop in after breakfast?' Elsie pressed before Ashton could open his mouth. She glanced at Jessie. 'The lighthouse has only recently opened to the public. Someone bought it last year, and they sell local art. We could pop in, and you could walk to where your grandparents picnicked and take some photos. Maybe we can persuade Phoebe, Murphy and Bear to have a run?'

'How about I stay behind and take the dogs to the beach so they don't get in the way?' Ashton offered.

Elsie narrowed her eyes. 'It'll be a lot easier if you drive us all in your Land Rover.' She smiled sweetly and, despite the fluffy pink hair and small frame, she reminded Jessie of a sergeant major. 'I remember taking you up there for the first time when you were sixteen. It was still a working lighthouse. That look on your face. You'd lived in Indigo Cove your whole life, but you'd never once just stopped and enjoyed a view.' She grinned and the younger man flushed.

'It was pretty good,' he said quietly.

Jessie wondered why Ashton hadn't visited before that. Had it been something to do with his parents? She knew very little about the man, and a part of her suddenly wished she knew more.

'Dorothy and I definitely went.' George bobbed his head.

'Then that's decided. Come on, get stuck in.' Elsie pointed to the plates of snacks as she took in both their faces and frowned. 'Have another cocktail. This evening is all about relaxing and reminiscing.' She flashed a smile at George. 'Talking of walking down memory lane, didn't you say you wanted to see the foxgloves?' Elsie jerked her head towards the right of the garden and winked. 'There's a fabulous display in the flowerbed over there.' She rose again and held out her arm. 'Let's go before it gets dark.'

When Jessie started to get up, Elsie shook her head. 'Not you. You stay with Ashton.' Elsie gave George a sober stare.

'It won't be dark for ages.' George reached for a handful of cheese and pineapple sticks, looking confused.

'I really think we should go now,' Elsie insisted, widening her eyes.

Her grandfather looked at Elsie for a moment, then he glanced at Jessie before his eyes slid to Ashton and he dipped his chin. '*Ahhh.* You'd better not be another *nitwit*,' he growled, rising and hooking an arm through Elsie's offered elbow. 'We won't be long, so don't do anything I wouldn't,' he added sternly, following Elsie along the grass.

Ashton picked up the jug of old fashioned and filled Jessie's glass. Then he poured the final dribble into his own and drank it down in one. 'Well...'

'Yep.' Jessie nodded as she watched the couple who were now a few metres away. Her grandad kept glancing back at them, clearly making sure Jessie was okay. 'Don't make any sudden moves in my direction – we're being watched,' she whispered.

Ashton didn't laugh. Instead, he gazed at her. 'I was very mixed up that night. It wasn't you—'

'Please don't embarrass us both by finishing the "it's not you, it's me" excuse,' Jessie snapped. 'Let's just move on.' She shook her head, irritated. 'The earth didn't stop spinning on its axis when you ran. I don't even know why I remembered that day.'

She did, and it was obvious enough that Ashton's rejection had hurt, but she didn't want to be humiliated any more. Had no idea why she'd expected a resolution or answers because they might make her feel better? Fix whatever was broken inside? That was stupid and childish. She had wounds, and it wasn't Ashton's job to mend them. She was going to have to do that for herself. Being in Indigo Cove was the first step to doing that. Perhaps the first phase of taking charge of the rest of her life?

Jessie began to rise, feeling weary. 'Please can you tell Elsie I have a headache?'

Ashton reached out a hand and placed his palm over hers. 'Don't. Please,' he said ardently. 'I'm sorry I upset you and I understand.' He cleared his throat. 'I don't even blame you for wanting to leave. But Elsie has been cooking all day and she'll be hurt.' His eyes bored into hers until she nodded and sat.

'You're right,' she sighed, shaking herself out of her mood as she looked around the garden. 'Fine, I'll stay.'

'Thank you...' He paused. 'I was worried if you left, I'd have no one to talk to about Tamagotchis.' He gave her a half-smile that suggested the joke was an attempt to clear the air.

Jessie took in a deep breath, grounding herself. 'Well, I know next to nothing about them, so you'll be doing all the talking.'

Ashton smiled. 'That's okay, I could probably bore you on that particular subject for hours.' He paused. 'Thank you for staying and for being so...' He spread his palms.

She shrugged. 'It's okay.' It would be so much easier to dislike Ashton if he didn't care so much about Elsie. Even easier if he didn't look quite so good in that shirt. Jessie let her eyes trace the stubble on his chin and the dark patch of hair that peeked from the top of his collar before jerking her eyes back up as Elsie and George came to hover beside the table.

'Ready to move into the dining room?' Elsie asked, pointing towards the house.

'Of course,' Jessie said, watching as her grandfather took the older woman's arm and started to lead her towards Look Out House.

Jessie rose and glanced at Ashton who was watching her with an odd expression. Something in her chest squeezed and she shook her head. She had to keep her head – she wasn't looking for romance or connection, especially not with the very first man who'd broken her heart.

10

'Cock-a-doodle-do!' Peaches shrieked gleefully, hopping his way across the lawn and probably waking every one of Ashton's neighbours within half a mile.

Ashton swiped a hand across his bare chest and took a long sip of strong black coffee as he stood gazing at nothing at all. He hadn't slept, so had got up early and pulled on a pair of loose sweats so he could watch the waves ripple on the sea and pace the garden. He'd spent too many hours staring at the ceiling last night as he'd thought about what Jessie had said to him the night before.

Despite Elsie's attempts to leave them alone together multiple times during the evening, the younger woman had managed to avoid him, then had made her excuses before retiring. Ashton shook his head, casting his mind back to that fateful night fourteen years ago, wondering how Jessie had got things so wrong. He'd been kissing her, losing himself in those soft lips, then he'd pulled back and looked into her face. When he'd seen the need in her eyes and recognised the returning call in his chest, he'd run. After seeing the disaster that was his parents' marriage, he wasn't prepared to feel those things for anyone, ever. He'd been too young to think too much about how she might have felt. He'd assumed Jessie would have decided it was just a lucky escape from a bit of a weirdo.

Guilt churned in his gut as he wondered how he could make it up to her. He wasn't used to feeling wrong-footed, probably because he did his best to avoid getting close to anyone, but he was going to have to explain himself or it wouldn't feel right.

He heard the squeak of a shutter opening and twisted around to see Jessie standing by her bedroom window in a pair of short silky pyjamas that almost took his breath away. She was scrutinising the sea with a sad look on her face, and for a nanosecond, Ashton wished he could ask her what was wrong before choking down the thought. He turned back towards the view, aiming to remain as still as possible so she wouldn't spot him.

'Am I supposed to call you Romeo?' Jessie suddenly enquired. Ashton looked up to see her head poking from the open window above.

He cleared his throat. 'I'm not climbing up a drainpipe if that's what you mean.' Even if it might go some way towards making things up to her.

Jessie gave him a sad smile. 'They do say romance is dead – I for one think they might be right.'

'Was it ever alive?' He grumbled. 'If you come downstairs, I'll make coffee. That's my best offer at this time of the day.'

She patted a hand against her chest and let out a swooning sound. 'As offers go, I think that might be the best I've heard in a while. Give me a minute,' she added, before disappearing.

Ashton forced away the smile working its way onto his face. Murphy barked beside his feet and Bear wandered up to check what was going on before flopping back onto the grass. 'If you can find Phoebe, we'll all go running in a minute,' he warned and was rewarded with a couple of loud doggy groans.

Jessie beat Ashton to the kitchen because he needed to

change clothes. She'd put on a skirt and T-shirt in record time and was leaning against one of the black marble counters, waiting for the kettle she'd put on to boil. 'I thought you'd made another run for it, so decided I'd better start without you.'

Jessie watched as he switched off the kettle and unhooked the water container from his fancy coffee machine.

'Sorry,' she said quietly, when he didn't respond. 'I know that joke's getting old. I often say the wrong thing when I'm nervous – and if I'm honest, I say the wrong thing most of the time. I told you last night that I didn't want to hear your explanation and I still think that's for the best.'

Ashton turned towards Jessie, but she'd already spun away and was pacing the kitchen in her bare feet, running fingertips over the countertops and chrome fittings. She was so tall, almost regal, with long limbs that were effortlessly graceful. She looked good in a skirt, her legs tanned and toned.

'This kitchen is really wonderful,' she said, stopping to admire one of the grey shaker-style cupboard doors.

'The whole thing is Elsie's design.' Ashton shrugged. 'Everything was so old when I bought the building, it was falling apart, so I had to replace it. Elsie took one look in the showroom and fell in love with those cabinets, chose a cooker and fridge to go with it – then spotted the accessories. He groaned. 'After that, I was toast...' He smiled at the memory: the man who'd been serving them had actually skipped on his way to the card machine.

'You're good to her,' Jessie said, watching him carefully. 'Seems a little out of character.'

'What, for a heartless Lothario who used to lurk on beaches to break the hearts of teenage girls?' he asked dryly.

Jessie flushed and pushed a lock of wavy hair from her eyes. It was the first time Ashton had seen her wear it down – it was a pretty shade, with highlights crossing the colour spectrum from brown to blonde. He suspected her hair colour was natural, and that Jessie probably had no idea how lovely it was.

She folded her arms. 'Sorry, that was rude. You'll have to forgive me, it's been a bad month and I've lost what filter I usually have.'

'Why?' Ashton asked, turning back to finish making their coffees before handing her a mug. Jessie took it and wrapped her hands around the bone-china, drawing his attention to her long, slim fingers and neat, unpainted nails.

She stared at him for a minute. 'I'm supposed to be on my honeymoon. I'm guessing Elsie didn't share that news with you?'

Ashton shook his head, shocked. 'What happened to your groom?' he asked.

She sipped some of the coffee, then nodded her approval, and something inside his belly skipped. 'He was having an affair...' Her shoulders sank and Jessie swallowed. Even from where he was standing, Ashton could see her eyes had filled. She looked down into the drink, clearly fighting back tears, making everything inside him go cold and then hot.

'How long were you together?' he asked gruffly, because he wasn't sure what else to ask.

'Six years.' Jessie blinked. 'I didn't realise he was unhappy. I had no idea...'

'Were you happy?' Ashton asked gently.

Jessie pressed down on her bottom lip, and it was obvious she'd never asked herself that question. 'I... I don't know. Maybe... at least at first.' She sighed, her forehead pinching. 'Perhaps not so much in the last few years.'

'So that's it, it's over?' he probed, his stomach knotting as he waited for her to respond. His reactions made no sense to him – it wasn't like he cared.

She nodded. 'The funny thing is, I think Brendon thought I'd just forgive him and stay friends. He honestly couldn't fathom why I wouldn't. I actually think he thought I was lucky to be near him in any way.' Her voice lifted at the end, and Ashton could hear raw emotion in her tone.

He normally ran the other way when people began to unload, but he found himself rooted to the spot, found he wanted to know more. 'That's... really...' he murmured, feeling anger sweep from his toes to the top of his head, prickling his skin. It was as unexpected as it was unwanted and he tamped it down.

Jessie snorted out a laugh and nodded. 'It really is. I don't think I could have put that better myself.' Her eyes met his, and her smile was endearingly lopsided. 'I was coping well with everything, but then I arrived in Indigo Cove and one of the first people I bumped into was the boy who kissed me when I was seventeen and ran off. It was an old wound I thought had healed...' She screwed up her nose. 'What's the opposite of serendipity?'

'Life,' Ashton said, taking a long sip of his drink.

She nodded. 'You really are a soppy romantic, aren't you?' she teased.

He put his mug onto the counter and folded his arms. 'I'm going to tell you once and for all: the way I behaved then really had nothing to do with you. I was in a bad place.' He nodded, not used to explaining himself, but after everything Jessie had just confessed, he knew he had to. 'You... affected me.'

'How?' She tilted an eyebrow but didn't look particularly concerned.

Ashton frowned. 'I think I liked you a little too much. My parents were...' He took a deep breath. 'Let's just say being around them didn't give me the best insight into how healthy relationships work.' He sighed. 'And suddenly I had this girl in my arms and I was kissing her and I wanted to kiss her more. I didn't like the way you made me feel. At the time, running seemed like the best way of dealing with it.' He paused, looking for the right words to explain himself and came up empty. 'I was an idiotic teenage boy. That's really my only excuse.'

Jessie stood looking at him for a moment and something flickered across her face. Ashton wondered if she was going to smile and hoped she would, hoped she'd forgive him.

'And that's it?' she asked, staring at him. 'I've got to say I wasn't expecting that.' Jessie screwed up her nose. 'What happened dented my confidence, now you're saying it had nothing to do with me?' She linked her fingers when he nodded. 'That's going to take some time to process.'

'I'm sorry,' Ashton said quietly, meaning it.

'Tell me how you'd deal with it now?' she asked finally.

Ashton shoved his hands into the pockets of his jeans. 'Oh, I'd probably kiss you again.' He watched her eyes widen. 'But I'd run faster next time.' The smile she finally gave him made everything inside him sing. 'Is there any way I can make it up to you?' he asked, wondering why making Jessie feel better was starting to matter to him so much. Perhaps he just felt guilty and wanted to put things right?

'Nope.' Jessie blinked and her blue eyes bored into his. 'You'd really kiss me again?' She sounded so surprised.

He took a step forward. 'I really would.' His voice deepened and he wondered what she'd do if he pressed his lips against hers now. Would she taste the same: like candyfloss and lemon, that odd mix of sweet and sharp?

'Are you two almost ready to go to the lighthouse?' Elsie asked suddenly from the kitchen door, breaking whatever spell had started to weave its way between them.

Ashton took a step away from Jessie. He'd been so close to finding out.

11

The Lighthouse Gallery had high ceilings and the walls had been painted a soft green colour. Hundreds of photos and paintings in various sizes filled every available space. Each piece had a small placard underneath giving its name and details about the artist, along with the price.

'I remember that view!' George said, admiring a pencil drawing of a bench underneath a tree that faced rolling hills, tall grey cliffs and the sea.

'That's Sunset Point. It's a popular place for couples.' Elsie grinned. 'I might have been there a time or two with husband number three.' She winked.

'I definitely had a photo in my album from there,' George said, looking closer. 'Is it close to Indigo Cove?'

'Just a quick hop, skip and a drive from the high street. Perhaps you could visit tomorrow?' Elsie suggested. 'If you come to the café in the morning, Lila will tell you the best place to go.'

'That's a good idea.' George looked at Jessie. 'Then we could take the camera and get some photos of the views?'

Jessie nodded.

'Oh, aren't those pictures beautiful and so clever,' Elsie gushed, stopping abruptly in front of a series of framed collages made from jigsaw pieces. 'There's a dog, and a coastline and oh, do you see that, Ashton?' She nudged him in the stomach. 'It's a plate with a cup and saucer. See here.' She pointed to the placard. 'It's called "Pieces of Cake". That picture would be perfect in The Beach Café. I'm going to buy it for Ella.' She put Peaches on her hip as she burrowed in her handbag for her purse.

'Let me get it. I've had enough free coffees from that café to buy this artwork three times over,' Ashton said. Besides, it was another small step for him reconnecting with the locals. He motioned to a salesperson at the end of the room who signalled that he could lift the picture from its spot and followed Elsie to the counter. It was crafted from a series of old oak barrels which had been painted grey. 'Could you wrap this please? It's a gift,' he asked the blue-haired woman who was serving behind it.

'Can you tell me about the artist?' Elsie asked. 'Are they local? We've got a puzzle club at a café in the village, and I was wondering if they'd like to come along.' Her smile brightened when George and Jessie wandered up to join them.

'I know he's local,' the woman said, picking up a shoe box from the floor and shuffling through an array of rectangular business cards. 'Sorry, all his cards have gone.'

'Do you know his full name?' George asked. 'It just says *AT* on the sign.'

'Yes, it's...' The woman scratched her chin. 'Art something.' She frowned. 'That's not right.' She squeezed her lips together. 'Arundel?' She made a hissing sound. 'No...'

Ashton turned the frame over and pointed to the back. 'It says Arthur Tremaine.' He peered closer. 'There's a mobile number.'

'Oh, he never answers that.' The woman waved a hand. 'I leave the man messages whenever he sells anything, but he doesn't pick them up. He usually pops in to see me every week on his tour of the local galleries. I think he enjoys the face-to-face time. Once here, he always stays for ages to chat. I don't mind. He's really very...' She raised an eyebrow suggestively at Elsie. 'Charming. Do you want me to put him in touch when he next comes in?' She took Ashton's debit card so she could ring the purchase up on the till.

'Yes please!' Elsie said. 'Or could you ask him to pop into The Beach Café by the harbour? He may not have heard about The Puzzle Club – but he could come along and see his work on display. There's always someone around to chat to.'

'No problem.' The woman nodded and handed Ashton back the card before wrapping the picture in brown paper. She picked up a black diary from the shoebox and started to write. 'The Beach Café, got it. I'll mention it the next time Arthur's here.'

'Shall we go for that walk?' Elsie asked, as Ashton picked up his purchase and put it under his arm.

'If we take it slowly, I'm at least fifty per cent sure I can make it up the hill,' George said. 'I'll recognise where Dorothy took her picture as soon as I see it.'

'Are you sure, Grandad?' Jessie took his arm. 'It's really steep and I'd probably remember it too. Didn't we walk up there when I holidayed here with you both?'

'We did, love, but we went to a different spot. I'll be okay, I'd really like to go.' He looped his arm around his granddaughter's, and they wandered through the door and collected the dogs who'd been tied up outside. Ashton put the picture into the boot of the Land Rover before following. Murphy was bouncing around like a lunatic, and Phoebe charged ahead, nudging Bear who seemed reluctant to walk at all. The air was hot, so he knew they wouldn't be able to stay out for long.

'It's not far,' Ashton assured them, taking his dogs off their leads so they could join Phoebe who was already running free.

He watched Murphy and Phoebe dart ahead of Elsie before bounding in front of Jessie and George. 'If you get to the top, I'll give you a treat,' Ashton shouted, pulling a tin from his pocket and shaking it.

Bear obviously understood because he stilled and sniffed the air, then the dog started to charge. If Ashton hadn't seen it for himself, he'd never have believed he could move so fast. He watched as Bear leaped up the path, overtaking Elsie, then charging past George and Jessie and reaching the top of the hill where he joined the other two dogs. As soon as he arrived, he began to bark.

'Now I know how to get you to run.' Ashton laughed as he caught up with Elsie and rattled the treats.

'Bear always did love his food.' Elsie chuckled. 'Jeff used to spoil him – he loved dogs.' She sighed. 'I do miss that man, I'd almost forgotten how much.' She smiled sadly, watching George as he progressed slowly up the hill beside Jessie who was hovering at his side, guarding him to make sure he didn't fall.

Elsie took the tin from Ashton and shook it too. Bear let out a sudden howl and sniffed, his eyes fixed on the treats in Elsie's hand. Murphy and Phoebe barked and began to run towards them, then Bear started to charge down the dusty pathway too – hurling himself downwards at a ridiculous speed. He sped past Murphy and Phoebe, his ears and furry belly wobbling as he sprinted at full speed. It was only when he reached the halfway point that Ashton realised that he was bearing down on Jessie and George.

'No!' Ashton yelled, seconds before the golden retriever hit them and they both went flying.

'Grandad!' Jessie cried, grabbing for the older man's hand just before he hit the ground with a sickening thump.

Bear bounded right past to Elsie, jumping up and making a grab for the tin. He almost knocked her over too, but Ashton grabbed Bear and caught him by the collar just before he did. He felt sick, what if George was badly hurt?

'Naughty boy,' Elsie admonished, before she ran towards George. Jessie had made it to her feet and Ashton watched, holding Bear back, as she knelt beside her grandad who was lying prone on the floor. She looked terrified.

'How is he?' he yelled moving closer, feeling a twinge of panic when the older man didn't move and Jessie didn't respond. Although she might not have heard him because she was too focused on her grandfather.

'Are you ok, George?' Elsie panted.

'I'm thirty-five per cent sure I am,' the older man finally assured them, his voice tense, as Ashton drew up beside him too. Ashton watched George wince as he tried to move.

'Don't get up.' Jessie brushed a hand over her grandad's arm. 'Where does it hurt?'

'Don't fuss,' the older man said, levering himself onto an elbow as Phoebe came to nudge him. 'I'm really fine. It was just a shock.' He stroked the dog, grimaced and dropped onto his back.

'What's wrong?' Elsie crouched beside him.

'My hip is hurting – I'll be fine in a minute, don't worry,' George croaked. Bear wandered up to join them and sniffed one of George's pockets. 'Sorry to disappoint.' He patted the dog's head. 'But there's no food in there.'

Ashton let out a relieved breath, amazed the older man could make a joke at a time like this.

'When we get to Look Out House, I'll pack up everything and drive us to Sea Glass Cottage so you can lie down,' Jessie promised.

'I'm not sure I'll be able to manage the steps, love,' George said, wincing.

'There's no point in your grandad moving today,' Elsie jumped in. 'He'll be more comfortable staying where he is. He can rest that hip and enjoy the views from his bedroom, you know there's plenty of room.'

'Elsie's right,' Ashton said. He was worried about George too but had to admit to himself that he might just have wanted Jessie to stay longer. He quickly brought himself back to the immediate present, aiming to work out how they might get George up. 'Does anything hurt?' he asked. 'I need to be sure before we try to move you.'

'Just my pride, son, and in truth, my hip is very sore.'

Ashton took his arm and along with Elsie and Jessie they helped the older man to his feet. He wobbled a little and Ashton tightened his grip as they tested walking. They dodged a large stone in their path, then ducked around Bear and Phoebe who were both still hovering.

'If I'm staying longer, I'll need more things,' George said, as they got to the car and Ashton opened the door and helped him inside. As soon as the older man was sitting, colour started to return to his cheeks.

'I was going to ask Ashton to drop Ella's picture into The Beach Café this afternoon,' Elsie said. 'Perhaps you could drive Jessie to Sea Glass Cottage afterwards to pick up more clothes for you both?' She raised an eyebrow.

'I'll get some stuff for Grandad, but I'd rather stay at the cottage tonight if that's okay?' Jessie asked her grandad. 'I don't like the idea of leaving it empty again just in case someone on the beach sees.'

Ashton folded his arms. It was on the tip of his tongue to tell her that it was a bad idea because he liked the idea of her being in Look Out House, but he managed to stop himself and nodded instead.

George shrugged. 'If you'd be happier there, love, but I'd like Phoebe to stay with you – it'll put my mind at rest. With any luck, I'll be able to join you tomorrow night, so it won't be for long.' He looked up the hill and pulled a face. 'We couldn't take the photo...'

'We could come back another day?' Jessie suggested.

'Why don't you do it now?' Elsie asked. 'I'll get your grandad some water, and we can sit in the car and enjoy the view. Ashton could come with you and give the dogs a longer walk. They'll only get up to more mischief if they don't run their energy off.' She pointed to Murphy and Phoebe who were still charging around them; Bear had joined in although he was panting heavily now.

'Are you sure, Grandad?' Jessie looked worried.

He nodded. 'I really want that picture, Jess, and at this rate, I might not be able to walk up that hill before the end of our holiday.' He sighed. 'If *you* take the photo, then it'll be almost the same as Dorothy doing it. You got all your talents from her...'

'Nothing I take will be as good,' Jessie warned. 'You know how rusty I am.'

'You'll never know if you don't try,' George said firmly.

'We should go quickly so George and Elsie don't have to wait around too long.' Ashton pointed up the hill and the dogs immediately sprinted ahead, reading his mind.

Jessie sighed as her grandad handed her the camera. 'You really don't need to come,' she said to Ashton, striding ahead of him.

'I'm not saying no to Elsie,' Ashton joked, breaking into a trot so he could catch up with her. 'Besides, she's right – I suspect I do know the best place to go. You probably don't want to leave your grandad waiting for too long.'

It took them ten minutes to reach the top of the hill again and they didn't speak because they were going at such a pace. The air was baking, but there was a pleasant breeze. They stopped at the top and took in their surroundings – the sky was cloudless and the sea was dark blue and calm. They didn't get too close to the edge of the cliffs, but the ground leading to it was a mixture of dusty bare rock broken up by tufts of lush grass. Ashton watched Jessie swipe hair from her neck as she gazed through the viewfinder of the camera.

'I remember this place... it was one of my favourite pictures from my grandparent's honeymoon album,' Jessie said, standing perfectly still as she gazed through the camera lens. 'I used to be able to do this without thinking,' she huffed after a few moments, sounding frustrated. 'It's like every time I try to line up a photo, I get in my own way.'

'I don't know anything about photography, but I'm guessing if you don't take any photos, you'll have no chance of getting it right,' Ashton suggested.

Jessie frowned and took a quick snap, checked it and frowned again, then she took another three and when she looked at those, Ashton saw the tiniest tilt at the edge of her mouth. Was Jessie smiling? It was odd how much that pleased him.

'Those are okay, I suppose. I used to prefer taking portraits when I was at university. It was so interesting looking at faces up close, at how different they can appear depending on the background, light or composition. How so many things factor into what works.'

'Have you really forgotten how to take portraits?' Ashton asked, watching her. 'Or have you just been too afraid to try in case you don't like what you see?'

'Blunt,' she said, considering the question. Then she angled the lens towards him and snapped. 'I guess not.' Jessie checked the picture. 'As I suspected – you're not entirely hideous.' She frowned. 'Could you try harder not to be quite as photogenic, though? I feel like I want to muss your hair or something.'

Ashton flushed, surprised by the compliment.

Jessie tipped the camera again and brought it closer to her face so she could study the image. 'It's not that great technically – you can tell I'm out of practice.'

'Were you once a photographer by profession? You look like you know what you're doing.' Ashton wandered nearer to the edge of the cliff and called to Murphy and Phoebe, who'd strayed a little too close.

Jessie shrugged. 'That was always my plan. I studied photography at Uni and got a job in a studio straight after.'

'You didn't decide to go it alone?' he asked.

She frowned. 'I didn't have the confidence and I needed the money to live on. My stepmother didn't want me living with her when I graduated. The job was grunt work mainly. I loved it, but I started to wonder if my work was good enough to stand out. I met Brendon, and it made more sense for me to get a job working in the same insurance company as him. We decided to move in together, and I needed to bring in more money than I was. Being a photographer was only ever a fantasy anyway. I didn't have my grandmother's talents...'

'Is that what she thought?' Ashton asked.

Jessie pursed her lips. 'No, but she was just being nice.'

She moved to a new spot and snapped again, then spent time adjusting the camera and taking more shots, considering each picture before choosing to keep or delete it. Her movements were unhurried and measured – Jessie was obviously an expert, whatever she said.

'I'm self-aware enough to know I was never as talented as Dorothy.' She checked the pictures and Ashton could tell Jessie liked what she saw. It was almost imperceptible, but had her shoulders straightened? Was she standing a little taller now?

'So you gave up?' he guessed.

'No. I...' Jessie turned to him and frowned, her forehead creasing. 'Paused. Then I forgot to restart. Brendon thought I was wasting my time and—' She shrugged. 'I suppose I decided he was right.' She pulled a face as if something had just occurred to her. 'How stupid was that?'

'Very stupid,' Ashton said seriously, and this time she laughed out loud.

'My God, you're just as brutal as me,' she gasped, grinning.

'You could practise taking some more portraits of me while you're here,' he blurted, wondering where the idea had even come from. 'I mean, as you say, I'm not entirely hideous and...' It would mean he'd get to spend more time with her. To help make up for how he'd made Jessie feel all those years ago. That was the only reason, there couldn't be more.

'I appreciate the offer, but I'm sure you've got better things to do.' She turned away and took another photo of the view.

Ashton felt a wave of disappointment but decided not to ask again. Instead, he fiddled with the mobile in his pocket. He liked watching Jessie work. He didn't spend a lot of time observing people – computer code was so much easier to decipher, and it didn't keep changing. It wasn't opinionated, or confusing, and it definitely didn't disappear overnight unless you hit delete. But there was something about Jessie that fascinated him.

Ashton grabbed the mobile from his pocket and took a quick picture. Jessie must have seen him from the corner of her eye because she spun around and frowned. 'I told you I don't photograph well,' she said, her cheeks flushing.

He looked at the picture and shook his head. 'Well, you're not entirely hideous...' he joked, twisting the mobile around so Jessie could see the screen. 'You look...' He searched for the right words. 'At peace. Like you're doing something you love. It's put a light inside you.'

She considered the image and her eyes rounded. 'I look just like my grandma.' Her gaze met his and she looked overwhelmed and a little shell-shocked.

'You okay?' Ashton took a step forward just as she nodded and turned away, swiping a hand across her cheek.

'Maybe you could send that to me?' Her voice was uncertain. 'I might take you up on your offer, after all. I'd enjoy taking portraits of someone who doesn't mind being a guinea pig. Besides, I guess with that face it would be difficult to get it wrong.'

The compliment had him blushing again. 'Tonight?' Ashton asked a little too eagerly for his own liking. 'I could drop you at Sea Glass Cottage after we go to The Beach Café, take your grandad's clothes to Look Out House and come back.'

Jessie frowned. 'But then I won't have a car.'

'If you keep the dogs, I'll drive the Ford Anglia back to the cottage later, and I can walk around the beach with the dogs once we've taken our pictures. It's my usual route – which is why I bumped into you the other night. There's a pathway up the cliffs straight into my back garden.'

He watched as Jessie processed the idea and nodded.

'Fine.' She turned around and snapped a few more shots. 'I think I'm done. Hopefully, there'll be something there that Grandad's happy with.'

'I'm sure he'll love them,' Ashton said, as Jessie called Phoebe, then started to make her way back down the hill with Murphy and Bear following. Ashton brought up the rear, realising he'd just arranged to spend another evening in Jessie's company, knew he should be cancelling the plan, he just wasn't sure he wanted to...

12

'Oh, I love it!' Ella gushed, her eyes glittering with bubbles of tears as she ripped the brown wrapping paper and tugged it back to reveal the pretty jigsaw montage from the Lighthouse Gallery. '"Pieces of Cake"!' she read. 'It's just perfect.'

She trotted out from behind the counter of The Beach Café, where she'd just placed two mugs and a takeaway box filled with slabs of chocolate cake for Jessie and Ashton. Then she swung the artwork in the air, weighing up where she should position it, before dancing over to each of the café's four walls so she could hold it in place.

'Ashton, you're a darling man, regardless of what you'd like everyone to think. I knew there was a heart beating in there somewhere and you've finally shown it to me.' She winked at Jessie.

'I can assure you,' Ashton said sternly, 'that the picture is a present from Elsie, not me.' He shoved his hands into his pockets.

'That's not entirely true. Ashton paid for it,' Jessie jumped in, ignoring the irritated look he gave her. She enjoyed teasing him, but he deserved some credit too. Why did he look so uncomfortable about taking it?

'Well, if that's the case, thank you,' Ella said, reaching out to peck Ashton on the cheek, triggering a tsunami of pink to sweep up his face which Jessie found endearing.

'I owe you for all the coffees and cakes you keep giving me for free,' he ground out, taking a deliberate step away from Ella as he pulled his wallet from his jeans pocket. 'What do I owe for today's?'

'Oh, there'll be no charge for those,' Ella insisted, twisting around to peruse her surroundings again, ignoring the offered debit card. 'I have to find the perfect spot so all the customers will see the picture as they come in. The artist is obviously brilliant, and this is a wonderful way to promote The Puzzle Club. I'd love to meet them…'

She turned towards the entrance as a bell rang and the dark-haired teenager Jessie had met a few days before sauntered into the café looking at his phone.

'Brilliant timing!' Ella winked at Jessie. 'Darren's just started working with me in the afternoons during the summer holidays.'

'It's mainly for work experience.' The young boy pocketed the mobile and shoved his hands into his jeans, mirroring Ashton who'd put his wallet away but still looked self-conscious. 'Dad says it'll be good for my UCAS application.' He rolled his eyes.

'And as well as your wage, there's as much cake as you can eat while you're working, remember?' Ella sang. 'So there's plenty in it for you too.'

Darren sniffed. 'I don't mind, I suppose. I get to do puzzles in my breaks. They're not *all* boring, so long as they have all the pieces – and the music in this place isn't as bad as the stuff Lila plays at The Pottery Project. I just wish more of my friends came – I don't see them so often now I don't do pottery anymore.' He huffed as he looked around at the tables. 'It's even less busy than yesterday afternoon and it was dead then,' he grumbled.

'Thank you, Darren,' Ella said lightly, 'for telling it how it is. I'm expecting the crowds to arrive in a few hours. It's still early and a little hot out there.' She laughed quietly as the teenager wandered towards the counter and almost tripped.

He seemed too big for his body and had obviously undergone a recent growth spurt, so his feet were now too long for him to control. Jessie remembered that stage, how her limbs had lengthened so quickly her brain had struggled to keep up. She'd been gawky and self-conscious, which Maria had taken great delight in pointing out. At the time, Jessie had taken it to heart, but now, watching Darren, she realised clumsiness was normal. A rung on the growing-up ladder – nothing to be ashamed of. How many more memories had been marred by her stepmother?

Ella scratched a hand through her dark ponytail and pointed to the far wall where a picture of a set of cliffs had been hung. 'Can you take that picture down and put this one in its place please, Darren? In a moment, I thought we could clean some of the cupboards in the kitchen and put on Kate Bush really loud to motivate us while we do it.' She wriggled her narrow hips.

The young boy mulled over the request before nodding. 'It's better than doing nothing, I suppose,' he said.

'You're so right,' Ella said patiently. 'As it's not too busy, now it's a good opportunity for us to do a spring clean: there's plenty of cake out back too.'

Darren shrugged, then took the cliff picture down from the wall before replacing it with the jigsaw artwork. He took a moment to straighten it, then leaned closer to get a better look. 'That's clever, how it's made from puzzle pieces. I'd love to try something like that myself.' He cocked his head. 'I know I should have gone to bed earlier, the cherry on top of that cake looks like it's staring at me.' He frowned, peering closer. 'I'd better get started on the cleaning before it blinks too.' He glanced back at the picture again and shuddered before heading towards the counter at the back of the café.

'He's a real gem,' Ella said, when he'd disappeared into the kitchen. 'Hard to read at first, but he's got a heart of gold.' Her eyes flickered to Ashton before she looked back at Jessie. 'He's a typical teenager, but he works hard despite all the eye rolling. I think he's lonely now he can't spend time with Lila and Gryffyn or his friends at The Pottery Project. He loved crafting there.' She shook her head, looking annoyed. 'It's a real shame his dad doesn't understand. I think it's dented his confidence a little.'

'I can relate,' Jessie said. 'It's hard living up to other people's expectations.' Maria had wanted her to be so many things – none of which Jessie had achieved.

'It's hard when they don't have any for you either,' Ashton interjected, surprising Ella and Jessie. He must have regretted sharing because he shoved his hands into his pockets and spun around so he could study the jigsaw picture on the wall.

Ella watched him for a moment and then raised an eyebrow at Jessie. 'I can't afford to pay Darren much,' she said as if Ashton hadn't spoken. 'But he likes cake and I think he secretly enjoys getting out of his house. I was hoping having him work here might attract some younger customers, but according to Darren, cafés and puzzles aren't a teenage thing.' She put the last two words in air quotes. 'I thought everyone loved cake, who knew?' Her eyes shifted to Ashton. 'Have you two got plans?'

Jessie shook her head. 'Ashton's driving me back to Sea Glass Cottage so I can pack some clothes for Grandad. He fell today and hurt his hip and he can't manage the steps,' she explained.

'That's awful,' Ella said. 'I was worried because that stair-case is so steep. Can I do anything to help?'

Jessie shook her head. 'I'm hoping he'll be okay after some rest.' She didn't want her poor grandad stuck in bed for the rest of the trip.

'Well, if he's not, and if you need to find somewhere else to stay that's easier for him, please shout. I've had so many people calling over the last few days trying to find somewhere in Indigo Cove. It would be easy enough to rent it out, and I'd be happy to refund your grandad,' she promised. 'I don't want him living somewhere he can't comfortably get to.'

'You're both welcome to stay at Look Out House for as long as you want,' Ashton offered quietly. 'There's plenty of room.'

'Oh, I don't know...' Jessie gulped, shocked Ashton had offered, especially since he hated having visitors. Did he really want her living there, or was he just being polite?

'Elsie, Bear and Murphy would love it.' He shrugged, spinning around to look at the picture again, but Jessie caught an odd look on his face – almost like he was surprised by the conversation.

Something clattered in the kitchen. 'I probably need to go – will we see you both at The Puzzle Club tomorrow?' Ella asked.

'We'll be here,' Jessie promised. 'At the moment, it's the safest place for Grandad. He's been loving doing the puzzles. He's really sociable but spends far too much time on his own these days.'

'That's exactly what The Puzzle Club was started for.' Ella's eyes twinkled. There was another noise from behind the counter, and she pulled a face. 'I'll see you tomorrow. Hopefully, some of our regulars will be here. And if you want me to find new tenants for Sea Glass Cottage, just let me know...'

'Is Grandad okay?' Jessie asked two hours later, when Ashton arrived back at the cottage after dropping her off and then taking a rucksack of her grandfather's clothes back to Look Out

House, before returning again with the Ford Anglia. He was carrying a casserole dish and a bag. The three dogs, who he'd left with Jessie earlier, all clambered to the door to welcome him, barking.

'Don't worry. He's sitting in the garden with his feet on a stool,' Ashton said. 'Elsie's in her element. She sent food for the dogs, plus a beef Bourguignon that she told me we had to eat. I had to fob her off before she gave me a flask filled with old fashioneds too.'

He placed the dish and bag onto the counter and pulled out a handful of packs of dogfood and a large flask.

'Looks like she sneaked the cocktail in when I wasn't looking.' He shook his head and turned so he could glance around the kitchen. 'This is nice,' he said, walking the floor. He'd changed into new jeans and a shirt and had obviously brushed his hair, and Jessie fought a wave of attraction.

'Your grandad asked if you could take some photos on the beach. He told me he had some pictures of seashells in the missing photo album – I wasn't sure what he meant.'

'I know.' Jessie nodded. 'Grandma and Grandad used to go seashell-collecting in the evenings. Grandma took some close-ups of the pretty ones and there are a few of Grandad picking them up. I don't know how I'm supposed to recreate those, though, since he's not here...'

'Ah.' Ashton sighed, and his expression cleared. 'I understand now. Your grandad told me that in his absence I'd do. I had no idea what he was talking about at the time – I figured he'd just drunk too many of Elsie's cocktails.' He ran a hand across his forehead. 'If I knew I'd be modelling this evening, I'd have blow-dried my hair.' He grinned.

'Grandad said that?' Jessie checked, wondering what had got into him.

'Well, you did say I wasn't entirely hideous,' Ashton said, wandering to the doorway which led to the bedrooms before turning back just as Bear made his way into the corridor. 'Come back,' he snapped, starting to follow.

'He's fine, you can leave him.' Jessie gulped. She didn't want Ashton making his way into her bedroom. What if he saw her pillow boyfriend? She'd be mortified. 'The dogs need a walk, especially Phoebe,' she quickly said. 'I'll put the oven on now, and we can take them out while the casserole is warming.'

She switched on the stove and put the dish inside just as Bear wandered back out of the hallway carrying a pillow in his mouth. The sunglasses she'd propped on top clattered to the floor.

'What's this?' Ashton asked, picking the glasses up and wrestling the pillow from Bear.

'Nothing.' Flushing, Jessie snatched them from Ashton and put them on the sofa. 'I guess we've got about forty minutes. Then I need to be back to put on some rice. We should get the pictures done before it gets dark.'

She picked up the camera from where she'd left it on the sideboard and pulled her trainers on before heading down the steps onto the beach.

Behind her, Ashton called Bear, who was now sulking by the sofa, and all three dogs charged past, almost knocking her over as they galloped onto the sand, heading towards the shore. Ashton caught up with Jessie as she began to run.

'There are shells all over this beach,' she said, stopping when she spotted one and picking it up. 'Look at the pink and silver in this one – it's beautiful. The shells in Grandma's photos were like this.'

She studied the shell intently. Then she put it back into the sand and searched her memory for the exact composition of her grandma's photo before taking three quick pictures. They looked about right – she'd got the shells in the right place, although the light wasn't perfect. Maybe she could fiddle with the photos on her computer later? It had been a while since she'd played with images, but she'd been good at it once, talented at teasing out what she wanted.

If only life could be cropped and adjusted so easily – turned into something pretty with all the ugly shapes and shades cut out. She'd have chopped Maria out years before, and edited Brendon out sooner too. Eradicating all the memories that had left dents in her confidence – dents she couldn't seem to smooth out. She'd want to keep Ashton in her past though, but what did that mean?

She picked up three more shells and placed them at angles beside the others, smoothing the sand around them before taking a few more snaps. 'I remember the photo and it looked something like this,' she said.

'Have you managed to match it?' Ashton asked, wandering over to join her.

'I think so, they're not bad – I've got the gist.' Jessie said, rising to her feet and scrolling through the shots so he could see.

'They're really good. You're talented,' he said simply, making Jessie's chest swell even as she tried to fight the rush of pleasure.

'I'm just copying the pictures my grandma took which makes it easier,' she said. 'They're almost the same, but it's been a long time since I saw the album. I do remember the colours of the shells, though.' She looked up at Ashton. 'Are you ready be Grandad now?'

He nodded. 'Those are big shoes, but I'll give it a try.'

'Could you stand over there please and look towards the horizon?' Jessie pointed to a spot on the beach a few metres away. 'I'll take a few of you from behind.'

'That is my best side,' he said, giving her a lopsided smile, which told Jessie that Ashton felt a little awkward.

He wandered to the area Jessie had pointed to and put his hands into his pockets.

'That's not right,' she said, narrowing her eyes as she tried to recall the exact way her grandfather had been standing.

She wandered right up to Ashton so she could pull one of Ashton's hands out of the pocket and let his arm dangle to the side. Then she angled his head, scratching her fingertips over the stubble on his chin, drawing away when her finger-pads began to tingle.

'That's perfect,' she said, catching a hint of his aftershave on the wind. She gulped and took another step away from the feelings he was starting to evoke. She didn't want them – he'd hurt her once and she didn't want to put herself in the same position. Even if she did, Ashton wouldn't be interested in her.

Jessie cleared her throat. 'Now you're stood here like Grandad, everything's coming back about this photo from the album... Hmm, your hair's too tidy – can I muss it up?'

'Sure,' he said gruffly.

Jessie tousled some of the thick, silky strands of his hair and saw his jaw tense. Was Ashton uncomfortable with her touching him? 'Try to relax, think of it as just some fun,' she said, and his jaw loosened.

He was taller than her grandad and his shoulders were broader, but if she took the picture from a distance, he'd almost look the same – and the image would always be a reminder of the evening George had spent with Dorothy picking up shells.

'You look good from the back, it's *definitely* your best side,' Jessie teased, aiming to dispel the bubbles of awareness popping across her skin. She took a few shots, moving as she took them from a variety of angles. She'd show the results to her grandad and let him choose his favourites. Then she'd crop and play with the colours so they'd be ready to print along with the others she'd take at Indigo Cove.

Ashton turned when Jessie had finished and reached for the camera.

'Let me take one of you.'

She shook her head. 'I don't think—'

'I'm guessing there was at least one photo of your grandma in that album?' Ashton asked, searching her face and making the breath pause in her throat.

Jessie blew the breath out. 'A few,' she admitted grudgingly.

'Don't you think your grandad would want one of those too?' he asked. 'The other day you told me you looked like Dorothy in the picture I took.'

'Fine...' She shut her eyes. 'I can remember one of the pictures. Grandad would have taken it, but I'm guessing Grandma played with it afterwards because it wasn't too bad.'

'So you can do the same.'

Ashton wriggled his fingers until Jessie reluctantly handed over the camera. Their fingers brushed, setting off a new wave of tingles that made her knees wobble and the hairs on the surface of her skin arch.

'You have to press that button.' She pointed to the top of the camera and one of Ashton's eyebrows winged.

'I think I can handle that,' he said dryly.

'We have the same length hair, but I remember that in the photo Grandma hadn't styled it and she wore it down.' Jessie took her ponytail out and shook her head, letting the strands fall around her face. 'Also, I think she was kneeling.' She walked to where Ashton had been standing and got onto one knee before looking back at him. He was staring at her with that odd expression again, and the camera was still dangling from his hand. 'It works better if you look through the viewfinder,' she said.

'Sorry.' Ashton shook himself and swallowed, then held the camera up and started to take pictures while Jessie picked up seashells, trying to recreate what Dorothy had done in the photo she remembered.

She hated being in front of the lens, so as soon as she thought Ashton had taken enough, she rose. 'I'm sure I'll be able to work with one of those.' She reached for the camera again.

Ashton didn't hand it to her; instead, he scrolled through the images. 'You really are stunning.' He looked up as if he was surprised.

'I'm really not,' she snapped, but her pulse skidded. 'You don't need to say that.' She waved a hand, swiping at the words as if they were floating between them, polluting the air. 'I know what I look like. I came to terms with it years ago.'

'You have no idea,' Ashton said, quietly glancing around. 'You know I think we're almost exactly where we were that first time we met.'

'When you ran?' Jessie asked, taking in their surroundings too. She'd hardly noticed, but it did look familiar – then again, didn't all beaches look the same?

'I told you I was sorry.'

'You also said you'd kiss me and run again,' she said.

Ashton reached out a hand and held it millimetres above Jessie's arm. It was like he was afraid of touching her, scared of the connection – or maybe she'd read too much into it.

Embarrassed, she stepped back, almost tripping over the seashells she'd been posing beside. 'Are you worried I'm expecting something from you? Because I'm not.'

Ashton laughed, but the sound was hollow. 'That's not what I'm afraid of, Jessie,' he said, sounding surprised.

'Then what is it, why do I think you're about to run?' she asked, hearing the pain in her tone. She swallowed it down, felt the bubble sink into her stomach like a dead weight.

'Because I don't want to feel,' he said, the honesty of the words obviously startling him because his eyes widened. But instead of leaving, which Jessie still expected, he stepped closer until his feet were mere inches from hers. He was so tall – he didn't tower above her, but she had to tip her chin to look into his eyes. What she found there confused her because he looked conflicted.

He moved a hand as if he planned to place it against her

cheek, but before it got there, he dropped it back to his side. She watched the spark in his eyes that she'd originally read as annoyance flare. Felt a shiver in her chest as she responded even as she tried to fight the feelings. Jessie couldn't put her heart in anyone's hands again. It was too fragile, too damaged. But her pulse still began to pound as Ashton's eyes skated over her mouth as if he were learning the shape of it.

'The thing is, I have a feeling you could rip emotions out of me that I buried long ago,' he said, his tone low. 'I don't want that.'

'So, why are you standing so close to me?' Jessie complained, wanting to kick herself for drawing attention to their position. She didn't know if she wanted Ashton to stay where he was or to move. Didn't know what she wanted anymore. Her whole body was shaking, and she could feel her toes pushing upwards as if they were determined to move her mouth closer to his.

'I've no idea,' Ashton grumbled, just before he moved and suddenly his lips were pressed against hers.

Jessie had often wondered over the last fourteen years if she'd imagined the way it had felt to kiss Ashton. Had somehow dreamed her skin had felt like it was burning while her pulse had galloped so quickly she could barely hear anything above the rush of blood.

She could feel her knees begin to shake and pressed her palms to her sides, pushing them into her hips so she didn't reach for him. She knew she should stop this, knew falling into a kiss with Ashton again was a terrible idea. He'd scarred her young heart once, so why was she leaning into him? Why was her mouth opening and allowing his tongue to tangle with hers – to begin a slow slide taking whatever this was between them from tentative to something more meaningful? Jessie knew this wasn't just lust.

There were fireworks going off in her ears and a rainbow of

colours swirled behind her eyelids. Her pulse beat a tattoo until she could hardly catch her breath. She moved her hands then, knotting her fingers into Ashton's T-shirt so she could tug him closer, feeling the contours of his well-defined muscles and heard herself moan.

The sound was alien, the feelings he was inspiring terrifying. All her ideas of protecting herself, of staying away from this man – from any man – had been jettisoned from her mind. Jessie's kisses with Brendon and the boyfriends before him had been gentle affairs – there had been none of this heat, none of this need searing its way across her skin, licking at her insides, making her want to drop her clothes onto the sand and sink to her knees. She'd always assumed it was because she didn't inspire that kind of reaction, didn't have that capability for desire in her, but what if it had never been true? What if all along it had been to do with who she'd been tangling with?

'Damn.' Ashton pulled back and rested his forehead against Jessie's. She was still holding onto his shirt and could hear his short, choppy breaths – guessed he was as surprised by this moment as she was. 'Why does that happen when I kiss you? I feel like I'm eighteen again and scared witless.' He stepped away, holding his hands up as if he were nervous about touching her again. 'We should...' he panted, moving further away and pointing back towards Sea Glass Cottage.

'Stop?' Jessie suggested, easing herself down from her tiptoes. 'You think?' She laughed although it was more from nerves than humour. 'You know this is a terrible idea?' she said, more to herself than him.

Ashton frowned and shook his head. 'Maybe,' he said faintly, linking his fingers in front of him as if he were afraid of what they might do if he left them to their own devices. His mouth pinched and he stared into her face looking confused.

'Aren't you supposed to be running?' Jessie asked after a long pause. She wasn't sure if she wanted this. Was she ready to open her heart again – especially to a man who'd broken it so thoroughly years before? 'Because I think the best route out of here is somewhere over there.' She pointed down the beach.

Ashton's lips quirked. 'I know I told you I would, but I'm not running this time, Jessie.' He closed his eyes and brushed a hand across his forehead. 'I don't know what's happening,' he said, opening them again and staring at her, his eyes a maelstrom of emotion. 'I don't want this...'

Jessie raised an eyebrow. 'Would you rather we called it a mistake and try to forget it?' She heaved out a breath wondering if she could, if she really wanted to. Or whether it was even her choice. Then she called the dogs and pushed past Ashton, heading back towards the cottage.

It was only when she was a few metres away that she heard him murmur. 'I'm not sure I can...' as he echoed her thoughts. Stunned, Jessie slowed but continued to pace forward. Wondering exactly what Ashton had meant and if she was really ready to find out...

13

Jessie pressed the mobile against her ear as Rose yawned on the other end. 'What time is it?' her friend asked, and Jessie checked the clock beside her bed and immediately regretted calling when she realised the small hand had barely passed five. It was light outside: she could see the sun through the French doors in her bedroom, just about rising from where the sea met the horizon – but that didn't mean it was a reasonable time to call.

'I'm sorry, it's stupid o'clock. I didn't check. I'll call back later,' Jessie promised.

'Don't hang up, I'm awake now.' Rose yawned again and Jessie heard the shuffle of bed clothes and guessed she was sitting up. 'You have news – I can feel it. Is it male-flavoured?' she asked seriously.

'I met him again,' Jessie blurted.

'Who?' Rose shot back.

'The boy – the one from the beach, only he's a man now,' she explained, needing to talk to somebody...

'The one who ran? Tell me more.' Jessie heard the squeak of

springs and wondered if her friend was bouncing on her mattress in excitement.

'He's...' Jessie tugged the sheet closer to her chest.

'Built and drop-dead gorgeous – with Isaac Newton's brain and the body of Magic Mike?' Rose filled in, her voice excited.

Jessie looked at the pillow she'd flattened beside her and sighed as she adjusted the sunglasses so they were sitting in the correct place. 'He's not like anyone I've dated before. He's smart and funny but strangely sad, and he holds himself back.' She swallowed. 'We kissed again last night, and it was just as amazing as before. I'm not really sure how it happened...'

'Well, it usually involves lips and sometimes – if you're lucky – a few body parts too...' her friend said dryly.

'It's not a joke,' Jessie complained. 'I came here with Grandad to get over Brendon. I'm supposed to be working out what I want to do with my life. I should be married now. Why aren't I still lying in the foetal position sobbing? Shouldn't I be devastated?'

'Jess stop looking inwards and blaming yourself. Maybe it would be better if you really thought about Brendon and whether he was ever right for you at all,' Rose said. 'Sometimes, we hold onto people for the wrong reasons...'

'I went out with him for six years – we got engaged – so he must have been perfect for me once.' Jessie scraped a hand over her eyes.

'Or maybe he just filled up all the holes Maria left inside you. Only he didn't really... He just made loads more,' Rose said quietly. 'And now he's no longer in your life, perhaps you've had the time to realise that. Maybe those holes are starting to fill up.'

Jessie paused. 'I don't know... It doesn't explain why I've immediately locked lips with someone I barely know.' Or why it had felt so good – better than any kiss with Brendon ever had.

Rose blew a raspberry into the receiver. 'I'd say that's obvious. You met this new guy before your ex and never forgot him.

Jess, this is a clear case of unresolved attraction. You're not shallow, but you never had the right feelings for Brendon. Wake up and smell the chemistry. I've told you before, you settled for the man because he was easy and he was there. I'd never blame you for that.' She sighed. 'Brendon proved Maria was wrong, that someone *could* love you – and that you were worthy of it. But you didn't need him to show you that – you're amazing, beautiful and people adore you. Besides, Brendon was never the one,' she added softly. 'And he's in your past now. The cheater's moved on – not in the right way, but he did you a favour. Jess, it's time you moved on too. If you need someone to help with that, then fate's just delivered the one person who can. What's his name?'

'Ashton,' Jessie muttered. 'But... I'm so confused...'

'Jess,' Rose replied softly. 'I'm fairly certain you know exactly what to do.'

When Jessie arrived at The Beach Café with Phoebe later that morning, she immediately spotted her grandad and Elsie sitting in the far corner at a table next to Lila and Gryffyn. They were all chatting and laughing, and George had Peaches nuzzled under one arm.

Elsie and her grandad were partway through a new puzzle and the four of them had plates piled high with slabs of lemon cake and mugs of hot chocolate on the tables beside them, along with a pile of jigsaw boxes they'd obviously chosen their latest from. Her grandfather looked so happy. Jessie stopped between the tables for a moment to watch.

'Jess!' George swung an arm in the air as soon as he spotted her. 'Come and join us. Elsie and I are seeing if we can finish a puzzle in record time. Peaches is assisting – I had no idea a cockerel could be so helpful at finding the right pieces.' He carefully stroked the bird's head before leaning

down to greet Phoebe as she scampered across the floor to
join him.

'Good morning!' Lila said, waggling her fingers, while
Gryffyn didn't look up from the puzzle he was poring over.
'How did you sleep?'

'Fine,' Jessie lied, sliding into a seat opposite her grandad as
Phoebe nuzzled his hand. In truth, before her conversation with
Rose, she'd spent the night tossing and turning, thinking about
Ashton and their kiss. She had no idea what she wanted, but the
thought of staying away from him seemed impossible now.

'How's your hip, Grandad?' she asked, checking him over
carefully and deciding he didn't look too bad. She'd texted a
couple of times last night and again this morning, but he'd
simply responded each time with a: 100%.

He wriggled a little on the high-backed chair and winced.
'Better than yesterday, but I still don't think I can manage a long
walk. It was hard enough getting from the Land Rover to the
café this morning.' He pulled a face. 'I'm so sorry, Jess, but
would you mind if I stayed at Look Out House for a while
longer? I really can't face all those steps.'

'Of course I don't mind,' Jessie soothed, thinking about the
empty cottage. It was beautiful, but she didn't relish the idea of
staying there alone for much longer.

'I'm wondering if it might make sense for you both to move
in to Look Out House for the rest of your break?' Elsie asked
quietly, looking up from the puzzle and meeting Jessie's gaze.
'It's a shame for you to be staying in different places, and there's
plenty of room. I know Ashton wouldn't mind.'

'He mentioned it yesterday,' Jessie said. Although she'd
expected him to change his mind. Did that mean he'd meant
what he'd said on the beach? That he couldn't leave things? Is
that why he wanted them at Look Out House?

'Of course,' Elsie promised. 'And Ella's had four calls
already this morning from families looking for last-minute

holiday accommodation. She could easily rent it to someone else. Your grandad could rest his hip, and I can cook and keep George company. Just think about it,' she added, when Jessie frowned.

'What do you think, Grandad?' Jessie asked quietly.

'I'd love to stay at Look Out House, but only if you're comfortable with it,' he said, rubbing Phoebe behind the ears. Even the dog was looking at her with an imploring expression, almost as if she could understand the situation.

The idea was tempting. She'd sleep better, her grandad would be happier, and the accommodation would be easier on his hip. But the biggest reason was the one circling the centre of her chest: if she was living with Ashton, she might get the chance to explore the chemistry pulsing between them again.

Perhaps Rose was right, and she did know what she wanted, after all? Perhaps for the first time in years, she'd get to feel truly sexy and beautiful. Would that change her, mend some of the insecurities? It could never amount to anything long-term – Ashton was too emotionally distant and too far out of her league. But was this her opportunity to move on? Should she grab it before it was too late?

'Okay,' she said, and knew she'd made the right decision when her grandad cheered in response.

'That's brilliant news!' Elsie agreed.

'You just leave the arrangements to me – I'll talk to Ella,' George said, his grin widening.

'I'm sure Ashton will be happy to help you to move your things,' Elsie promised. 'He said he'd drop by later to pick us up and then he's going to take you to Sunset Point.'

'He is?' Jessie asked.

'Of course, that was the next place your grandma and I visited. I definitely want a picture from there for the album. Speaking of photos, how did the ones of the shells turn out – and was the boy a suitable stand-in for me?' George leaned forward, breaking into her thoughts. 'He's a little taller – but I like to think I was just as handsome once, at least from here.' He patted the back of his head and chuckled.

'They came out well, I think,' Jessie said tentatively. 'I'll show you once I've had a chance to crop them and adjust the colours.' She wasn't ready to share them yet, but was itching to play with them on her computer later. Perhaps she would once she'd moved into Look Out House.

'I also wanted to talk to you about taking some pictures for me!' Lila jumped in. 'Your grandad mentioned you're talented with a camera. I've got four cats at The Pottery Project, and I'd like portraits of them all. I'd also like some pictures for my website. One of the outside of the building and perhaps a few of people doing lessons and some of the artwork they made too...'

'Oh, I'm just an amateur really...' Jessie shook her head.

'You never did give yourself credit, love,' George grumbled, sounding frustrated. 'My granddaughter is brilliant, she should never have given photography up. Well, it's true – you shouldn't have. Dorothy always said you were a talented photographer...' he said sternly, when Jessie started to argue. 'It was the knuckle-head's fault, he made you feel like you were never good enough at anything.' He looked annoyed.

'Grandad...' Jessie complained. 'Brendon didn't say I couldn't be a photographer, I just...'

'Ah, but he never told you that you *should*,' he said, sounding annoyed. 'Which is one of the reasons why I want you to help me to retake my photos now.' The creases at the corners of his eyes deepened. 'It's a waste to turn your back on all that talent, and if I can in some small way help you find your love for photography again, well...' He put a hand on his chest. 'My work will be done – and I know Dorothy would be delighted to know she'd continued to inspire you.'

'So Jessie, I wondered if you'd be able to come up to The Pottery Project today so you can meet the cats and plan the shots?' Lila asked. 'Perhaps then you can come back later in the week to take the photos for real?'

'I've just messaged Ashton – he's happy to pop back to the café now so he can drive George and me to Look Out House with the dogs,' Elsie promised. 'He said he'll take you to The Pottery Project and then on to Sunset Point. Don't forget you were going to get that photo of the bench.' Her eyes sparkled.

'I can drive you back in the Ford Anglia. Ashton doesn't need to come, but shouldn't I wait to take more photos until you're feeling better?' Jessie asked her grandad. Things were moving faster than she'd intended, and she needed time to catch her breath.

George waved a hand. 'This hip is going to be sore for a few days. I need to rest it and if I use my maths professor skills and add you plus Dorothy's camera together, I know you'll get the right result.' He winked.

'You can pack everything up from Sea Glass Cottage on your way back and move into your old room before we all have dinner at Look Out House,' Elsie declared. 'Which reminds me, how did you enjoy the cocktails and casserole last night? Ashton didn't mention it, and I was in bed when he arrived home.' The older lady grinned as she slid another piece of puzzle into the jigsaw on the table.

'They were very tasty, thank you,' Jessie said. Clearly, Ashton hadn't mentioned that he hadn't eaten with her. Instead, he'd followed her as she'd walked back to Sea Glass Cottage, then as far as Jessie knew he'd continued his way along the beach to Look Out House.

She'd parked herself on the decking with Phoebe for the rest of the evening, then downed three cocktails and eaten only part of the small bowl of casserole she'd dished out before losing her appetite. The kiss had confused her, the feelings it had drawn out, but after speaking to Rose, she knew what to do.

'Finished!' her grandad yelled suddenly, thrusting his arms

in the air as he beamed at the completed jigsaw. 'And all the pieces were in the box this time.'

'That only took us a couple of hours,' Elsie said, checking her watch and punching the air too. 'It's definitely faster when we work together – although we'd never have done it without Peaches. He spotted the bit that had dropped onto the floor.' She reached out and stroked the bird who was still happily ensconced under Jessie's grandfather's arm, then waved towards the door. 'Ashton's here!'

Jessie turned and watched as the man in question wandered into the café with Bear and Murphy who were tied up on leads. He didn't look directly at Jessie, but he did pull up the chair beside her so he could sit while Phoebe shuffled under the table to greet her new friends.

'Good morning,' he said, his voice low. 'I hope you slept better than I did.' His tired eyes and messy hair confirmed he hadn't had a good night.

'Not particularly.' Jessie sighed as Ella wandered up to join them too.

'Coffee and lemon cake for my favourite customers?' she asked.

'Yes please,' they choroused.

'This is ridiculous,' Gryffyn complained. 'There's a piece missing from this puzzle too.'

'I'll put it to one side. There are seven more puzzles from the pile that got donated which haven't been made up yet,' Ella said.

'It's odd that someone would bother giving us something that can't be used. I don't understand.' Lila frowned.

'Perhaps they didn't realise some of them had pieces missing?' George suggested, as Gryffyn opened a new box and tipped the contents onto the table.

'I expect that's what happened,' Lila said. 'Do you know how many of them are incomplete?'

'No, but I'm thinking of asking Darren if he can either count the pieces or make the puzzles all up,' Ella said. 'Speaking of Darren, he left a maths paper here for you, George. He asked if you could take a look at it.'

Jessie's grandfather nodded. 'I would be one hundred per cent delighted to!' he exclaimed, almost tipping his chair with excitement.

Jessie leaned back in her seat and watched the pleasure light up her grandad's face. This summer was full of surprises. She glanced at Ashton and saw he was staring at her. Felt her whole body warm and wondered if there might just be something unexpected around the corner...

14

———

Ashton pulled his Land Rover to a stop on a large gravel driveway, and Jessie sat for a moment staring at a pretty cottage with a blue front door which was opposite a large barn with a sign for *The Pottery Project*. A ginger cat scampered from somewhere behind the building, then narrowed its eyes at the car before dashing through the entrance which had been propped open, presumably to let in a breeze.

'You didn't need to drive me,' Jessie said for what felt like the hundredth time as she opened the car door, grabbed her grandma's camera and hopped out. After they'd had cake and coffee at The Beach Café, she'd driven her grandad's car back to Look Out House, following Ashton who'd insisted on transporting all three dogs, Elsie and George before bringing her here.

'I told you, it's Sunday: I don't have to work,' Ashton said. 'You said you needed someone to practise your portraits on and I already volunteered, remember?'

He'd been quiet in the car and neither of them had mentioned the kiss the night before, but the air had been oddly charged, and Jessie wondered if before long she wouldn't be able to stop herself from blurting out something. Although she had no idea what she'd say. *Kiss me again – make me feel the way you did last night? I need to know I can feel attractive, but I don't want to talk about it, and I know there's no way this thing between us can work out...*

She sighed as a bright green cabriolet Volkswagen Beetle drew up on the driveway beside them, spraying pebbles as it parked. Lila leaped out of the driver's side. 'Sorry I'm late, I was dropping my granddaughter Ruby at the Roskilly Brewery,' she said. 'She's dating one of the owners, Gabe.'

Gryffyn slowly got out of the other side of the Beetle and nodded at them before heading for The Pottery Project.

'Do you fancy a tour?' Lila asked, pointing to a hefty brown cat as it poked its nose from the studio entrance. 'This is Coffee – all four of my cats are named after my favourite cakes,' she explained, as she skipped towards the door. 'I'm not sure if I'll be able to find them all today, but if you want to take a look around, perhaps you can get some ideas for places to photograph them. I like the idea of them being snapped in situ and the pictures would work well on the website. Why don't you both come in?'

Lila fixed Ashton with her blue eyes, and Jessie wondered what the older woman was thinking. 'It's good to have you here, boy – I'm not sure you ever visited before, although I do believe I've invited you at least a thousand times.'

When Ashton flushed, she waved a hand. 'It's not a criticism, pet, but it's good you're finally out and about. Elsie's very fond of you and she worries a lot.' She narrowed her eyes. 'It doesn't do a person any good to hide themselves away from the world, especially not from a village like ours. We're all far too nosy, so it's not like you can get away with it forever, although you've managed for a lot longer than most.' With that, she entered the studio.

Gryffyn had already donned an apron and was working at a

pottery wheel. He'd switched on the record player perched on the white counter which hugged one of the walls and a cool jazz track was playing. Lila wandered over to see what he was working on, but he grunted and waved her away.

'Ignore him,' she advised. 'Gryffyn's a talented potter, but he's not very communicative when he's working, it's all part of his "bad cop" routine.' She rotated and spread her arms as if taking in the large studio.

It had high ceilings with Velux windows, which meant every inch of the space was flooded with sunlight. There were tables on both sides of the room, each with their own pottery wheel. A large desk had been placed at the top of the room, which Jessie guessed was the teaching table. Bright-white windowsills on the far left were cluttered with cacti and tomato plants bursting with fruit.

'Take a look around, get a feel for the space. The cats pop in and out all day. There are no lessons going on, so you can take as much time as you like.'

Jessie held onto the camera as she paced. It was a pretty room, and she could already see dozens of places which would be brilliant for catching a cat stretching, yawning or sleeping. Her stomach fluttered as her mind woke from years of inertia and filled with compositions and poses which she wondered if she could pull off.

'I can work with this,' she said, putting the viewfinder up to her face and swivelling around so she could take in the various scenes.

What would Dorothy make of the photos she was taking now? When Jessie was younger, she had spent hours with her grandmother exploring landscapes through a viewfinder on many an afternoon. Her grandma had always been so patient, had spent plenty of time explaining how things worked.

Jessie had forgotten how losing herself behind a lens had made her feel. Photography had originally provided an escape from Maria, then it had become the way Jessie wanted to spend all her time – a place where she could create the perfect reality she craved.

'Then why don't you pop up one afternoon next week? Friday? I'll give you both a go on the wheel, you can take photos of the studio and if we're lucky, catch all four of my cats?' Lila suggested, flapping a hand at Ashton too.

'I'm not sure.' He frowned, but the older woman waved away his obvious reluctance.

'Just for an hour or two, pet. You'll hardly even notice you're here. Now I've got you in my studio, I'm determined you'll come back.' She grinned.

Gryffyn looked up from the pottery wheel he was working at and served Ashton a weighty look. 'Don't fight it, lad, she's going to get her own way whether you argue or not.'

'I've a vague recollection that your mother used to do pottery – am I right?' Lila asked suddenly, her forehead squeezing as she cast her mind back. 'She might even have joined one of my beginner courses...'

'I don't remember,' Ashton said gruffly, as the colour leached from his face. He noticed Jessie watching him and turned around before pacing to one of the counters so he could study the vases, cups and bowls on display.

Lila obviously didn't realise he was uncomfortable because she continued to chatter as she wandered around the studio patting her tomato plants, picking up tea towels and pottery tools and tidying them away. 'Don't you have a sister somewhere, what's her name? Forgive me, it was a long time ago and it's only now you're here I'm remembering it all.' She returned from where she'd been depositing a plate in the kitchen, and it was then that Ashton turned too.

'Merrin,' he whispered, and Jessie wondered what she could hear in his voice. Ashton had mentioned a younger sister on the beach fourteen years ago but hadn't told Jessie her name. *What had happened? Why did he look so upset?*

'I'm so sorry, I didn't mean to stir up bad feelings,' Lila said, reading Ashton's face.

'It's okay,' he replied and gave her a lopsided smile. 'Apologies,' Ashton said after a few more seconds. 'I think I've left my phone in the car.' With that, he marched out of the door.

The studio was quiet for a few moments and then Gryffyn grunted. 'I think you just upset the boy.' He shot Lila an accusatory glare.

Lila wiped her hands on her bright green smock and glanced across at Jessie, looking worried. 'Is his sister okay?' she asked.

Jessie shook her head. 'I've no idea.' She glanced towards the exit. 'Look, I'd better go – but I'll come back on Friday like you said, and we can take the pictures then.' With that, she waved at the older couple and walked out into the driveway. There was a story here, one Ashton obviously didn't want to share – but would he if she asked?

Ashton didn't talk in the car for the whole drive to Sunset Point. Jessie left him alone with his thoughts and watched out of the window as they sped past laybys bursting with vibrant summer flowers that quivered in the breeze, and she marvelled at the occasional peek of the sea beyond the hedgerows. When he pulled up in a small sandy car park, he sat for a few moments in silence before turning the engine off.

'Before you ask, I don't want to talk about my parents or Merrin,' he said without looking at her. 'It was a long time ago, and they're no longer a part of my life.' Ashton opened the door of the Land Rover and climbed out, tracking around to open the door to help Jessie onto the ground even though she didn't need assistance.

Jessie let out a long sigh. 'So you're happy to share lips but not life stories?' She should probably respect his wishes, but had never been good at keeping her mouth shut – and somehow guessed Ashton needed to talk about his sister, even if he denied it. He was still pale, and she could almost feel the sadness seeping from his skin.

Ashton grunted and took Jessie's hand. The casual intimacy of it surprised her. He led her across the car park to a small track that wound upwards. It was framed by trees and summer flowers, but the vegetation was sparse enough that she could see the sky. The sun was still high, and the sky was an almost unreal cyan blue. The scene would make a beautiful photo, although the matching one in her grandad's honeymoon album had been snapped closer to dusk.

'There's a bench up here. I think this is where George and Dorothy must have gone. Couples have been visiting it for years – I've heard it's very romantic,' Ashton said.

'Have you been?' Jessie cleared the sudden ball of envy from her throat.

'I've walked Murphy and Bear up here a few times, but I've never brought a date.' He dropped her hand and opened a gate which led to the narrow pathway before letting her walk through it first.

'Seems like a waste,' Jessie said, ignoring the tingles charging through her fingertips and holding the camera up to her face so she could hide any telltale signs of jealousy and frame a quick shot.

'I'm not a monk, Jess, but I've never wanted something serious – I don't do "romantic", that's always seemed dishonest to me.' Ashton frowned, turning so he could look at her. 'You're the only girl I ever met who drew out feelings I didn't want to have.' He continued to stare at her as if he were trying to figure out why. But Jessie couldn't help – men like Ashton didn't fall for women like her. 'I never looked to repeat them, I don't particularly want to now.'

His words skewered her, but Jessie chose to move on. 'Because of your sister?' she guessed.

'What bit of "I don't want to talk about it" did you not understand?' Ashton let out a frustrated sigh. 'It's up here,' he said, charging ahead.

'I understood,' Jessie said, and despite her long legs had to scramble to keep up. 'I'm just going to ignore it. Everyone has to talk to someone.'

'Says who?' he asked, as he reached the top, panting heavily.

Jessie was about to respond, but then her attention caught on the view. 'Wow,' she said. 'It's not often I'm rendered speechless, but that's really something. Even Grandma's photos didn't do it justice.' They were surrounded by so many colours – there was the sky, and the hint of sparkly blue sea in the distance, which looked indigo from where they were standing. The ground was dusty and had a slight orange hue while the trees were a lush emerald colour, despite the recent lack of rain. Wild flowers were peppered in between the trees, providing random splashes of pink, white and blue. In short, it was stunning.

Ashton let out a long breath. 'You're right,' he said quietly, shifting around to take in the panorama. 'I've lived here my whole life, but I can't say I've ever really noticed how striking the scenery is. Familiarity breeds contempt, I suppose.'

'Or perhaps you just haven't taken the time to appreciate things,' Jessie said, gently taking a couple of quick snaps and then offering him the Nikon. 'Look through here, the camera has a way of narrowing the attention – of blocking everything else out. It can both show us the truth and misrepresent it.'

'How do you know if you're seeing the truth then?' Ashton asked.

Jessie shrugged. 'Instinct. I used to know – at least I did until I met Brendon. Then I stopped looking through the camera, which is probably why I couldn't see it anymore.' She sighed.

Ashton paused and then took the camera and looked through the lens, taking his time to slowly sweep his way across the landscape. Jessie watched the bunch of taut muscles on his forearms as he gripped the Nikon. Then he shifted around until he was staring straight at her. She faced him down until she began to feel uncomfortable and dropped her gaze, starting to pick at her pink T-shirt. It was old and she probably should have put something better on, something more flattering.

'I know you don't like people looking at you.' Ashton dropped the camera to his chest, waiting until she moved her gaze up to his face. 'Is it because of the ex, or the evil stepmother?'

'You remembered Maria?' Jessie said, surprised and oddly touched. He shrugged, then she narrowed her eyes as she realised what he was doing. 'We're not talking about me today, Ashton, I'm bored of me. I want you to tell me about Merrin.'

'I'm not talking about her,' he said flatly, but he took a step forward and his eyes darkened. 'Shall we talk about the kiss last night instead?' Ashton's voice had deepened to a pitch that made Jessie's nerves vibrate.

She flushed but couldn't seem to move. Jessie knew Ashton was changing the subject again but somehow couldn't call him out on it. Perhaps because she wanted to talk about it too?

'You didn't run,' she said slowly. 'You did go home, though.' Was that the same thing?

'Because I thought you wanted me to – and because I needed to think.' Ashton took a second step – now they were so close she could feel the warmth of his breath on her cheek. 'I didn't want to run. I don't know what I wanted but...' His mouth pinched and emotions flitted across his skin. 'This makes no sense.'

'What, you finding me attractive?' Jessie asked quietly, but her voice didn't betray the sharp stab of hurt.

Ashton sighed. 'You know what I saw when I looked through that camera?'

Jessie looked up at him. His cheeks were flushed now, and there was a look in his eyes. She swallowed. 'I've no idea.'

He slowly shook his head as he stared at her. 'A very attractive woman, who has no concept of the power she has over a man. Someone with a talent she's denying herself because...' Ashton shrugged. 'I don't know, because she doesn't think she deserves it, or some...' He frowned. 'Let me use one of your grandad's words – *some bozo* – made her feel like she wasn't capable. Probably because he realised exactly how far out of his league she was.'

Jessie opened her mouth and closed it. She could feel her hands shaking, perhaps with emotion, or maybe because she wanted to touch him and wasn't sure if she should. She cleared her throat. 'You're talking rubbish, but I appreciate the sentiment.'

Ashton shook his head. 'You just told me a camera can misrepresent or show the truth. I know which one I saw, and my instincts are sound. Which is probably why I want to kiss you again.'

'You do?' she gasped.

'Can I?' he asked, echoing the question he'd asked on the night they first met.

'Sure.' Jessie gulped because even if she wanted to, she couldn't have refused. 'But you should know when we stop kissing, I'm going to ask about Merrin again.'

'I wouldn't expect anything else, but you should know I won't talk about her,' Ashton said, before closing the distance between them.

This kiss was as powerful as the ones they'd shared twice before. A part of Jessie had been hoping their chemistry had worn off or dulled overnight – fireworks went off and fizzled out, didn't they? Even volcanoes fell dormant after erupting, although that could take a few years. But it was like the laws of nature didn't apply to them. Ashton's lips were soft and warm, and he was pushing the camera out of the way, wrapping his arm around her waist and pulling her tight to his groin and all she could think was, *dear God, please let me get closer.*

Jessie sighed a little and pressed a hand against one of Ashton's shoulder blades so she could press her chest into his pecs. Then she tangled her other hand into his hair, looping her fingertips through the soft strands so she could tug his face closer, crushing their lips together so fiercely they bumped teeth. Is this what it felt like to want to climb inside somebody? She could almost feel the ball of need at her core, as if her id had claimed her brain rendering all sensible parts of her character obsolete.

She could feel the sun beating down on her head, like it was the only link with reality that was left. She tried to hold onto it, even as Ashton slid a palm under her thigh and hoisted it to his hip so he could press himself closer to her centre. Jessie responded with a needy moan and ground herself into him just as a dog barked in the distance, crashing her back to earth. Ashton must have heard it too because he slowly let go of her leg, holding her up as her knees wobbled. She swallowed as he encircled her in his arms.

'It's okay, it's just someone walking their dog, they didn't see anything,' he whispered, and she pressed her nose into his neck and breathed in his musky scent until she heard the walker pass by. 'If he'd come by just ten minutes later, I'm not sure I could have said the same thing.' Jessie was shaking when Ashton stepped away, but he continued to hold gently under her elbow as if he couldn't bring himself to let go. 'I'm sorry, that was...' He breathed. 'I was going to say unexpected, but that would be a lie. I knew that would happen again, I just didn't know when.'

'You've got nothing to apologise for,' Jessie said, regaining control over her voice. 'I was as much a part of that whole thing as you, and I... I loved it. I'm not going to lie. I felt... things I've not really felt with anyone but you. Things I want to feel again.'

Ashton's eyes met hers and he jerked his chin. 'I don't want to rush into something we might regret.' He grimaced, his eyes glittering. 'I told you about my parents, about their relationship. Getting close to people has always ended up negatively for me. This is exactly the type of thing I've spent my life avoiding.'

'And it's something I've been looking for, but never thought I'd find,' Jessie admitted. Ashton's eyes flared. 'You probably don't want to hear that, but, you know me, I'm nothing if not candid.'

'Being honest isn't something you should ever apologise for, Jess,' he said, his voice intense. 'Let's sleep on it, shall we, see how we feel tomorrow?'

'I know I'm going to feel the same,' Jessie said, pinning him with her eyes. Was he trying to back out? She couldn't really tell, but she braced herself for disappointment.

Ashton sighed, but he nodded. 'I know I will too, but let's give ourselves the time anyway – I'm hoping I'll come to my senses. This is complicated, and it's going to get messy.' He stepped forward and pressed his face into her hair, dropped a soft kiss onto her forehead before stepping away. 'You should take your photos. I happen to know Elsie's got a banquet planned for us all later, and we still need to go back to Sea Glass Cottage to pack up your stuff. We don't have to take the lot tonight – it'll take Ella a few days to get new tenants into the cottage.'

'Okay,' Jessie said, reaching a hand out for the camera, shuddering when their fingers brushed as he handed it to her.

'Damn,' Ashton said, pulling his hand away. 'Let's head for the bench and do me a favour, will you?' His gaze was penetrating. 'Don't let me touch you again.'

'Until tomorrow,' Jessie said, and felt something inside her shift when he nodded. It could have been excitement, she wasn't sure, but she did know whatever happened in the next twenty-four hours, she wasn't going to change her mind or back out...

15

Buzz, buzz, buzz.

Jessie groaned and turned over in bed as the ringer at the front gate of Look Out House went off again. She checked her watch and winced when she spotted the small hand was now hovering over the number three. How long had she been in bed? It felt like minutes. After her visit to Sunset Point with Ashton, she'd moved the bulk of her and George's things to Look Out House, shared a meal with Elsie, her grandfather and Ashton in the dining room before heading to bed just after eleven. But she hadn't been able to sleep – her head was in a turmoil thinking about tomorrow. What would it bring?

A door opened upstairs, followed by the loud thump of footsteps. 'What's going on?' Jessie yawned, rolling onto her other side and putting her feet onto the floor. Then she grabbed her dressing gown from a nearby chair and tracked to the bedroom door.

She peered outside just as Elsie shouted. 'Don't worry, I've pressed the button, the gates are opening.'

'Do you even know who it is?' Ashton yelled, as his feet hammered on the stairs.

Jessie wandered out of her bedroom onto the landing, rubbing sleep from her eyes, and peered over the banister just as her grandad appeared from his bedroom, limping with Phoebe at his heels. 'What's going on? I'm a hundred per cent convinced that's not the milkman.' He yawned, mussing his hair until it was poking all over the place.

'Just a visitor!' Elsie replied breathlessly. Jessie trotted downstairs to join them just as the older woman swung open the front door. 'They didn't give a name, but whoever it is said they needed to speak to Ashton urgently. It's all very thrilling, but I hope they don't wake Peaches, or he may decide it's morning already.'

Murphy and Bear appeared from the kitchen and bounded out of the doorway, then Phoebe abandoned Jessie's grandfather and followed them as a set of lights flickered on, illuminating the drive. They all huddled together to watch a tall figure walk towards them, flanked by the three dogs. As they drew closer, Jessie could see the person was female with long hair that had been tangled into a messy plait. The young woman was wearing jeans and a blue shirt and was hunched into an odd shape. She followed the driveway around a curve and Jessie spotted the backpack she was carrying and the basket looped through her right arm.

'Are you all right?' Elsie cried, making her way onto the porch.

'Does Ashton Reynolds live here?' the girl asked, as she reached them and put the backpack carefully onto the floor, holding the basket closer to her chest as she straightened her shoulders. Then she stared at them expectantly.

'Why do you want to know?' Ashton stepped forward and shoved his hands into the pockets of his jeans. His white T-shirt was crumpled and Jessie wondered if he'd slept in his clothes or had tugged the whole ensemble on before leaving his room. He looked good – better than he had a right to, considering it was the middle of the night – and Jessie wondered if she'd dream about him when she went back to bed. She was sure the answer was yes.

'Because I need to talk to him.' The girl flicked her plait over her shoulder.

'It's very late. Did you think about calling first?' Ashton asked grumpily.

'I've been doing that for weeks,' the girl shot back, narrowing her blue eyes.

'Ah, so you're our mystery caller,' Elsie whispered, putting a hand to her chest. 'I've had such a strange feeling about those calls. I just knew they were going to be important. It's good you're finally here.'

'Do you know something I don't?' Ashton asked Elsie.

'You're Ashton...' the girl interrupted. 'I would have recognised you anywhere from your eyes.' She looked less self-assured as she stared at him, and he silently gazed back.

'What do you want?' Ashton asked, but Elsie waved his question away.

'Do you want to come in?' Elsie indicated towards the hallway. 'Someone will bring in your backpack, and we can go into the kitchen to talk.' She cocked her head. 'You're a little young to be out on your own this late.'

'I'm seventeen – old enough to be here and old enough to do what I want.' The girl frowned. She was tall, almost the same height as Jessie would have been at the same age. She was prettier, though, with high cheekbones and arresting blue eyes, all topped off by an adorable heart-shaped mouth. Her clothes were loose and unflattering, and she tried to tug the T-shirt over her jeans, hunching her shoulders again.

'I think we've met,' Elsie said, considering her. 'Do you remember me?'

'I don't understand...' Ashton said, sounding confused. 'Why would she recognise you?'

Jessie studied the girl's face, wondering why she felt the same.

The girl's attention flickered to Ashton and then she looked at Elsie again. 'I don't know you. I live in a small village in the Scottish Highlands called Lockton. If we'd met, I'm sure I'd remember you.' The girl took a tiny step into the hallway. Then she checked left and right as if deciding if it was safe. She turned and watched Ashton as he mulled over what to do before picking up her backpack and lugging it inside.

'You'd better come in.' Ashton sighed. 'Is there anyone else out there waiting for you?' He peered back into the empty driveway.

'It's just me.' The girl watched as Ashton shut the door and placed her backpack to the side of it. Then she carefully put the basket beside it.

'Are you looking for Ashton because you want to rent a room?' Ashton asked, his gaze switching from the young girl's to Elsie's as if he were trying to puzzle something out. 'This is a private house, not a hotel or hostel,' he continued. 'But you should stay until the morning obviously.' His cheeks flushed. 'I don't want you out there alone...' He shoved his hands into his pockets again as he focused on her, perhaps taking in her age. 'Where are your parents?'

The girl's forehead pinched. She looked younger now she was under the bright light from the chandelier and less sure of herself. What had she been doing out there in the dark on her own? 'I'm not here for a bed, I wanted to see you.' She shoved her hands into her pockets, mirroring Ashton like a cantankerous mini-me.

'Why?' He looked suspicious.

The girl gulped. 'Because...' she swallowed again and blinked, 'I think I'm your sister, Merrin.'

Jessie saw Ashton's eyes widen, then flicker over the young girl's face before he took a deliberate step away from her. So his sister was alive? After he'd refused to share any information about her, Jessie had thought the worst.

'As I suspected,' Elsie said quietly.

Ashton cleared his throat, colour draining from his cheeks. 'No, you're not, you can't be.' His voice was low and deep, like it was coming from somewhere far away. 'She's...' His mouth twisted. 'Gone. She moved away with my parents years ago, I've not seen her since she was three. Is this some kind of scam – are you looking for money? How do you know about her anyway?' The words shot out like bullets, his voice odd.

Jessie took a step forward, unsure as to whether she needed to throw herself in front of the girl to protect her, or comfort Ashton as he looked so shaken.

Merrin wrapped her arms around herself and jerked her chin. 'Do I need to show you something to prove I'm me?' the girl asked, glaring at him. When Ashton looked at her blankly, she shuffled in the back pocket of her jeans. 'I've got ID: I needed it for my bus pass to get to college.'

She shoved a plastic card under Ashton's nose, but he didn't look at it. Elsie took it from her hand instead. 'It says Merrin Jones,' she said softly.

'My sister would be a Reynolds, not a Jones,' Ashton shot back.

The girl's mouth pinched. 'Dad changed our names when we moved.'

'Ashton, she's telling the truth. I knew it the moment I opened the door. She looks just like you did at the same age,' Elsie said quietly. 'I've had a feeling for a while – all those mystery phone calls and hang-ups, but I wasn't sure...'

Ashton shook his head. 'You're mistaken. My sister's gone.' He stared at the young girl, his face a storm of emotions. Jessie could see the tension in his shoulders, though, could tell this whole situation had thrown him and he had no idea what to do.

'Well, okay.' Merrin blinked a couple of times. 'At least now

I know how you feel. I guess I should have believed our dad.'
She swallowed. 'He told me if I ever tried to find you, you
wouldn't be interested and would probably try to pretend you
didn't even know me.'

She glanced at the basket and backpack which were still sat
near the door frame. 'You should have picked up your phone: it
would have saved me a long trip. It's fine, I get it, you don't owe
me anything and you definitely don't need some random sister
turning up on your doorstep. Everyone for themselves, that's the
Reynolds/Jones mantra, isn't it? I almost forgot.'

She straightened her shoulders in a gesture Jessie recognised, and she knew that despite the outward show of bravado,
the girl's heart was breaking into tiny shards – pieces it might
take her years to put together again. 'It's fine.' The girl blinked,
and Jessie saw her eyes were glistening. 'You don't need to
worry. I can see myself out.' She began to head back towards the
door but stopped when Jessie spoke up.

'Please, don't...' she said, recognising the feelings of rejection and fighting her own waves of emotion as they threatened
to consume her. Why wasn't Ashton saying anything?

'I think we'd all be happier if you stayed until the morning,
Merrin,' Elsie said kindly, giving Ashton an assessing look.
'Why don't we find somewhere comfortable to talk? I for one
would like to hear more about you. George—' She nodded at
Jessie's grandad as he yawned and his shoulders sagged. 'Why
don't you go back to bed and we can fill you in in the morning?
You need to rest that hip or you'll be off your feet for even
longer. You wanted to go with Jessie to The Pottery Project
tomorrow, remember?'

'I'm fine...' His eyelids began to droop, and he rubbed a
hand across his side.

'Grandad...' Jessie protested.

'I wonder if Merrin would be more relaxed if she wasn't
surrounded by so many strangers?' Elsie whispered.

George pondered that for a moment, then nodded. 'You're right, that I can understand.' His chest heaved. 'You can fill me in tomorrow. Phoebe, time for bed.' He gathered the dog and waved before slowly limping back down the hallway.

'I'll bring you a hot chocolate and your painkillers as soon as I wake up,' Elsie shouted after him. 'Can I interest you in a mug now?' she asked Merrin, hooking an arm through the young girl's elbow, tugging her in the direction of the kitchen. 'I keep my marshmallows in a special hiding place so Ashton can't steal them.' She winked. 'The boy's always had such a sweet tooth – I don't suppose you remember because you were so young. If I don't keep my wits about me, he'd eat everything sugary in the cupboard.' She chuckled.

'If you're hungry after all your travelling, I made a chocolate cake today and there's a bit left.' She stopped for long enough to take in the girl's face and her eyes softened. 'It's not a surprise you don't remember me – I rarely got a chance to see you face-to-face, but when you lived in Indigo Cove, my house was next door to yours. I used to bake cupcakes for you sometimes. You were such a lovely child...'

'I'm sorry, I don't remember.' Merrin chewed her bottom lip, then she glanced at Ashton who'd stopped a careful distance behind. 'I don't think I should stay. *He* doesn't want me here. He doesn't even believe I'm me.' Her eyes filled again, and she swiped at them.

Ashton stared at her, then shook his head. 'I need to think,' he said, before turning on his heels and disappearing towards the back of the house with Murphy and Bear. Jessie wanted to hate him for running, but he was obviously hurting, and she wasn't going to judge until she had more facts.

Merrin stared after him, then she swallowed before turning her shining eyes to Elsie. 'I should leave.'

The older woman shook her head. 'You need to give your brother time. He's a good man, but you arriving like this is a big shock.' Elsie led Merrin into the kitchen before depositing her beside one of the bar stools. The teen sat, then put the basket on the table within easy reach. Jessie took the seat next to her and leaned her hands on the breakfast bar. 'Stay there and we can talk. How did you get here?' Elsie enquired setting a large piece of cake on a plate and putting it on the counter in front of the young girl before going to heat milk on the stove.

'I got the train and then hitched a couple of rides.'

Jessie winced. Where were the girl's parents – surely they wouldn't want her out alone like this? Why wasn't Ashton in touch with them? The whole thing was a mystery. Jessie watched Merrin stare at the cake before she attacked it with so much gusto Jessie guessed she hadn't eaten for a while.

'It was okay, everyone who picked me up was friendly.' Merrin licked chocolate from her fork, furtively checking the room, perhaps searching for hints of her brother. She must be trying to figure him out.

'I can assure you, it's not okay,' Elsie said sternly, as she stirred cocoa powder and sugar into the milk, shaking her head. 'Why did you decide to come here this evening? Is there a reason why you chose today?'

Merrin shovelled in another piece of cake and chewed slowly before swallowing. 'I've been calling for a while, but no one picked up. Mum and Dad...' She winced. 'I call them Genni and Christian – they're our parents – went on holiday yesterday and left me to take care of...' She scrubbed her forearm over her mouth, cleaning off a chocolate moustache, and then lifted the blanket from the top of the basket. Three tabby kittens immediately sprang up to look over the side.

Merrin stroked one of the cats under its jaw and her expression softened as it began to purr. 'This is Pavlov.' She tapped a bitten down fingernail above his head. 'This is Newton and this is Lovelace. Science is my favourite subject,' she explained. 'I found the litter a few weeks ago by the side of the road close to where we live. I've been hiding them in my bedroom, and Genni and Christian didn't know about them until last night.' She swallowed. 'I was supposed to stay home and watch the house – and they told me to get rid of them while they were away. But I can't.' She looked into the basket, frowning. 'I've been thinking of leaving for a while; I realised then I had to move out now.'

'Why did you want to move out?' Elsie asked.

Merrin frowned. 'I hate living with them, they're hardly ever home, and if they are, they're always arguing or criticising me.' She sighed. 'It just got to the point when I thought, it's time.'

'How did you find Ashton?' Elsie asked softly.

Merrin shrugged. 'I found a photo of him a couple of weeks ago in the shed when I was looking for a basket for the kittens to sleep in.' She sighed. 'I've been dreaming about him since before I can remember. When I asked Mum and Dad if the dreams meant anything and if I had a brother, Genni told me I was just making stuff up. But when I showed Christian the photo, he said I did have a brother and that he'd left us.' Her forehead creased. 'That caused a big row. Another one...' She sighed.

'What happened then?' Jessie leaned forward.

'Christian told me Ashton had moved out when I was three and had cut off all contact with us. He said he didn't want a sister, and that I annoyed him.' Jessie could hear hurt in the girl's voice. 'But I remember him playing with me – he used to take me to the park. Was I imagining all that?'

'Ashton used to take you everywhere with him,' Elsie soothed, as she placed a steaming mug of hot chocolate piled with marshmallows in front of Merrin. 'He didn't leave, it was the other way around. Your parents went one night without a word when he was nineteen.'

Elsie's eyes flickered to Merrin, and Jessie saw sympathy in them, and felt the same sympathy reflected in hers. So that's why Ashton hadn't wanted to tell her about his sister. If it were true, it was no wonder he avoided getting close to people.

'He never got over losing you,' Elsie added softly.

'That's...' Merrin shook her head looking confused. 'But why didn't he try to find us?'

'He searched for months,' Elsie said.

Merrin picked up her mug, blew on it before taking a small sip.

'He went to the police, but there was almost nothing they could do.'

'So he just gave up?' Merrin put the mug back onto the table and slid it away, even though it was still half-full. 'I'd *never* have stopped looking. He can't have cared that much.'

'Ashton searched for three years and found nothing,' Elsie said. 'He'd tried everything by then, and I honestly didn't think he'd ever find you. I told him he had to stop because the whole thing was tying him in knots. He couldn't eat, sleep, work – it almost destroyed him. I thought your parents must have taken you out of the country.'

'Just Scotland.' Merrin's lips thinned.

'Do they know you planned to come and find him?' Jessie asked.

Merrin shook her head. 'I haven't spoken to them since they left for Portugal. I know they were planning on staying out there for a few weeks, but they haven't actually told me when they're due back. I searched Christian's office when they were out – broke into a box he keeps locked – and found Ashton's birth certificate. Dad had put it together with mine. That's when I discovered we had the same surname: Reynolds.' Her eyes widened. 'But I always thought I was Merrin Jones. Now I know I'm a whole different person, a Reynolds just like him.' She shrugged. 'I looked my brother up on the internet, found a number in company's house.'

'Clever,' Elsie said softly.

Merrin lifted a shoulder, looking embarrassed. 'I'm good at problem-solving, at least that's what all my teachers say. Christian says I'm a show-off.' She looked towards the door where Ashton had been standing earlier. 'I've been calling and calling, but he never picks up. I think you did once, but I wanted to talk to him.' Her eyes shadowed. 'What's the point in having a phone if you're never going to answer it?' She shrugged. 'I thought I'd come to find him myself. I know I should have expected his reaction – he doesn't want a sister.' Her eyes darted around the room. 'I'm *so* stupid.' She nibbled her thumbnail and screwed up her nose.

'You're not stupid,' Jessie said, feeling the girl's pain to her core. She understood about not being wanted. How much the rejection hurt and coloured how you felt about yourself.

'Give Ashton time,' Elsie pressed. 'This has come as a shock. Why don't you finish your hot chocolate, and you can choose a bedroom to sleep in? There's plenty of room for the kittens, and you'll have your own bathroom too.'

'Seriously?' Merrin's eyes expanded. They were the same blue as her brother's and just as stormy and sad.

Elsie nodded. 'I'll fish out some tuna to feed the cats. In the morning, I'll introduce you to Peaches – my cockerel. I suspect he'd like to meet the kittens too. He's surprisingly good with animals. Do you like puzzles?' She waited while Merrin grabbed her drink and swallowed the rest down, then climbed from the stool.

On her way out of the kitchen, Elsie stopped by one of the cupboards and pulled out a large torch, and a flask before filling it with the leftover hot chocolate and handing it all to Jessie. 'Why don't you see if you can catch up with Ashton?' she said, as they left. 'I've a feeling the boy could do with someone to talk to.'

'I... um. Am I the right person?' Jessie asked, rising from her chair. She wasn't sure Ashton would want to see her. He hadn't wanted to talk about Merrin earlier today; she guessed he'd be even less open to it now.

'You're exactly what he needs. Try the beach first. Take a sweater so you don't get cold. There's a path down from the end of the garden by the cherry tree. You can't miss it.' With that, Elsie pointed Merrin in the direction of the hallway, and they were gone.

16

Fifteen minutes later, Jessie found Ashton standing at the edge of the sea, staring into the flurry of waves rocking by his feet. Murphy was racing with the bubbling foam of white horses, while Bear sat surveying the horizon, perhaps hoping it might deliver his next meal with the tide? Ashton had already set a small fire a few metres back from the shoreline – it had a couple of large rocks resting beside it which looked big enough to sit on. A blanket was laying on the sand beside one of the boulders, and Jessie wondered if Ashton was planning on staying here for the rest of the night.

It had taken her a while to find the right pathway down from the garden – and even longer to traverse the rocky cliffs using just the light from her torch. She'd taken it slowly because any ambient moonlight had been blocked by the surrounding shrubbery and she'd been worried about tripping over her own clumsy, big feet.

All the while Jessie's mind had been racing as she'd tried to piece together everything she'd heard this evening. How Ashton had been abandoned by his parents, how they'd stolen his sister from him, leaving him bereft and alone. A million feelings bubbled inside her – a new understanding for Ashton and sympathy for Merrin, the girl who'd also been deserted by her parents and then rejected by her brother all in the same week. So many of those emotions Jessie could relate to, but she knew she had to talk to Ashton, to find out more about his side of the story now.

She shone the light from her torch onto the ground, and it picked up the shimmer of powdery white sand. Both large and small seashells glittered under its beam, parading their colours like models on a catwalk. Had her grandparents ever ventured this far to take pictures and collect shells? The shapes and colours were similar to some of the photos in her grandparent's album. The idea of them having been here made her smile, despite the difficult situation they were all now plunged into.

Jessie took in a deep breath, inhaling chilly air which filled her lungs with salty courage. As she approached, Bear's ears pricked up first and he turned and began to bark and wag his tail but didn't move from his spot. Murphy hopped around and came bounding over to Jessie – just as Ashton saw her and frowned.

'So now you know why I didn't want to talk about my sister,' he said under his breath, before twisting back to stare at the waves. 'I still can't believe she's turned up on my doorstep after all these years... or that she's up in the house now and I'm just standing here.' He swiped a hand over his eyes.

'Elsie asked me to come to find you. I think she was worried you might try to make a swim for it.' Jessie nodded towards the sea and watched as Ashton shook his head.

'Are you going to tell me I'm a terrible person?' he asked, scratching a hand through his hair. 'Because I already know it. I don't know what she wants from me,' he said, his voice tortured.

'Perhaps she just wants to get to know her brother – is that really so bad?'

'That depends...' Ashton looked down and kicked at the

sand with his boot. The bottoms of his jeans were wet, and Jessie wondered how long he'd been standing there for. 'I still remember the night they took her.' His voice had deepened. 'She was mine, she'd always been more mine than theirs. I often wondered if they'd just taken her to hurt me. I don't know why I'm telling you this...'

'Because I'm here. Because I think you need to talk to someone.' Jessie held up the flask Elsie had given her. 'I have provisions. We can drink and talk, play the silent game, or you can stay there. It's up to you.' She turned and tracked back to the fire and sat on one of the rocks. It was more comfortable than she'd expected and the warmth from the blaze was comforting. She didn't watch for Ashton but heard his footsteps above the crackles of the flames and could feel him when he sat on the boulder beside her.

'I used to come to this spot a lot when I was younger.' His words were almost drowned by the crackles from the fire. He pointed left. 'If you walk in that direction, you'll find the place we met the other night, a few hundred metres from Sea Glass Cottage...'

'Scene of our kissing crimes.' Jessie sighed as the memory of them shot through her. A gust of wind blew past making her lips tingle like someone had just brushed a feather over them. The sensation set off something low in her belly, a fresh flood of desire.

'The beach used to be where I went to think, to escape.' Ashton stared into the flames and Jessie opened the flask and poured a cup of hot chocolate, trying to get her errant body back under control.

'No marshmallows, they're all gone,' she warned, offering Ashton the mug.

'Where's Merrin?' He took a sip and let out a soft moan of pleasure before offering it back to her.

'Elsie's making her comfortable. She's going to stay the

night.' Jessie watched as Ashton processed the information, then pinched the bridge of his nose.

'That's good – she's too young to be wandering the streets on her own,' he said. 'At least I didn't scare her off. She deserved a better welcome, but seeing her again was a surprise and I... I needed time to think, to figure out what I'm going to do now.'

'Tell me what happened?' Jessie asked, sipping the drink before handing him back the mug.

Ashton finished the hot chocolate and put the mug in the sand. Bear made a beeline for it but was obviously disappointed to find it empty because he whined. Ashton scrubbed his hands on his jeans. 'I wasn't going to tell you. I've tried to put the whole thing behind me.' He sighed. 'I was sixteen when Merrin was born.' He stared at his hands.

'I remember you talking about your sister,' Jessie confessed.

He nodded. 'Up until she came along, it had been just me and whichever dog I'd decided to adopt. My parents used to hate me bringing them home, but I liked the company and as long as I took care of them myself, they put up with it. It was probably just easier. The path of least resistance and all that...'

Jessie didn't point out that Merrin had done the same when she'd adopted the kittens. Had she needed the company too?

'I remember my parents fighting when Genni found out she was pregnant with Merrin. Christian was furious with her, as if the whole thing was just her fault.' He shook his head. 'They never really wanted kids – I was fine when I was small and cute and didn't argue back, but as soon as I got big enough to have my own opinions, they pretty much washed their hands of me. They liked the child benefit payments, so they didn't chuck me out and they weren't really cruel, they just...' He shrugged. 'It was like I didn't exist. Mostly they fought and we lived side by side. Half the time, I'm not even sure they remembered I was there.'

'How did you get by?' Jessie asked. Maria had been unkind,

but she'd never ignored Jessie, and Jessie had always had food and clothes even if they'd often come with strings attached. So long as she wore the right clothes, didn't emphasise her height, put on weight or share too many of her opinions, peace reigned. She'd learned to behave, to hide all those sides of herself – at least until she'd gone to university when she'd made more of an effort to embrace her real self via her photography. But when she'd met Brendon, her need to fit in had surfaced again.

'I had to fend for myself. I was pretty much feral until I met Elsie,' Ashton said.

'You told me once she'd saved you...' Jessie remembered. Now she understood.

Ashton nodded. 'I'll always owe her and Jeff for that.'

'Tell me more about Merrin,' she pressed.

Ashton's forehead pinched and Jessie studied his profile. He looked so unhappy – she wanted to touch his arm, to comfort him but didn't reach out. Perhaps she was afraid of what might happen if she did? She knew what she wanted, but Ashton's sister arriving complicated things. What if this situation made him change his mind? What if he no longer wanted to explore what was happening between them? It was obvious his desire to keep people at arm's length was linked to losing his sister. Now she was back, would it make him shut down again?

'I loved my sister from the minute she was born and tried to give her everything I didn't have. My parents were good to her, though, better than they were with me.' Ashton picked up one of the sticks laying by his feet and threw it onto the fire, watched as it blackened and disappeared. 'I think they preferred girls – perhaps they thought she'd be less argumentative, or maybe she was just prettier.' His lopsided smile briefly returned. 'I was always difficult, apparently. I used to work in the evenings to help support us, and one night when I got back from the bar I worked at, they'd just... taken everything and moved on...' Murphy wandered up and rested his head against

Ashton's leg, perhaps sensing the conversation was difficult for him.

'That's awful. What did you do?' Jessie asked.

He sighed. 'Elsie and Jeff helped me go to the police, but they couldn't do much. My parents had left debts, but between us, we sorted them all out. I was nineteen – if they wanted to up and leave, apparently that was fine.'

'You tried looking for them?' Jessie asked. 'Elsie said you had.'

'I wanted to find Merrin – I wasn't bothered about my parents – but I was a lot younger in those days and didn't have the resources. Now I know they changed their surname and moved to Scotland, I understand why I couldn't find them. I could track them down easily if I looked today with that information.' He wiped a hand over his face.

'But you stopped looking,' Jessie said, pulling her cardigan tighter. She hadn't changed out of her pyjamas which was probably a mistake because the silk was wispy and too thin even for a mild summer morning. Yet more honeymoon clothes she'd brought in an effort to feel sexy. But she didn't need clothes for that, she just needed Ashton to look at her.

He let out a breath. 'Maybe it was easier. Searching for Merrin was screwing with everything. On one hand, I was scared that if I did find my parents, they'd reject me all over again and Merrin wouldn't want to know me either. On the other, I hated feeling so helpless and when I stopped looking, stopped thinking about her altogether, things became bearable. I could get on with my life. I suppose I wanted to move forward...'

'Alone?' Jessie asked.

'I'm not sure that was a conscious decision, but it's how it worked out.' Ashton picked up another log and threw it into the fire. It crackled and spat a cloud of orange and red.

'When someone hurts you, it's hard to pick yourself up and move forward,' Jessie said. 'When they make you feel like you

don't matter, or that you're somehow not good enough, sometimes it's easier to just shut down.'

'Is that how I made you feel?' Ashton asked, turning to look
at her, his eyes unreadable in the reflected light from the
bonfire.

'Perhaps. Fourteen years ago, you devastated me, then when
I first saw you in The Beach Café, I felt angry and confused.
But not now,' Jessie admitted. 'Now I... well, you know what I
want.'

In retrospect, Maria and Brendon had done far more
damage and Jessie understood Ashton now, realised in many
ways that they were the same. Two people who'd been rejected
and made to feel like they didn't matter. He'd told her once he'd
learned to stop caring, but was that true? From where Jessie sat,
she could see he cared far more than he wanted to. The knowl-
edge made her like him even more.

'The thing is you've got a young woman – your sister –
sitting in a bedroom in your house thinking she doesn't matter to
you. That you don't want to know her. She's travelled hundreds
of miles and she's just as alone as you. Are you honestly going to
turn your back on her?'

'Of course not,' Ashton exhaled. 'But how am I supposed to
be a brother to a girl I barely know? What if I screw it up and
she leaves again? In case you hadn't noticed, I spend most of my
time trying to avoid connecting with people.' His forehead
creased. 'I think I've forgotten how.'

Jessie pressed a hand on Ashton's forearm and edged a little
closer. She could feel the heat from the fire had warmed his skin
and she wanted to melt into him. 'You let my grandad and I stay
in Look Out House even when you wanted us miles away. And
you did it because it made Elsie happy, and it meant an old man
could relive some of his special memories. You brought Ella the
jigsaw picture in the Lighthouse Gallery and tried to pretend it
wasn't you. You kissed me yesterday and I think we're both

ready to see where that might lead...' She felt the muscles in his arm flex, but he didn't pull away. 'You don't give yourself credit for the man you are. I'm guessing there are a lot of messages swimming around your head that you need to dismiss. Perhaps if you let Merrin stay, you'll discover in time that there's room in your life for her, after all?'

'I don't know what to do with a teenage girl...,' Ashton grumbled, his voice rough. 'I can barely take care of two dogs. It was easy when she was small. A couple of pushes on the swing, an ice lolly and me being around was everything she needed.'

'I'm pretty sure you don't need to do much,' Jessie said. 'As far as I know, teenagers will ignore you or tell you exactly what they want if you just take the time to listen, or wait until they're ready to talk. I don't know much, but I'm guessing like all of us they want to be loved. I'll bet Merrin just wants some of your attention and the chance to know her brother. You were close once and she mattered. I've a feeling she's a lot more vulnerable than she's making out. Perhaps she's just another misfit, like us?' She nudged him with her shoulder. 'It doesn't sound like she's wanted at home...'

Ashton looked up and his eyes held hers. 'My parents used to adore her. I always thought it was only me they didn't want...'

'Perhaps they don't know how to love? Not everyone does.' Jessie paused. 'I'm not sure it matters. The only thing that does is what you can offer her now.'

Ashton puffed and looked into the fire. 'Depends if Merrin wants to stay.'

'I'm pretty sure she does.' Jessie reached out and rubbed his shoulder, felt the heat from his skin under his T-shirt and let go when her palm started to tingle. 'You just need to talk to her, show her you're open to having a relationship. I think you'll be okay, and you'll have Elsie here to help if you're not.'

'And you and George too?' he asked hopefully.

'If you like...' Jessie said, touched.

Ashton shut his eyes. 'I'm going to need all the help I can get. I've had about three conversations in The Beach Café with Darren, and during two of them he rolled his eyes. That's all the experience I have of teenagers since I was one myself.'

'All teenagers roll their eyes – it's in the handbook,' Jessie said. 'We need to keep Merrin busy, find places you two can bond. Maybe she can come with us tomorrow to The Pottery Project. Think she'd like to go to The Puzzle Club too?'

Ashton shrugged. 'The only thing I know about my sister is she used to love cats, ice cream and swings.'

'It's a start.' Jessie reached out a hand and touched his arm. 'You know you're going to have to talk to her?'

Ashton nodded. 'I'm not going to let her down again.' He turned to her, and the flames cast shadows across his face. 'Thank you,' he said softly. 'For... I don't know. Making me feel like I can do this.'

Jessie's insides warmed. 'Us misfits need to stick together,' she said quietly.

'You're not a misfit, Jessie.' Ashton's voice was low. 'I've never met anyone who fits as well as you. Your grandad and Elsie adore you – you've only been here a week and Ella and Lila do too. I could see Merrin connecting with you almost as soon as she entered Look Out House.'

'Well, that's...' She swallowed and felt her cheeks flame. 'We'll see,' she said. Then she rose from the boulder and pulled her cardigan tighter around her. 'Do you think we should head back?' Jessie looked towards the house.

Ashton shook his head. 'Why don't we wait an hour, watch the sun rise, take another picture for your grandad's album?'

'I forgot the camera,' Jessie said, spreading her hands. 'But I'll sit with you, make some memories of my own.' She slumped back onto the boulder beside him, felt him tentatively reach out and place a warm palm over her hand.

'What we talked about yesterday,' he said, staring forward as Bear let out a sleepy whine.

'Mmmmmm...' Ashton was going to back out, Jessie could feel it, was surprised at how much it hurt.

'I'm going to need a few more nights. I don't want to get into something at the moment. I've got to focus on Merrin, figure out what I'm going to do...'

'Which leaves no room for kissing.' Jessie swallowed. 'I get it.'

She heard Ashton sigh. As the silence stretched, Jessie stared into the fire trying to convince herself it was probably for the best – that he was out of her league, after all...

17

Ashton could hear voices as he made his way down the stairs from his bedroom the following morning. He stopped in the hallway as he heard a girl laugh and his stomach lurched when he recognised the familiar timbre. A million memories flooded through his mind. Merrin had such a pretty laugh and had always been so quick to share it when she was a baby – his sister had been so open and loving, the opposite of him.

Ashton had lain awake for the last few hours, thinking about the months after Merrin had been ripped from his life. How he'd vowed to never let anyone get close to him again. Years later, he'd brought Look Out House as a place to escape, a fortress which would protect him from his feelings. But now they were vibrating under his skin, determined to run free – feelings for Jessie and now his sister he wasn't sure he was capable of ignoring, no matter how much his head told him he should.

He found Elsie, Merrin, George and Jessie all sitting around the kitchen counter sipping hot chocolate and he paused just inside the doorway, feeling out of place.

'We're just having a quick drink before we head to the café

for breakfast,' Elsie said, spying him. 'Merrin's decided to stay for another few days.'

The girl's mouth flattened as she turned to stare at him through narrowed eyes. There was a basket on the table, and Merrin reached a hand inside and Ashton saw it was filled with kittens. Was she using the pets to soothe herself? 'Unless you want me to leave?' she challenged. 'Because I know where the nearest bus stop is.'

'I'm sorry about yesterday,' Ashton said, taking a step into the kitchen, feeling something inside his chest squeeze when he saw Elsie smile and Jessie nod. 'It was a shock to find you on my doorstep after all this time. I didn't think I'd ever see you again and...' He blew out a breath, ignoring the almost overwhelming urge to escape. It would be so much easier if he walked away. But he wouldn't. Instead, he stepped further into the room and rested his hand on the counter close to where Merrin was sitting. 'I *am* happy you're here.' He felt the tightness across his chest ease.

'Elsie said you run your own business as a cyber security consultant which means you don't trust anyone.' Merrin gazed at him with eyes the same shade as his own. 'I suppose I can understand that. But I'm not here for your money.' She swallowed, her cheeks flooding with pink.

'I know that.' Ashton jerked his chin. 'And you're welcome to stay at Look Out House for as long as you want.' He folded his arms, saw Elsie frown and unlinked them.

'I'll stop for a couple of days and see how it goes.' Merrin's expression shuttered. 'I've got other places I can move to, people who want me.' She dropped her eyes to the table and drew her hand away from the basket so it wasn't close to his.

'It's always good to have options, Merrin,' Elsie reflected. 'But I hope you'll agree to stick it out. It would be good for the two of you to get to know each other again. We were planning on going to The Puzzle Club this morning, then Jessie's visiting The Pottery Project to take photos of some cats.'

His sister gaped. 'Cats?' she said reverently, and Jessie nodded. 'I like cats...' There was so much Ashton had forgotten about his sister or blocked out, but it gave him hope that he still remembered her love for cats at least.

'I might have to pass on The Pottery Project,' George said, rubbing a hand against his thigh. 'I was hoping to join you, but unfortunately my hip is still bothering me, and if I add up all the pros and cons, I think it'll be best if I rest it today.'

'I'll stay in The Beach Café with you,' Elsie offered. 'There are plenty more puzzles we can test our record with – I've a feeling we can do it even faster with more practice.'

'Look, I've got to make a call.' Ashton started to turn, suddenly desperate for the solace of his office, the security of the computer where he could lose himself for a while.

'You'll come to The Puzzle Club, though, won't you?' Elsie looked at him knowingly. 'And of course Lila is expecting you at The Pottery Project too.' She watched him hopefully and when Ashton looked around the table, he saw Jessie was gnawing on her lower lip while Merrin's mouth had thinned, suggesting she was expecting the worst.

He drew in a breath. Change was hard, but if he didn't try now, he'd be on his own for the rest of his life. A few weeks ago, that would have appealed, but it didn't now. 'Sure,' he promised. 'I can take a break for a while.'

Ashton opened the door of The Beach Café and stood aside to allow Jessie, George, Merrin with her basket and Elsie with Peaches, and the dogs to go in ahead. Ella was standing behind the counter piling clean mugs on top of one another, and Darren sat in one of the far corners doing a puzzle. 'This one has pieces missing too,' he complained.

'Good morning,' Elsie sang, making them both jump.

'I'm so glad you've arrived.' Ella waved her hands at an empty table. 'Darren, why don't you see what our customers would like to eat and drink?' She jerked her eyebrows towards them.

The teen pushed a lock of his dark hair back from his eyes and started to get up. Then his gaze locked on Merrin and his eyes twinkled. Ashton felt an unexpected surge of protectiveness.

'Hello. Who are you?' the boy asked, straightening to his full height and puffing out his chest as he moved away from his table towards them.

Ashton watched Merrin slowly blink as she took in the teenager's long limbs and untidy dark hair. She put the basket of kittens on the floor and wrapped her arms around herself. 'No one,' she mumbled, looking uncomfortable.

'This is Merrin Reynolds.' Elsie pulled out a chair as George sat at the table closest to her and selected a new puzzle before tipping out the pieces. 'She's Ashton's sister and she's visiting. I think she might enjoy jigsaws. Perhaps you could show her where everything is?' The boy nodded eagerly, and Ashton had a sudden urge to jump between them.

He watched his sister's shoulders hunch and her cheeks flush. She wore jeans and another T-shirt that was far too big for her again. He'd heard Jessie offer to lend her one of hers when they'd been getting ready earlier, but Merrin had refused. Now, Ashton was glad she had.

'Can we all have one of your special cream teas each, please?' Elsie asked, dispelling the awkward atmosphere.

'I'm not hungry,' Merrin said quietly. 'But I'll have a diet coke, please.'

'Why don't you sit over there? Underneath the picture.' Darren tentatively pointed to the table midway between where George was sitting and where he'd been working on his puzzle.

'I'll get your order.' He glanced across the café at Ella who gave him a surprised shrug before he sprinted towards the kitchen.

'I don't think I've seen that boy move so fast since he started working here,' Ella whispered to Merrin, giving her a slow wink. 'I think you might have to come back again tomorrow, you're obviously a good influence.'

His sister's cheeks went even redder, and Ashton frowned, watching as she gazed at the table Darren had suggested.

'Are you any good at puzzles?' Ella asked, going to pick one out of a large pile at the back of the café. 'Because I've tasked Darren with completing all of these – they were donated to us recently and some have bits missing, so I need him to make them up, to check. If you can help, I'd appreciate it.'

Merrin frowned. 'I've not done a jigsaw since I was a kid – we don't have any at home,' she said nervously, her eyes darting to Ashton, and he suddenly recalled the Barbie jigsaw he'd bought for her third birthday. His parents had abandoned it when they left. But after they'd gone, it had taken him over four years to part with it.

Merrin glanced at Elsie who gave her a warm smile. 'You'd better get started. If you're a fast puzzler, maybe you and the boy can make up a team in the Jigsaw Championships we're hosting here?' The older woman tipped a new puzzle onto the table and began to sort its pieces into piles.

Ashton watched his sister walk up to the table where Darren had been sitting. She took a few moments to stare at the framed jigsaw picture he'd bought for Ella before she stroked a finger over the glass.

'Everything okay?' Elsie asked, looking up from the pieces she'd been studying.

His sister shrugged. 'That picture's weird.' She shook her head. 'I feel like it's following me around the room.'

'I know, right?' Darren said loudly, appearing from the kitchen with a tray piled high with drinks and cakes.

'Teenagers...' Elsie let out an amused sigh.

'Maybe they're just seeing something we're not,' Ella whispered. 'Oh, before I forget.' She turned to Jessie. 'I got new tenants for Sea Glass Cottage – would you be able to finish getting your things out by the end of this evening so I can clean it first thing? They'd like to move in tomorrow if possible.'

'I can pick it all up later,' Jessie said, her eyes darting to her grandfather. 'There's not much to collect. I'll walk along the beach with a backpack this evening. I'm sure Phoebe would be happy to join me for a walk.'

'I'll come with you, bring Murphy and Bear,' Ashton found himself offering.

'If you go late enough, you could see the nightfall,' Elsie pondered, tapping her chin.

'I had a very romantic photo of the sunset in my album, do you remember, Jess?' her grandfather asked.

She nodded as her attention darted to Ashton. 'I'm sure we can recreate it...'

'You're here!' Lila bounded out of The Pottery Project as soon as Ashton drew the car up on the gravel driveway. She was wearing a bright red smock today with matching Dr. Martens and had an array of pottery tools poking from her bun.

'You must be Ashton's sister!' She ran to the car to greet Merrin with a hug and helped her out of the car with the basket of kittens. 'Elsie called this morning to let us know you'd be coming along today too. I understand our Darren's taken quite a shine— Oh,' she said when Merrin's cheeks glowed, 'I don't want to embarrass you, but we're very fond of the boy here. His dad won't let him come to The Pottery Project anymore, and I miss seeing him.'

She took the teenager's hand and lead her into the studio while Ashton waited for Jessie to get out of the car. 'You'll never

believe I was asking your brother about you just yesterday afternoon – Elsie's been talking about you recently and she had a
funny feeling you might turn up.' Lila's voice grew fainter as she
entered the studio.

'Looks like Merrin's made a friend,' Jessie said, as they made
their way into the bright building and watched as the girl put
the basket onto the counter and proceeded to introduce the
kittens to Lila. 'She's really starting to open up. I can see a
difference in the way she holds herself already. She's quite shy,
isn't she?'

'She wasn't when she was younger,' Ashton said sadly,
remembering the outgoing toddler she'd been. Merrin had been
afraid of nothing and would talk to anyone whenever they
went out.

Lila scooped up her large brown cat from the windowsill
before turning to Jessie. 'I herded all the cats into the building
this morning, and they're in the studio somewhere.' She
marched around the room searching the corners and underneath chairs. 'Lemon's probably snoozing beside the kiln, she
loves it there because it's extra warm. Ginger was on my wheel
earlier...' She bent to look under another one of the tables but
rose again shaking her head. 'She's disappeared again, but I'm
sure we'll find her catnapping somewhere.' She pointed towards
Merrin. 'Do you enjoy pottery?' she asked, as she continued to
pace the studio, searching for her pets.

'I don't know, I've never tried it.' Merrin reached a hand
into the basket she was carrying again so she could stroke the
kittens. 'I like drawing, though.'

'So you're a creative.' Lila clapped her hands. 'I knew we
were going to get along. Why don't I give you and your brother
a quick pottery lesson while Jessie here finds my cats? Perhaps
you could get some pictures of me teaching them?' she asked
Jessie.

'My granddaughter, Ruby, has been nagging me to update

the business website and you two would make a very attractive focal point. I love the idea of siblings working side by side, and you two look so alike.' Lila skipped into one of the back rooms and came out holding a large clump of clay wrapped in plastic.

'There are aprons by the kitchen,' she said to Merrin. 'Put the basket back on the counter where your kittens will be safe. Wash your hands, help yourselves to snacks and drinks, then set yourself up at a wheel.' She put the clay on her table and pointed to a pottery wheel on her right before nodding to Ashton. 'You can set up over there.' She pointed to one on her other side. 'We're going to start easy; I want you to get a feel for the clay. If you take to it, perhaps you could both come back and try something more ambitious another day.'

Ashton watched his sister pick up two aprons from hooks beside the kitchen before putting one on. 'I think we'd better just do as she asks...' Merrin whispered, her voice filled with humour.

'You're probably right. I've a feeling Lila is not going to take no for an answer,' Ashton said. 'I'm far too scared to try.' He pulled a silly face.

Merrin chuckled and then looked surprised. She turned away and Ashton felt a pinch in his chest – an arc of connection. Was Merrin starting to warm to him? The idea appealed, even as he fought it – the thought of letting himself get close to her, and then losing her again, terrified him.

He quickly shrugged on the apron and looked down at the clay Lila had placed on the wheel in front of him.

'Jam your hands in that. See what the clay feels like when you handle it,' she demanded. 'I love pottery because it gives me such a sense of control in a world where we often have so little. That doesn't apply once it goes into the kiln, of course.' Lila studied Merrin who was tentatively pressing her fingers into the soft material. 'Go on, girl, don't worry about getting your hands dirty. That's one of the best bits!'

Ashton watched his sister continue to poke and play, her face a picture of concentration as she started to manipulate the clay. A memory flickered at the edges of his mind, of her putting stickers into a book he'd got her with that exact expression on her face. When his parents had taken her, he'd found the half-finished book in her bedroom. He'd kept it in a drawer in his house until he'd found it by accident years later, but it had brought back so many unwelcome feelings, he'd burned it in the fire.

'Aren't you even going to try?' Merrin asked, and Ashton realised he'd been staring.

'Sure.' He cleared his throat and stuck his fingers into the firm material, wishing he was back in the safety of his living room poring over code. Instead, he started to work it into the shape of Murphy, adding the dog's ears, short legs and paws. He heard a click and turned to find Jessie staring at him through the barrel of the camera.

'That'll be one for the website,' Lila said, as she started to grapple with a piece of clay on her pottery wheel too. 'Go on both of you, don't give up. How are you getting on with the cats, Jess?'

'I got a great shot of the yellow one by the kiln, but I'm waiting for the others to show up,' she said, putting the camera back to her face and taking another snap of Ashton before turning to Merrin, but his sister held up a palm.

'I'm not very photogenic.' She pulled a face. 'You should just take more of him.'

'You look very like your brother.' Lila gave Merrin a measuring look. 'You both make a pretty picture, and I'd really love to have photos of the two of you.' Her eyes twinkled. 'I've a feeling you'll be good for business.'

The teenager looked surprised. It was clear from her reaction that she wasn't used to being complimented. Ashton glanced at Jessie and saw her frowning too, but she held the camera up and took some snaps of Merrin.

'I'll take a few photos of the outside of The Pottery Project as well,' Jessie said to Lila. 'Then I'll track down the other three cats and take their portraits while these two are finishing up their work.' Jessie's attention caught on Ashton's handiwork, and she raised an eyebrow, then giggled. Merrin directed her gaze to his crafting too and she started to laugh.

'Okay, so I'm not very good at pottery,' Ashton grumbled, oddly touched by their teasing.

'We'll have to book you in for an emergency lesson, pet,' Lila said gravely, coming up to examine the clay he'd been working on. 'Next time, I think we're going to need Gryffyn to assist with the teaching. He's got a talent for bringing out the best in our clients.' She pulled an amused face. 'No matter how creatively challenged they are.'

Merrin snorted, then placed a hand over her mouth to hide her laughter. Her eyes darted to Ashton with a mixture of humour and dread. Was she afraid of how he'd react to the teasing?

'I guess you got all the creative genes.' He nodded at her work and winked. Her quick jerk of surprise both surprised him and made him feel sad. But for the first time since Merrin had arrived the evening before, Ashton realised he wanted her to stay, after all.

18

Jessie stood in front of the mirror in her bedroom in Look Out House and frowned at her oversized shirt, wondering if she should change into something new. She heard a knock at the door, went to open it and was surprised to find Merrin standing there.

'I'm sorry,' the teenager flushed, looking back into the hallway as if she were worried about being seen.

'Do you want to come in?' Jessie asked, stepping aside. Merrin wandered in and put the basket of kittens on the floor, then took her time looking around the bedroom.

'It's pretty here,' she said after a pause. 'All the rooms are so nice. I can't believe Ashton owns the whole thing, it's huge.' She walked to the window so she could gaze out. 'Where we rent in Scotland is tiny, so all this almost doesn't feel real. I keep looking at Ashton and thinking is he really my brother, am I really here?' Her voice was wispy. 'It's like a dream and I keep expecting it to end.' She sighed.

'I don't think Ashton would do anything to have this end, and definitely nothing to hurt you,' Jessie said. 'Do you remember living in Indigo Cove?' She sat on the bed when she remembered she'd made another pillow boyfriend last night and had forgotten to hide it. She pulled the duvet higher, relieved she'd accidentally left her sunglasses in Sea Glass Cottage, otherwise it would be more difficult to disguise.

'Not really.' Merrin shrugged before turning and folding her arms. 'Darren asked me to go on a date with him tomorrow,' she blurted, her cheeks turning luminous.

'While you were in the café earlier?' Jessie asked, surprised.

She nodded, her eyes wide. 'I had to talk to someone because I don't understand why.' She looked down at herself. She wore the same jeans as the ones she'd arrived in last night and a black T-shirt that was so huge it swallowed her curves. The effect wasn't flattering, but Jessie understood about hiding yourself.

'Did you say yes?' Jessie asked, as Merrin slumped onto the bed beside her. The teenager started to nibble the edge of her thumbnail and obviously thought better of it because she dropped her hands into her lap.

'How can I.' Merrin looked down at herself. 'He's so... And I'm just...' She waved her fingertips at herself.

Jessie pursed her lips. She wasn't sure if she could find the right words, but she understood insecurity, how easy it was to feel like you weren't good enough.

'Do you think you'd feel more confident if you had some-thing else to wear?' she asked, wondering if the girl had anything in that backpack of hers that wasn't three sizes too big or black. 'I mean, you might feel better if you stop hiding yourself.'

She held up a hand when Merrin started to protest. 'I'm not saying you should dress for anyone but yourself – but I used to wear baggy T-shirts, huge dresses. I constantly concealed myself because I felt ugly.' She looked down as Merrin raised an eyebrow at her billowy pink shirt. 'Okay, maybe I still do sometimes,' she admitted. 'What I'm saying is: you don't have to because you're beautiful.'

'I'm not,' the teen snapped, colouring. 'Don't say that. I'm too tall and my feet are too big. Christian always tells me my looks are funny.'

'Does he?' Jessie hissed. Annoyed, she rose and went to pick up her camera, then scrolled through the photos until she found the one of Merrin at The Pottery Project before turning it round. 'You might not believe me,' she said. 'But perhaps you'll trust what the camera says.'

She waited as the teenager stared, her face filled with distrust. 'You just got me at a good angle,' she mumbled. 'Why don't you take one of me now?' She raised an eyebrow, her expression challenging, although there was a sprinkle of hope mixed in there too.

Jessie took a step back, framing the shot, placing the teenager dead centre with all the cushions and bedclothes behind. The girl's outfit wasn't flattering, but there was something about the way she was sitting, all that embarrassment and raw courage bubbling under the surface, the rigid set of her shoulders, which contrasted so perfectly with the softness of her pretty heart-shaped mouth. Jessie took a couple of snaps and checked them, knew the edges of her lips had twitched upwards as she showed them to Merrin. 'What do you think?'

Merrin shrugged but moved closer.

'I didn't doctor anything. That's all you,' Jessie said, flicking through the images so the teenager could see herself multiple times. She didn't say much, but Jessie could tell Merrin liked what she saw because there was pleasure in her mouth as it curved.

Something hard inside Jessie peeled away as she acknowledged how good it felt to make the young woman feel that way. Jessie had lost confidence in her skills with the camera, had doubted and dismissed her talents. Had forgotten how she used to see life so much more clearly when she looked through a lens. All the lessons Dorothy had taught were starting to fill her mind again. As if a barrier had been removed, even though the barrier had been her own feelings.

'You look so like your brother. If I'd been even half as gorgeous at your age...' She trailed off and stepped away as she realised that she'd just revealed her own insecurities. 'I'll send the snaps to your phone if you like?'

The teenager's brows drew together, and she held out a palm. 'Can I take some of you now?' Merrin rose from the bed. 'It only seems fair that you get to experience how it feels to be on the other side of the camera.'

'That's not necessary, Merrin. Your brother took plenty of pictures of me the other night,' Jessie said in her most reasonable tone, remembering how shocked she'd been that she looked so much like her grandmother. She held the camera to her chest, feeling strangely exposed. But the teenager stared her down. 'Fine...' She knew she was being ridiculous. It couldn't hurt.

'Why don't you stand by the window?' The teenager asked, staring through the lens and tracking Jessie as she strode to where she'd pointed. She should have worn something else, should have put on make-up or brushed her hair. Instead, she took a deep breath and stood facing the camera. Her stomach was doing somersaults, but she'd begun to feel better about herself since arriving in Indigo Cove, had started to realise she wasn't as flawed as she'd always believed. Perhaps it was time to let herself be exposed?

Merrin took some snaps, dropped the camera from her eye to check the pictures and nodded. 'Okay, so maybe you'd like to take a look at these.' She tramped up to join Jessie and they both stood in silence as she scrolled though the shots.

'You know,' the young girl said after a few beats of silence. 'I've changed my mind, will you lend me some of your T-shirts please? I will go on that date. I think I'll shower first and practise doing something with my hair.' With that the teenager picked up the basket of kittens and strode out of the bedroom, closing the door behind her.

Jessie didn't acknowledge her leaving; instead, she stood rigid, staring at the small screen. The woman in the image was tall, with long slender limbs. Her shirt was baggy, but the light shining from the window highlighted the gentle curves of her slim figure, and the long elegance of her frame. She had an unusual face – it wasn't conventionally beautiful – but if she had to find a word, she'd have called it interesting. The long angular nose wasn't really wonky or huge – it dominated her face but served to enhance the size and depth of her eyes, the way her lips grew fuller in the centre.

She gulped, recognising the image for what it was. This was someone people would notice if she walked into a room. Not 'beauty' in the traditional sense, but the eye – artistic or not – would seek it out for all its faults. She let out a long breath, releasing a myriad of muddy feelings she barely understood. Why hadn't she seen this before? Why had she never listened to Rose – and why had she given Maria and Brendon so much power over her self-esteem? She shook her head and put the camera down, realising for the first time in her life that she, Jessie Levine, wasn't ugly, after all.

19

It was dusk by the time Jessie and Ashton got to the coastline just down from Look Out House. The three dogs charged ahead towards the shoreline while Jessie held tightly onto the camera, clutching it to her side.

'I can't believe the change in Bear since he met Phoebe,' Ashton reflected, as they made their way along the beach side by side, then he shook his head as the dogs hit the waves and began to frolic in the surf. 'It's like he can't stand the idea of being parted from her so he runs to keep up – he's already lost weight and I don't have to watch him constantly for fear he'll start to eat something he shouldn't. It's a miracle.'

'Sometimes, I think we need something or someone new to come into our lives to change it for the better,' Jessie observed, thinking that's exactly what being in Indigo Cove had done for her.

'A new perspective,' Ashton said, reaching for her hand and wrapping it in his. 'Like the ones we see through your grand-mother's camera.'

Jessie swallowed. 'I suppose,' she said, feeling the tingles from their contact climbing up her palm. What did it mean that

Ashton was touching her? Had he changed his mind about pausing what had been happening between them? How did she feel about it? The warm bubble in the pit of her stomach told her she was fully on board.

'Merrin looked happy this evening too,' Ashton said, as they continued to meander along the beach. The sun was starting to drop, and Jessie knew she'd have to stop soon to take some snaps, but they hadn't reached the right spot yet. 'I noticed she'd borrowed one of your T-shirts. It suited her. I want to thank you for staying and for helping my sister to settle in. For making sure she feels welcome and comfortable. She's only been here for a short time and already she's blooming.'

Jessie wondered exactly how Ashton would feel if she told him his sister was planning on going on a date with Darren, and decided to remain quiet. She'd enjoyed watching the exchanges between the siblings, the way their relationship had begun to thaw. Merrin was smiling more, initiating conversations and, while the kittens were always close to her side, she was reaching for them less often now. But the biggest change had been in Ashton – he seemed less closed off and was definitely laughing more.

'She's a special girl – I can't imagine how much you've missed her,' Jessie said instead, swiping a strand of hair from her face as a gust of wind caught it.

She wondered if Ashton would notice that she'd changed too. Tonight, she'd put on make-up, jeans and a silky shirt that traced the contour of her body, emphasising the figure she'd spent most of her life trying to hide. Usually, her head would have been full of Maria's unkind words or Brendon's lack of interest as she worried about what she was doing wrong. Instead, now she felt... confident.

She turned to look at Ashton's profile at the exact moment an orange thread of light from the setting sun caught the side of his cheek. She grabbed the camera and held it up so she could take some shots.

'I thought we were here to take photos of the sunset,' he complained.

'We are but...' She shucked out a breath. 'I wanted to get another portrait shot of you and... that light is really something.'

Ashton nodded, but his eyes didn't leave her face. 'It is beautiful,' he murmured. 'You are too.' He held up a palm. 'I know you don't like hearing that, but it's true.'

Jessie blinked and shrugged. 'Perhaps I don't mind it so much when you say it,' she said, turning away so he wouldn't see the flush climbing her cheeks. She followed the dogs as they trotted parallel to the shoreline.

'What's changed?' Ashton asked, sounding surprised.

'I don't know, perspective – seeing myself in a different way. Knowing you'd tell me the truth no matter what. Maybe it pays to be blunt sometimes...' she admitted. 'Oh that's it,' Jessie yelled, hopping from side to side as the sun dipped further down towards the horizon. She stepped closer to the waves and got the camera ready. 'This is almost exactly like the photo my grandmother took. The sea was shimmering just like that, and the sky was filled with all those same oranges and pinks.'

She took her time setting up the shot and then taking a series of snaps as Ashton pressed a palm onto her shoulder. 'I always wondered where Grandad was when Dorothy took it. I imagined he'd be standing beside her watching the whole thing – like they were both part of the picture, only a part we couldn't see.'

'Sometimes, those are the most important parts,' Ashton said, stepping closer until Jessie could feel the warmth from his body across her back. 'George was right, this is romantic,' he whispered, dropping a kiss onto the back of her ear, making her knees liquify.

'Are you seducing me?' Jessie groaned as Ashton's mouth

travelled to the side of her neck and she moved her head to
allow him better access as heat pooled at her centre and her
body started to feel tender and heavy.

'Depends if it's working,' he whispered. 'I know I said we
should wait, that I needed to get my head together, but the
longer Merrin's here, the more I've had to accept that shutting
myself away from life – from people I could care about – is a
mistake.'

Jessie let the camera swing down from her face and turned
so she could stare at him. 'What do you mean?' she asked. She
needed reassurance, had to hear the words.

'I mean, I don't want to wait. I'd like to see where this thing
between us could lead.' Ashton's eyes were clear now and fixed
on hers, there was no question he meant what he said, and Jessie
felt something inside her flutter and uncurl. 'So what I need to
know is how do you feel?'

Jessie cleared her throat as the implications of what Ashton
was asking hit. 'You won't run?' She swallowed. 'Because I don't
think I could stand it if you did.'

He shook his head as he gently brushed a strand of hair
from her cheek. 'I didn't last time, Jess, I just asked for space to
clear my head.' His voice had taken on a deep, rusty tone. She
didn't think Ashton could be more attractive, but there was
something about this new side of him that turned her inside out.
He blinked, watching her expression as she decided, and a smile
lit his face when she nodded.

'We should walk to Sea Glass Cottage,' she said slowly.
'There's a hot tub on the deck which I'd like to try and a bottle
of champagne chilling in the fridge. We don't need to move out
until the morning, and there's plenty of room for the dogs, even
some food for them.'

His eyes travelled slowly across her face. 'Sounds perfect,'
he said, grabbing her hand. 'Know what I want to do first?' he
asked.

'No.' Jessie shook her head.

'I want to run,' Ashton said. 'But I want you beside me. I'm not going anywhere this time.' Then he tugged her along as he began to kick up pace, heading in the direction of Sea Glass Cottage.

The three dogs arrived first – the run had turned into a game as they all sprinted the mile and a half along the shoreline, although Ashton and Jessie couldn't catch up. Together they'd passed two couples walking hand in hand, another photographer setting up a sunset shot, and a family meandering towards the harbour ready for bedtime. Ashton raced Jessie up the steps to the decking, and they collapsed together on the pretty patio chairs, giggling and panting heavily.

'I've never met anyone who could keep up with me before,' Ashton said, as his breathing started to steady. 'Must be those long legs of yours.' He grinned and leaned down to undo his trainers and kick them off before walking to the hot tub and heaving off the lid. He dipped a hand into the water. 'It's the perfect temperature, but I'm a little sweaty: think we should shower before we get in?'

Jessie nodded and undid her sandy trainers too before rising and digging into her pocket for the door key. The dogs charged inside first, sniffing at the furniture while Jessie switched on some lamps and Ashton fed and watered them and then poured out two glasses of water before handing her one.

'I thought we should hydrate before opening the champagne,' he said, clinking his glass against hers. She watched him tip back his head and swallow the liquid in one, and had to stop herself from leaning in to nip at his collarbone and all the sexy skin he'd just exposed. Just watching him was making her body quiver.

'Shower's that way,' Jessie rasped, pointing towards the

hallway which led to her bedroom. She followed him down, heard the scatter of the dogs' paws as they trailed after. She found Ashton standing by the edge of her bed staring at the body-shaped pile of pillows she hadn't cleared away. The sunglasses she'd forgotten to take with her to Look Out House were peering over the top edge of the duvet. Mortified, Jessie put her hands to her cheeks and momentarily shut her eyes.

'Who's that?' Ashton asked, sounding amused.

'It's...' She gulped as warmth skidded across her skin. 'I know it's stupid, but he helps me sleep.'

'He?' There was a long pause before Ashton said. 'So, are you going to introduce me?'

'Funny.' Jessie edged towards the bed, intending to clear her pillow boyfriend away.

But Ashton got there first. He picked up the sunglasses and folded them carefully before putting them on the bedside table. Then he gathered the cushions and tossed them towards the headboard. 'I don't think you'll be needing him this evening, Jess,' he said softly and everything inside her began to fizz too. He pointed towards the en suite. 'Shower?'

'Um.' Jessie nodded, suddenly feeling shy. 'I'll use the other bathroom and get ready in Grandad's room. Shall I meet you in the hot tub in five?'

Jessie got there in less than three minutes. She'd already packed up her costume, so it was in a drawer in Look Out House. She'd been wearing some of her favourite underwear but didn't particularly want to get it wet, so she'd bolted out to the decking wrapped in nothing but a towel and had managed to sink under the bubbles in the hot tub seconds before Ashton wandered out of the kitchen. He was carrying two flutes filled with champagne and had wrapped himself in a fluffy towel – it hung low on his hips, and she felt the breath catch at the top of her throat as she watched him stride towards her. His frame was lean, but his firm muscles were all dips and peaks, taut arches and bows. It was exactly how she'd imagined he'd look under his clothes.

For a mad moment, she wondered how it would feel to run her mouth across his chest, to navigate each of those perfect inclines and hollows with the tip of her tongue. His smooth skin still glistened from the shower, and there was a light dusting of dark hair that trailed from his belly button and disappeared into the white cotton. Jessie swallowed a wave of lust and forced her eyes up to Ashton's face as he handed her one of the champagne flutes and dropped the towel. A wave of disappointment engulfed her when she realised he was still wearing his boxers. Then, in two quick strides, he was in the water with her and they were sitting side by side, watching the last traces of the sunset.

'I can't believe this is the first time I've used the hot tub,' Jessie said after a short silence, as the sun finally disappeared leaving a smattering of glitter on the waves and sand.

Ashton pressed a soft kiss to her shoulder and shifted closer, making her whole body purr. 'I'm glad you waited until I was here. I'm not sure how well your pillow boyfriend would have coped in this water – I'm guessing it wouldn't be his happy place.' His mouth moved slowly across her collarbone towards her neck.

Jessie swatted him and sipped some of the champagne as tingles glided downwards, making her skin pucker. 'I suppose your muscles are just a little more defined,' she teased. She suddenly wished she wasn't naked because she felt so exposed.

Then his hand skimmed across her cheek and he moved her chin so they were gazing at each other. His eyes were dark and hooded, despite the dazzle from the string of white lights dangling above them which had just clicked on.

'I'd like to take a photo of you right now to keep,' Ashton said, as his eyes traced her face before his attention dipped to the water. The bubbles were doing a good job of hiding what was below the surface, but Jessie suspected Ashton knew she wasn't wearing a thing.

'Why?' Jessie asked, feeling embarrassed.

'Because then you'd see how beautiful you look.' He stroked a curl of hair from her face.

She shrugged, feeling embarrassed. 'I'm not used to compliments, but I'm trying to change so thank you – but I think a photo of you would be better.' Jessie smiled, wishing she had her own camera beside her. She wouldn't take any of them on Dorothy's: she couldn't risk getting it wet.

'Then I'll say thank you to you too,' Ashton said. Jessie froze as he plucked the champagne flute from her hand and put it on the edge of the hot tub beside his own. Then he moved so he could press his mouth to hers. The kiss was hot and wet, and she leaned into him as tension squeezed her insides. There was something erotic about the combination of Ashton's kisses, and the swirl of hot water and bubbles pulsing against her skin.

His arm moved until he was circling her waist and he pulled her closer still as his kisses grew deeper and more sensual. The blood was pumping faster around Jessie's limbs, and the heat pooling at her centre as her skin tightened and grew more sensitive. She made a soft moaning sound, then hooked her leg over his thigh and lifted herself until she was sitting in his lap with their chests mashed together. Her core was pressed against his boxers now, and she moved her hips until Ashton let out a low moan.

'We need to go slower,' he protested, breaking the kiss even as his body continued to rock against her. 'It's been a while for me, and this is...' He blew out a breath and kissed Jessie again as she pressed herself harder against him, taking her pleasure and smiling against his mouth as he took hold of her thighs. 'I can't stop...' he said.

Jessie loved that Ashton was losing control, loved that she had this power over him. Things had always been so tame and repressed with Brendon – this felt different. It was like Ashton couldn't get enough of her. Jessie's legs were too long to hold in place, and she started to slip, felt herself sliding backwards – like she would have ducked under the water if he hadn't caught her in his arms.

'We might need to go inside,' Ashton said, pressing her back into his chest and touching his forehead against hers. 'I'm not sure how long it'll be before someone walks past on the beach and sees us.'

'Will it ruin your reputation?' Jessie asked, smiling.

'If anything, it'll enhance it, but I'm not looking to share you,' he said quietly.

'So you want to get out?' Jessie asked, climbing back onto Ashton's lap with her legs bent on each side of his hips, holding on gently. 'We need to finish our drinks before we do.'

She picked up her champagne flute and took a slow sip before leaning it against his lips, waiting until he accepted and drank. She'd dreamed about this, had never imagined anyone would want her in this way. She'd been blind, so consumed by her insecurities, by other people's words, that she'd stood in her own way and almost missed the chance of experiencing it. Instead, Jessie watched as Ashton's eyes held hers and the moment stretched – it felt intimate and sensual. She licked her lips, then put the empty glass back on the side and leaned forward so she could nibble at his mouth. He tasted like the champagne. Ashton let out a long breath and Jessie felt him shudder as he pressed against her centre again.

'We need to get out,' he growled, holding onto her forearms and pressing her back until she was standing. The water dripped from her body as she stood in the hot tub, her top half exposed, her skin puckering in the night air.

Ashton took the towel from the edge of the hot tub and quickly wrapped Jessie in it before climbing out, then he held out his palm so he could help her. He grabbed his own towel and dried his torso and feet before turning so he could help Jessie dry off too. He took her hand and marched them both across the decking and into the cottage, shutting the door and ignoring the dogs as the three of them shot to their feet, probably hoping for another walk.

'Not now.' His voice was tight as he led Jessie along the hallway and into the bedroom. Then he shut the door, switched on the light and turned towards her before dropping his towel. 'Now it's your turn,' he said, pointing to the one she was holding tightly around her chest.

'You want the lights on?' Jessie asked, surprised.

'I want to see everything,' Ashton said, watching her face. 'I want you naked.'

'So do I,' she agreed. 'So, what about those?' Jessie pointed to Ashton's wet boxers which were now clinging to his hips, outlining the solid planes of everything that was straining underneath.

He nodded and unselfconsciously pushed them to his feet, keeping his eyes fixed on Jessie's face as he stepped out of them. His body was as beautiful as the rest of him. She dropped her towel too and the glitter of appreciation she saw in Ashton's eyes wiped away any embarrassment Jessie was feeling – with just that one look he made her feel completely beautiful.

Then he stalked across the room and guided her to the bed, raising an eyebrow at the scatter of pillows leaning against the headboard. 'Mind if we move your boyfriend onto the floor? I'm feeling a little under pressure here with him watching,' he teased, pushing all the cushions off the bed before tipping her backwards and falling onto the mattress beside her. 'Slow or quick?' Ashton asked, moving up the bed until he was lying beside her.

Jessie turned onto her side so she could gaze at him. Reached out and let her fingertips trace the edge of his chest before they dropped lower, stroking slowly across his hips, dipping over the firm globes of his naked behind. Ashton shuddered and Jessie laughed, intoxicated by his reaction to her. She'd never felt this powerful, had always held back, had accepted things she never should have. But the old wounds were mending now, reforming and healing. She continued to explore the skin on his hip and then dropped her fingers to the dark hair on his belly, letting her fingers drift lower until he caught her hand.

'Quick it is,' Ashton whispered, pushing Jessie onto her back and dropping a kiss onto her lips before nibbling his way across her cheeks to her neck and then her collarbone.

Jessie was on fire – it was the only way she could describe it. Something was surging up from her belly as Ashton continued to move down her body, dropping soft kisses onto her skin, turning her into something wanton and wild. This was what she'd craved since she'd met him on the beach when she was seventeen.

She'd known from that moment what someone could do to her – how the smallest touch could turn her inside out, make her feel desirable. But she'd allowed herself to doubt it, until now. Jessie pulled at Ashton's hair, encouraged him upwards so she could nibble on his mouth, pushed her body so it was touching his.

'I don't want to wait,' she said, as the fire inside her flickered and glowed.

She felt like she was going to explode. The need she'd ignored for years, the expectations she'd supressed, grew teeth and roared. Then she pushed until Ashton was lying on his back and she was straddling him. Saw the flare of surprise in his eyes and the pleasure that chased it. He framed her cheeks with his large hands and tugged her face closer so their lips met.

The kiss started slow, then it grew hot and wet and Jessie moved slowly against him, took her time until she couldn't wait and then she tipped her hips and took him inside. Ashton broke

the kiss then and let her face go as they started to move. Their
eyes held and they rocked. Her teeth pinched into her lower lip
as she drew out her desire. But she didn't look away. Even as the
wave of pleasure flooded through her and Ashton gripped the
edges of her hips and moved until they both shuddered and
tipped over – their eyes remained locked. And Jessie knew, for
the first time in her life, that true beauty was rooted in how you
saw yourself.

20

'I did it,' Jessie confessed as soon as Rose picked up the phone. 'I made love with Ashton.' She gulped as she paced her bedroom at Look Out House.

'When?' Rose yelped on the other end of the mobile. 'I need details, what happened, when?'

'Just now...' Jessie brushed a hand over her face. 'Okay, last night.' She squeezed her eyes closed. 'I just got back. We were in Sea Glass Cottage moving all the rest of mine and Grandad's things. But then, well... things happened, and we only got out of bed when the sun rose.' They'd spent the next half an hour tidying the cottage before they'd left. 'I haven't slept.'

She let out an involuntary giggle. She'd never stayed up all night. She could still feel the tingles on her skin, the flutter of excitement in her belly. It was like she'd just emerged from a lifetime of dormancy – the oldest living caterpillar in history had just transformed into a butterfly.

'Dare I ask, how it was?' Rose sounded amused. 'Give me a minute, I'm going to put the kettle on, I need a mug of my strongest Yorkshire Tea for this.' Jessie heard the shuffle of bedclothes and thump of footsteps on the floor and guessed her friend had just got up. She knew the exact layout of the flat and that Rose would be in the kitchen in less than thirty seconds. Likely the kettle would already be full. Her thoughts were confirmed when she heard a hiss as it was switched on. 'Okay, I want to know more.'

'It was the most amazing night of my life,' Jessie gushed. 'I can't describe how it felt. After all these years to know how it should be – how real chemistry feels.'

'Sounds like the man knew what he was doing,' Rose said dryly.

'He knew.' Jessie sat on the edge of her bed. The first thing she'd done when she got back was tidy up her pillow boyfriend for the final time. The cushions were arranged beside the head-board along with the others – whatever happened she wouldn't be needing him again.

'How do you feel?' Rose asked softly.

'I'm not sure.' Jessie paused to examine her feelings. 'Different, excited, like the whole world's opened up. I don't know if I should expect anything to come of this. I mean, I'd like it to, but I'm not sure how Ashton feels.' She swallowed. 'But whatever happens, for the first time in my life I know what I want from a relationship. I won't settle again. I know I deserve it all.'

Jessie heard the tinkle of a teaspoon as Rose finished making the tea. Her friend had fallen uncharacteristically silent.

'Is there something you want to tell me?' Jessie cleared her throat. 'Because I thought you'd be hopping up and down, you've been telling me to do this for long enough.'

'Oh no Jess, this is the best news I've had all year.' Rose swallowed. 'It's just – there's something I have to tell you, and I was thinking this might be a good time.'

'About Brendon?' Jessie asked, her forehead drawing together.

'He's engaged – to her. It happened last week, when you were supposed to be on your honeymoon. I think your grandad would call that a typical *numbskull* move, and he'd be right,' she added. 'I don't want to hurt you, and I don't want to spoil today, but I wanted you to hear it from me.'

'No, it's okay,' Jessie said, swiping a tangle of hair from her face. She sat for a moment, waiting for the sickness in her belly to emerge, the sharp stab of pain. 'I don't know if this is because it hasn't hit me yet, but...' She sighed. 'I don't feel anything.'

She blinked. Had her feelings for Brendon been more about habit, more about settling for someone because she couldn't bear the idea of not measuring up? She swallowed as the full implications of it hit her and the blood rushed to her face. 'Rose, I'm not sure I was ever in love with him,' she whispered into the mobile.

'I've been trying to tell you that,' her friend said. 'I mean I can't say he's coming out of this whole situation smelling of anything but rotten socks, but...'

'Perhaps he sensed my feelings weren't what they should have been – maybe he decided he deserved better than that too.' Jessie put the mobile on speaker, then balled her hands and pressed them into her eyes. 'Brendon did deserve better. Do you think I owe him an apology?'

'I wouldn't go as far as that,' Rose said wryly. 'He did make you feel like you weren't good enough for the entirety of your relationship, encouraged you to give up photography, cheated on you for months before your wedding, then let you catch him out. He didn't have the decency to be honest with you, so, no, I don't think you owe him anything, Jess. I do think it's good you've finally realised that you and he weren't right for each other. I'm glad you've met someone who might be...'

'Might be?' Jessie queried.

Her friend let out a sigh. 'The jury's still out. This is the man who ran out on you fourteen years ago, this is the person who shattered your heart. He might have just been a boy then but...'

Jessie nodded, feeling the first pulse of fear. She'd been so absorbed in their night, so bowled over by her feelings she hadn't stopped to consider whether she could trust Ashton to stay the course. Although it was a little early for those kinds of expectations – she didn't even know where she'd be living in a few weeks. She had no job, no idea of what her future held. She had to figure that out before she added a new romance into the mix.

'I hear you,' she sighed. 'But I'm going to give Ashton a chance – see where this thing between us might lead.'

'Just keep a little part of your heart safe, Jess,' her friend said quietly. 'That's all I ask.'

'Are you sure I look okay?' Merrin asked for what felt like the hundredth time as Jessie parked her grandad's Ford Anglia in a parking spot close to The Beach Café. The teenager stroked a hand over the pretty pink T-shirt she'd borrowed from Jessie and fiddled with a curl of her hair.

'I'm not sure about the make-up – what if it makes me look like I'm trying too hard?' Merrin's voice was calm, but Jessie could hear an undercurrent of nervousness in it. Could hear it because she'd heard it in her own voice so many times.

'How do *you* think you look, Merrin?' she asked, turning towards the younger girl. Jessie thought she looked gorgeous – her dark hair tumbled around her shoulders, the natural curls seemed to have formed out of nowhere overnight. She had the same blue eyes as her brother, a pretty heart-shaped mouth. If Darren didn't lose the power of speech when they walked into The Beach Café, Jessie would have to check the teenager's pulse. But she knew better than to offer empty compliments. Confidence came from inside.

She flipped down the passenger visor exposing a mirror. 'Take a good look at yourself – how do you feel?'

The teenager spent a few moments staring at her face. She stroked a fingertip across her lips. 'Christian used to say my mouth was too big. Before he went on holiday, he told me Ashton got all the best genes.'

'I wonder if he'd say the same to your brother if he got the chance?' Jessie asked.

The girl's forehead pinched as she processed it. 'Why do people like to knock you down?'

Jessie shrugged. 'Who knows. Perhaps they're just unhappy with themselves and it makes them feel better? My stepmother used to tell me I was ugly all the time.' The shocked look on Merrin's face filled her with warmth. 'She died before I got a chance to find out why.' She looked into the young girl's eyes. 'But if I had to guess, I'd say she was jealous of my relationship with my father. I look a lot like my mother. My dad loved her right up until the end, and I don't think Maria could forgive him for that. Every time she looked at me, or heard me speak, I think I reminded her of it. Perhaps by hating me she was transferring all her negative feelings about the love she couldn't touch.'

Merrin pushed out her bottom lip. 'That's stupid.'

'Isn't it?' Jessie's mouth slid into a wide grin. 'I'm sad now that I listened to her for so many years. Let her affect how I saw myself. It was like she was a mirror, and I could only see myself in that. I took a lot of wrong turns because of it.'

The teenager sucked in a deep breath and took another longer look at herself in the visor before nodding. 'Okay – so I'm smart enough to know what you're trying to say and how it applies to me. But I think that's enough wise words for this morning. I also think I'm ready.'

She started to open the passenger door and stopped before turning back to Jessie. 'I know I haven't been in Indigo Cove for long but...' She gulped suddenly, looking younger. 'I like living with you, George, Ashton and Elsie.' She nibbled the edge of her bottom lip. 'Do you think my brother will let me stay? He hasn't said if he wants me to – I'm worried he'll expect me to go back.' Her eyes flashed. 'I'll be okay if he does. I don't need him, but I'm not going to live with Genni or Christian again. I'm never going back...'

Jessie gently touched her arm. 'I don't think your brother would let you go. I haven't known Ashton for long, but it's obvious he's got strong feelings for you. It's why he hasn't let anyone into his life for so many years. And those kinds of feelings don't go away.'

The teenager nodded and her expression softened, then she turned and got out of the car.

Jessie got out too and walked side by side with Merrin down to the harbour. She was sure Ashton would never let his sister go, but she wished she knew how he felt about her...

21

The Beach Café wasn't busy when they arrived. Jessie had offered to drive Merrin ahead of everyone under the pretext that she wanted to look in the souvenir shop. The teenager wasn't sure what Ashton would make of her dating and Jess didn't feel like she could break the confidence, even if it did feel like lying. Ashton had offered to drive George and Elsie to the harbour this morning, so as soon as he arrived, he'd probably work it out.

Darren rushed out from behind the counter as soon as the bell at the front of the café dinged. He was dressed in what looked like new jeans and he'd obviously ironed his T-shirt. He took a good look at Merrin and stopped, flushing to the roots of his hair.

'Bravo, I think we'll call that a bullseye,' Jessie whispered, as the boy half tripped, half stumbled across the café to greet them.

'Um,' Darren said under his breath. 'You look... um, nice. Um, I thought we could sit in the corner. Ella said when you got here, I could take a break. I saved us some chocolate brownies...'

Merrin half smiled. 'I like brownies,' she said, earning herself a dazzling smile.

'Also, there's a puzzle I promised I'd finish before we went out.' Darren wiped his palms on his jeans. 'Would you mind helping?' His eyes reluctantly flicked to Jessie. 'You can join us, I suppose.'

'You can count me out. I'm going to save a spot for my grandad and Elsie – but you go ahead.' Jessie pressed a hand to the small of Merrin's back, encouraging her to follow Darren, which she did after a moment of hesitation.

Jessie wandered up to the counter where Ella was waiting to give the pair some space.

'Young love...' the café owner sighed, looking sad. 'Why is it always so easy when you're that age? Is it just you two today?' She smiled when Jessie shook her head.

'Everyone else is coming soon. Can I have a cappuccino please and...' She perused the cakes. 'A slice of whichever one of those you recommend.'

She heard the bell ring again and turned, expecting to see Ashton. Instead, a man with dark hair and green eyes was standing by the entrance admiring the space. He was handsome with stubble scattered across his chin and wavy dark hair that had been artfully tied into a ponytail. His denim jeans were worn and comfortable-looking, and he had a way of standing that encouraged you to stare.

'Oh wow.' Jessie heard Ella gulp as the man spotted them by the counter and strode towards them, his rangy limbs eating up the space.

'Good morning.' The man's voice was deep but shy. His eyes fixed on Ella and Jessie noticed a spark of interest. 'Are you the owner of this place?'

'Was it the apron that gave it away?' she teased, nodding and batting her eyelashes. 'Ella Santo.' She held out a hand and he took it and shook.

'Arthur Tremaine,' he said.

'The artist?' Jessie asked, recognising the name. Ella gave her a questioning look. 'Do you make the pictures from jigsaw pieces?'

Arthur nodded, embarrassment flooding his cheeks. 'I do paintings mainly, the jigsaw pictures are a new thing.'

'Are you from around here? I don't think we've seen you in the café before,' Ella asked.

He shrugged. 'I've been living in France for the last five years and I've only just come back to the area. I've recently moved to a studio about ten miles from here.' He put his hands in his pockets and rocked back on his heels.

'My friend at the Lighthouse Gallery mentioned someone had bought one of my pictures and wanted to get in touch.' Arthur continued to scour the café, then grinned when he spotted the frame above Darren and Merrin's heads. 'Ah, there she is. I love seeing my work in the wild.'

'It's brilliant,' Ella said. 'Absolutely perfect for my café.'

'Were you looking to get more pictures made?' He swallowed. 'I hope I'm not overstepping, but is that why you wanted to speak to me?'

'It wasn't me who tried to contact you, but yes, maybe I do.' Ella's forehead creased. 'I'd like to hang more artwork around the café, perhaps sell some. Your puzzle pictures could be a really good fit. Maybe we could sit and have a chat in a minute?'

'Um, okay. Do you do espresso?' Arthur asked.

'Coffee or cake?' Ella joked.

He flushed. 'Both please. Excuse me.' He wandered away from the counter towards his picture, stopping on the way to take in the half-completed puzzles which had been left out on tables. 'Is there a reason these haven't been finished?' he asked, twisting around.

'Jigsaw Club,' Ella said, as she picked up a mug and started to do battle with the coffee machine. 'I'm expecting some of our members to arrive soon. I tend to leave the puzzles out because a lot of customers visit every day. Many of them just come for the company. They can do jigsaws and there's no pressure to talk. There's something about just sitting side by side and puzzling that works for people.'

The artist raised an eyebrow. 'I like that idea. Works if you're a little shy like me.'

'Everyone's welcome. Would you like to stay and make one up now?' Ella asked gently.

'Well... I could for a while. I've been stuck in my studio too much recently.' Arthur stood by the table where Merrin and Darren were sitting, just as the teenager groaned.

'This one has six pieces missing, what's the point?' He grabbed the bottom of the jigsaw box from the floor and started to shove the pieces inside.

'Just put it to one side with the others,' Ella instructed.

'Can I see the lid, please?' Arthur stepped closer to the teenagers.

'Sure,' Darren said, handing over the box. 'There's no point in making it, though.' He and Merrin continued to scrape the pieces from the table.

'Where did you get this puzzle?' Arthur tracked back to the counter and showed the lid to Ella, looking excited.

'Someone dropped in a big pile of them a few weeks ago.' She finished his coffee with a flourish before slicing a large piece of cake. 'We're always asking for donations and this man I'd never seen before popped in for a drink – said he had a whole load of old jigsaw puzzles in his car. Apparently, he tried to donate them to a local charity shop, but they didn't have room, so he asked if I wanted them instead.'

The artist blinked. 'How many puzzles did he give you?'

'I don't know – Darren,' Ella shouted across the café. 'How many jigsaws were donated to us?'

The teenager shrugged. 'Sixteen I think, we've made up fourteen and all but two have pieces missing.'

'Do you still have them?' Arthur sounded a little out of breath. Any hints of shyness had completely gone.

Ella nodded. 'They're piled at the back of the kitchen. I didn't have the heart to get rid of them because they're so old,' she confessed. 'Why don't you sit? We'll find you a puzzle with all the pieces and you can have your coffee and cake.'

'These are my puzzles.' Arthur hugged the box to his chest.

'How do you know?' Darren asked.

'They belonged to my grandfather.' Arthur turned to Ella. 'We were close. He was an artist too and an avid puzzler. He died recently. He was sick and that's why I returned to Indigo Cove from France. I've moved into his studio, and I've been using the pieces from his puzzles in my art.' He blinked. 'As a homage to him. He'd been collecting jigsaws all his life and I like to think that by including them in my work, I'm keeping his memory alive. Stupid, I know.' He blinked and Ella's expression softened.

'It's not stupid, it's lovely,' she murmured.

Arthur turned away again and strode to the puzzle picture hanging on the wall. 'That includes an eye from an Elvis puzzle my grandfather had.'

Darren groaned. 'That's why I thought it was watching me – I knew it!'

The artist nodded. 'I liked the idea of the cherry on the cake following people around the room.'

'It's a bit creepy,' Merrin said, screwing up her nose.

'I suppose.' Arthur nodded. 'For me, art's all about surprising people, giving them something they're not expecting. You'd be astonished to hear how few people notice the pictures are made from puzzle pieces. So many of us walk around blind to what's under our noses.' He gave Darren an assessing look. 'You saw it, though.'

'So, did Merrin,' the boy said, glancing at the young girl, his expression adoring. 'I pay attention to pictures – I love art.'

'He's very talented,' Ella said, walking out from behind the counter and wiping her hands on her apron.

'Are you studying it?' Arthur asked.

The boy drummed his fingertips on the café table. 'No. My dad wants me to do statistics at university, so I had to give it up. He's worried I won't make any money otherwise. He doesn't want me to be distracted from what's important.'

Arthur pursed his lips. 'My dad tried to do the same to me when I was your age.'

'What happened?' Darren asked.

'I moved in with my grandfather and became an artist anyway – and for a lot of years I was poor. But I never regretted my decision. For me, life isn't about money.' He shrugged. 'I make a decent living now – enough to get by. But I think in the end you've got to decide what matters to you. What's important.' He stared at the boy. 'Plus, there's no reason why you can't study maths and do art as well, is there? Perhaps you can even find a way of getting them to work in tandem.'

The boy jerked his chin. 'I suppose not,' he didn't sound convinced. 'Although Dad thinks I need to be focussed.'

'What do you think?' Arthur asked, echoing the question Gryffyn had asked the teenager before.

'I dunno,' he muttered.

'Sometimes, you have to do what *you* think is right,' Merrin said, looking intently at Darren. 'Go your own way. You can't always listen to other people because they're not always right.' Her eyes darted to Jessie, and she gave her a meaningful look.

'That's all true, but sorry, what about these jigsaws?' Ella asked, handing Arthur his espresso before putting the cake on a table close to him. 'You didn't tell us how the person who donated the puzzles got them?'

He pulled a face. 'It's a stupid story. I took a lot of my

grandad's stuff from his house to my studio after we cleared it so the estate agent could sell up. I've been putting a pile of things together I wanted to donate to charity. Some local artists I've befriended came over one afternoon. We've started to meet once a week,' he explained. 'It can be isolating when you're working in a studio on your own.' The tips of his cheekbones reddened. 'I had to make space for all of us to sit and put the jigsaws I was using for my art into another room.' He looked upset. 'I'd organised for a charity to pick up some of my grandad's stuff and when they arrived, they took his puzzles too because I forgot they were there. Stupid,' he berated himself again. 'Once I realised, I tried to track them down, but the charity had no idea what had happened to them.' He gulped.

'Couldn't they ask their volunteers?' Ella asked.

He winced. 'They'd had an influx of temporary helpers, and there was some kind of mix-up which meant their details weren't added to the computer. The charity tried to track the helpers down, but after a few weeks they told me the puzzles might be lost for good. They were very apologetic – but it wasn't their fault, I shouldn't have left them out.'

Arthur clutched the jigsaw box close to his chest again. 'I can't believe I've got them back,' he said. 'I've been struggling to create my pictures since they went missing – having these will change everything. If I can take all of Grandad's puzzles home today, I'd be happy to buy you replacements.'

'So long as the new ones have all their pieces,' Darren joked.

'I'm sure I can manage that.' Arthur laughed.

Ella eyed the artist for a few moments. 'Or you could do me a favour instead?' she said quietly.

'Anything.' He nodded enthusiastically.

'You mentioned you meet with a group of artists each week because working alone can be isolating?' Ella checked.

'Yes.'

'And you said you don't have a lot of room in your studio for your meetings?' she added earnestly.

'That's right.' Arthur dipped his chin. 'But I'm the only one with enough space to even consider it.'

'So, maybe meet here at The Beach Café instead and do puzzles while you talk?' she suggested. 'I could reserve tables. Provide drinks and cake. I want to give people a space where they can make friends – or just enjoy the ambience without feeling any pressure to socialise. And...'

'What?' Arthur asked, when Ella trailed off.

She looked uncomfortable. 'I want more people to know about The Puzzle Club and to take away any stigma from joining in. I was lonely when I broke up with my husband; one of my regulars Elsie needed company after hers died. I'd like more people to get the benefit, but it's been very difficult spreading the word... It's not like you can just advertise for lonely people. Perhaps you and your friends could help?'

'I'd love to be involved,' Arthur said, his eyes lighting up. 'It means I'll get to meet more local people, I won't have to keep reorganising my studio and...' He sipped his espresso. 'Your coffee is a lot better than mine.'

'Thank you.' Ella laughed. 'Also, while we're on the subject, we're hosting a Jigsaw Championship in a couple of weeks. Maybe you could help with that?'

'How?' Arthur stepped closer to Ella.

'Could I commission you to make us some special artwork for it?' Ella asked slowly. 'I know there's not much time but...'

'Sure, tell me what you need,' Arthur said.

Ella's attention darted to Jessie. 'I'll need you to be involved too.'

'Of course,' Jessie agreed, intrigued. 'Whatever you need.' She was starting to feel like part of the community now – starting to feel like she fit, had something valuable to contribute.

Whatever happened with Ashton, Indigo Cove was beginning to feel like home. She'd do anything to help out.

Ella grinned. 'Darren, please could you get us all some more coffees before you head off?' She pointed to their table when the teenager nodded and moved towards the kitchen with Merrin following behind. Ella drew in a breath. 'Please take a seat, I've got an idea I think you'll both like...'

22

'Bunch up please, just like that, that's perfect.' Jessie grinned at George and Elsie as she peeked through the camera at the older pair who were seated in the garden at Look Out House. They were drinking old fashioneds again and completing yet another puzzle from Ashton's collection. All three dogs were lying at their feet and the sun was beginning to set, which had given the background a stunning orangey hue.

Jessie took a couple of quick snaps and nodded. 'You're beautiful. Say "cheese and pineapple sticks",' she joked, earning herself giggles before snapping the beaming couple once again.

Then she took a picture of the sleepy dogs before flicking through the photos, taking time to peruse the other scenes she'd caught over the past week. Snaps of The Beach Café where Ella's regular customers pored over jigsaws while enjoying huge slabs of cake – some talking, some lost in concentration. Shots of Arthur flirting with Ella while his artist friends bonded and puzzled. A snap of George giving Darren a high-five when he'd got a hundred per cent on his algebra test. One of the teenagers fully absorbed as he sketched a beautiful landscape on the other side of the test paper as Arthur looked on.

Pictures of Lila and Gryffyn teaching at The Pottery Project; Elsie and Jessie's grandfather sharing a pint at the Roskilly Brewery in the same spot where her grandparents had done the same. A snap of Ashton and Merrin laughing on the beach. A couple of landscapes completed the photos Jessie had taken for the honeymoon album. She'd managed to capture Darren and Merrin on the beach holding hands too – the teenagers had been embarrassed, but had let her keep the picture, mainly because they agreed they both looked cute. Jessie even had one of Ashton sauntering sexily around her bedroom just before he'd pulled off his shirt. She'd deleted the rest of the snaps – she didn't want to share any of those.

But every time Jessie took a photo and checked it, she was stunned. Because the results astounded her. It was so obvious she had a talent for not just capturing a scene or face, but of narrowing the attention so you saw something you might not have with the naked eye – loneliness, connection, friendship, perhaps even love. She wasn't sure if it was the light, the way she framed the picture or perhaps just that she knew exactly where to look. Understood how the truth could be buried underneath a lifetime of judgements and how it could be teased out with the right perspective. And Jessie had to admit she was proud of the results – and even that maybe she was just as talented as Dorothy, after all.

'You look so happy when you're holding that camera, Jess,' her grandfather observed, beaming as he picked up his cocktail, tapped the glass carefully against Elsie's and sipped. 'It's like it was made for you to use. I want you to keep it. Dorothy always meant for you to have it anyway. I've been holding onto it: even when you gave up photography, I was hoping you'd find your way back to it again. Getting rid of the *putz* definitely helped...'

'Well, I think remaking your honeymoon album helped me more.' Jessie gripped the Nikon. She'd barely put it down in the past week – ever since Ella had given her the special project. A few months ago, she'd have refused. Passed up the chance because she didn't feel capable, but so much had changed… 'I'd love to have it, thanks Grandad,' she said, striding over to place a soft kiss on his cheek.

'I might need to borrow it soon, though,' he whispered. 'Elsie mentioned she hasn't been seashell collecting since before Jeff passed, and I thought we might take an early evening stroll with the dogs. My hip's been feeling much less sore the last couple of days, and I'm almost fully recovered from the hernia op. If we take it slowly, I think we'll be okay. I'd like to get some photos to remind me – I feel like my honeymoon album's evolved since we came to Indigo Cove. It's not just about the past anymore, there's the present and future in there too…'

His eyes drifted to Elsie and softened, and Jessie dipped her chin thinking her grandmother would approve. Dorothy would have hated the idea of George being lonely, deplored the thought of him spending the rest of his life alone. Life wasn't like a jigsaw: sometimes more than one piece could fit in the same spot. It might change the overall picture, but it could still work.

'Just be careful on the walk,' she said, thinking about the rocky track that led to the beach.

'I'm a hundred per cent sure your grandad will be fine,' Elsie joked, plagiarising his favourite expression. 'Even if he gets tired, Bear will give him a ride for the right incentive – and I happen to know of a shortcut which will take us to the road if the walk is too taxing.' She winked, her eyes sparkling. 'Don't worry.' She patted George on the shoulder. 'I'll look after him.'

'I know you will,' Jessie said softly, pulling away from her grandad and searching his face. He looked happier than he had in years, more rested, and there was a new excitement in his eyes. 'I want to get a quick picture of Peaches before he goes to bed, so I'll do that now and then I'm meeting Ella and Arthur, but I can give you the camera after that.'

She'd promised Ella and Arthur that she'd meet them at The Beach Café and show them her work in progress. Arthur had already started working with her pictures, and they were all excited about the results.

'We can take a walk now, maybe you could bring it to us when you're back?' Elsie asked and Jessie nodded. 'Any idea where Ashton is?'

Jessie felt her cheeks flood with warmth. They'd stolen an hour in her bedroom this afternoon before Ashton had driven off to check on Elsie's house. He didn't want the older woman to know it was almost ready for her to move back into. He'd said he wanted to surprise her, but Jessie suspected Ashton wasn't ready to part with his friend's company yet.

He'd changed so much too. He'd been teaching Merrin how to play chess each evening, had started cooking with Elsie and had even told her grandad he planned to put the bar back into the sitting room soon. He hadn't disappeared onto the beach alone either – usually Jessie accompanied Ashton on his dog walks now. No one was talking about what came next, but Jessie was starting to think there might be a place here for her. She had wondered about starting her own photography business, maybe even renting a flat of her own... If Indigo Cove were a puzzle, there was a Jessie-shaped space waiting for her to slot herself into. For the first time in a long time, she realised she'd fit.

She checked her watch. 'I don't think he'll be much longer. Let me get that photo of Peaches and I'll find you when I get back...'

'Take your time, love,' Elsie said, refilling her cocktail as Jessie skipped across the gardens on her too-big feet, feeling beautiful, excited and, finally happy in her skin.

23

Ashton spotted the battered red Audi that was blocking the gates of Look Out House as soon as he drove around the corner from Elsie's place. Tristan and his team had spent the last hour showing him the bungalow, talking over each other as they'd excitedly pointed out all the work they'd done. The new kitchen and bathroom were in, the carpets and tiles were down. Everything had been repainted and there was nothing else for them to do.

Ashton had stared at their handiwork, complimenting them on everything, while a part of him wished there was something else that he could ask them to rip out. He wasn't ready to part with Elsie, was happy with his busy house, with Merrin, George and Jessie there. He wasn't sure if he was ready to make it permanent, but was enjoying being part of this new eclectic family. He was happier now he wasn't alone – and he no longer felt quite so uncomfortable admitting it. Progress? Sighing, he turned off the road and pulled to a stop behind the Audi. Ashton didn't recognise the car. Perhaps it was just another ex-guest of the hotel wanting a tour down memory lane?

A man was sitting in the driver's seat and Ashton swallowed

down an odd sick feeling in the pit of his stomach as he took in the width of the man's shoulders. Memories flickered across his mind. He opened his car door and got out, feeling a new weightiness in his limbs, then his visitor climbed out too, and Ashton's stomach recoiled because suddenly he knew for sure. Perhaps he'd been expecting this to happen since Merrin had arrived?

'Son.' Christian Reynolds – or since he'd changed his name did that mean he was now Jones? – boomed as he watched Ashton approach. His father stood staring at him, sporting an expression Ashton couldn't read, his legs spread wide.

Ashton's insides tangled. He was filled with so many emotions – hurt, hatred, and most of all anger. But he wasn't ready to unpack those feelings or face them. Didn't know what he could do with them if he did.

'Why are you here?' Ashton asked, keeping his voice bare of any emotion. He could feel the anger fizzing in his chest – fury at the man for leaving the way he had and for depriving him of over a decade with his younger sister. But Ashton didn't let his feelings show. Revealing his emotions would give this man an edge, make his 'father' feel like he was the one with all the control – and Ashton wasn't going to let him have the upper hand.

'You know why. Nice digs,' Christian said, pointing idly towards Look Out House. 'I remember now just how many hours you spent at this place when you were growing up. I should have figured you'd find your way back here. Belong to a girlfriend, does it? You've still got your good looks – courtesy of my genes. Your sister wasn't so lucky, but I'm happy to see you've finally decided to use them to your advantage.' His knowing smile reminded Ashton of a reptile gearing up to pounce.

Ashton felt ill. The fact that this almost-stranger hadn't considered his son might own the house himself told him nothing had changed. He opened his mouth to tell Christian it belonged to him and stopped just in time. Was there still a part of him looking for his father's approval?

Disgusted, he simply said, 'Sure,' because if he admitted to owning it, Christian would want a piece.

Ashton shoved his hands into his pockets and studied the man biology deemed to be his father. He looked older: there were creases at the corners of his eyes and around his unsmiling mouth. On some people, these traits might add an air of age, a dash of wisdom, but instead, they gave him a cruel, calculating vibe. He was still as tall as all those years ago, but a lot skinnier – Elsie would probably describe him as a 'bag of bones', and then proceed to stuff his father with enough cake to remedy it. Now, there was none of the muscles Ashton remembered under the man's creased grey shirt. He looked sinewy and... older than his years, a little decrepit. But his eyes... they were just as mean as they always had been.

'Are you looking for something? Because there's nothing for you here. You should just go,' Ashton said after a long silence. He pointed right along the main road. 'If you follow that, it'll take you back to the motorway. Have a good trip.'

His father snorted. 'You're not even going to offer your old dad a cup of tea?' Christian leaned an arm onto the roof of his car, his expression languid and uncaring, but something nasty slithered across his face and Ashton wasn't surprised when he added, 'You know I'm here for Merrin.'

'I haven't seen her in years. You made sure of that,' Ashton said calmly, knowing it was pointless to lie. But it was damn well worth a try.

'I know your sister's here, so there's no point in playing games.' His father shrugged. 'She left enough clues: she'd used my computer to google this address. Anyone would think she wanted us to find her. Perhaps she did?'

'I thought you were on holiday in Portugal.' Ashton folded his arms and his father nodded.

'Your mother is still there, but... I had to come back to take care of some business. I realised Merrin was gone and figured she'd probably decided to find you. She only recently discovered you existed. I had no idea the girl had enough backbone to leave.'

He raised an eyebrow. 'I've got to say I was surprised when you didn't track us down after we left Indigo Cove – I always assumed she meant more to you than that. You gave a good impression of caring for her. Then again, you were always picking up strays. I guess you just replaced her with a dog?'

Ashton held his breath to stop himself from admitting that he had tried to find them and failed. He'd just be handing over ammunition: confirmation that Merrin mattered to him.

'Maybe you're more like me than I thought: you know what matters and what can easily be replaced.'

'Like a son you mean?' Ashton said. Hearing pain in his voice and shaking his head because he couldn't hide it.

Christian winked, looking pleased with himself. 'I told your sister you wouldn't be interested in meeting her.' His eyes narrowed to slits as he searched Ashton's face and the younger man tried not to move a muscle, not to give anything away. Then his father smiled nastily, and Ashton's stomach churned.

'Ahhhh, but you are interested, aren't you?' He blinked, obviously surprised. 'Now that's a shame because she's coming home with me. Unless...' He patted a hand on the pocket of his jeans. 'We can come to an arrangement.'

Ashton's heart started to pound. 'I'm not negotiating with you.' He'd happily part with the money but knew that wouldn't be the end of it. If his father saw a way to bleed him dry, he'd take it and Ashton wasn't going to give him the satisfaction.

'She's not going anywhere,' Ashton said, his voice firm.

At that very moment, he heard a car draw up. Jessie. He didn't want her to see his father in the flesh – didn't want her to see that he was related to someone so palpably evil. What would she make of him, would she think they were alike?

'And who's this?' Christian drawled, as Jessie got out of the car and strode towards them.

Ashton could feel a knot forming in the centre of his chest as nausea climbed his throat. This was what happened when you let yourself care about people – you were so much more susceptible to getting hurt. Suddenly, instead of being in control, the air was being knocked from your chest, the ground shifting under your shoes. The future you had mapped out, the safety of your daily routine and constancy of your emotions were in a maelstrom. You became vulnerable. And he hated it.

'No one,' Ashton snapped, watching as Jessie approached, suddenly, desperately wishing it was the truth.

24

Jessie didn't recognise the cool expression on Ashton's face as she parked the Ford Anglia and walked to the gates of Look Out House, chunks of icy fear sinking to the pit of her stomach. He looked tense and unhappy, but until she drew closer, she had no idea why. Then the man standing beside the red Audi turned to stare at her with dark, glittering eyes. He looked familiar, but she didn't think they'd met.

'My name's Christian Jones. Do you own this place?' the man asked, tipping his chin in the direction of the house. 'Because I think my daughter Merrin might be inside. She's just turned seventeen and she's run away from home. I'm very worried. I wonder if I could trouble you to let me in?'

So this was Ashton's father. His tone was glacially polite, but Jessie could tell he was lying about being anxious.

She glanced at Ashton to see what he wanted to do and watched his lips draw tight. 'I've told you, Merrin's not here,' he said. Jessie knew that was true because the teenager was on another date with Darren, probably walking around the harbour, catching up with his friends. 'Even if she was, I've said she's not going anywhere with you,' Ashton continued.

His father let out an irritated huff and shook his head. 'You have no idea about your sister. She'll do as she's told. She's as timid and stupid as those kittens she wanted to adopt. You're both so like your mother, sometimes I wonder if you have any of me in you at all – aside from those good looks.' He paused. 'Your sister might have come to find out more about her big brother, but it won't take long before she's back with us.'

'She's happy here,' Ashton said, then he immediately frowned as if he regretted giving so much away.

Christian took a step closer to his son, his wiry frame stiff. 'You think she's going to want to stay, you really think she cares for you?' The edge of his father's mouth contorted. 'You're just as soft and deluded as you always were.'

'Is that why you left me?' Ashton asked, his voice cold, but there was a hint of something underneath which told Jessie he really wanted to know. Perhaps to understand why he'd been abandoned, why he hadn't mattered enough to take with them.

Jessie took a step closer, but Ashton flinched as if she'd pressed a fingernail into an open wound, so she stopped where she was. She'd comfort him later, help him understand his father's actions had nothing to do with him. She'd learned that same lesson about how other people behaved since coming to Indigo Cove.

The older man shrugged. 'You were all grown up – it was time for you to move on and you weren't going to do it while you were obsessing over your little sister.' His mouth buckled. 'She wasn't even yours, she was mine.' He tapped a finger to his chest. 'But she stopped coming to me, it was always you she wanted. Always you she ran to when she wanted to play or fell over in the park.'

'So you took her from me.' Ashton's face paled.

'And I'll do the same again,' his father snapped.

'Is that why you hated me?' Ashton's expression betrayed

none of the emotion Jessie could hear in his voice – it was like he was studying an insect, one he wanted to squash.

The older man dismissed the question with a wave of his hand. 'I didn't have enough feelings for you to give it a name. I didn't want kids. You were an inconvenience. I tried to make you more like me but...' He hissed. 'Then that woman in the bungalow next door got hold of you and that was the end.'

'Elsie.' Ashton sighed and pinched the bridge of his nose. 'You're not taking Merrin,' he repeated, perhaps realising the argument was going nowhere, that there were no real answers for him here.

'We'll see,' his father said. 'I will say Merrin didn't miss you when we left before, and she'll forget you again as soon as we're back in Scotland.'

'You think so?' Ashton asked, his voice tight. 'You think you know her because you share the same DNA? You think she'll come with you just because you're her father?' He shook his head. 'There's a lot more to having a relationship than that. You have to earn love, you don't just get it, not once people grow old enough to know they deserve more.'

Ashton's voice was soft, and Jessie felt a glimmer of hope. Took another tiny step towards him, but he didn't turn. His knuckles were white, but it was the only sign he was finding the conversation difficult.

Then his father took a step towards him too, creeping closer until they were almost toe to toe. They were the same height, which meant the older man could look his son straight in the eye. Jessie watched Christian's mouth twist, waited for the punch of unkindness, but instead, the air suddenly hissed out of him, and he shook his head.

'She'll be coming back to Scotland, you'll see. There's enough of me in that girl to know what she's going to do. She's my family and she knows it too.' Satisfied he'd said his piece, he turned and wandered jauntily towards the Audi as if he didn't have a care in the world.

'You've got no idea about family,' Ashton said, looking shaken.

'And you do?' The older man turned, his voice dripping with sarcasm. 'Nobody wants you, nobody ever did, apart from an old woman with nothing better to do. Even your girl here will eventually see you're not worth keeping. No one will ever truly love you – you'll find that out.' Then he climbed into his car and fired the engine.

Jessie saw Ashton's expression turn blank and his shoulders sag as he watched the car skid backwards onto the main road in a cloud of dust.

'You know that's not true,' Jessie said. 'If that man hates you, it's got everything to do with him and nothing to do with you. You can hear what he says, but you don't have to believe it. Not if you don't want to...'

'We need to find Merrin,' Ashton snapped, watching as the Audi disappeared around the corner. 'I'm going to park the car and check the house – see if Elsie knows anything.' He strode to the Land Rover without looking at Jessie again and climbed inside before starting the engine. Then the gates swung open, and he was pulling onto the driveway before Jessie had even approached the Ford Anglia.

Her stomach felt cold, her limbs heavy, because there was something about the way he was behaving that felt wrong. Gone was the man she'd spent the last few weeks getting to know – now he was cold and detached.

She drove through the gate and parked on the driveway, then wandered through the open doorway into Look Out House. Ashton was already in the kitchen with his mobile pressed to his ear.

'She's not answering,' he growled. 'Elsie and your grandfather aren't here either.'

'They've gone to the beach.' Jessie linked her hands. 'I'm supposed to be taking them my camera.'

'Do you know where Merrin is?' Ashton looked furious.

'Somewhere around the harbour.' Jessie shrugged, walking to the other side of the kitchen counter, trying to put some distance between them because she couldn't stand how combative he was. 'She was going to meet some of Darren's friends.'

'Then why isn't she answering her mobile?' Ashton fired back.

'Perhaps she got caught up, maybe the signal isn't good. I don't know. Teenagers don't always answer their mobiles.' She spread her palms. 'We could drive there, see if we can find her?'

Ashton nodded. 'I've checked and the kittens are in the sitting room – she won't leave without them, whatever he says.' His eyes narrowed and he grabbed his keys.

'Ashton, Merrin isn't going to want to go anywhere,' Jessie said.

His expression was bleak when he turned back to look at her. 'Are you sure about that?' he asked flatly, before marching away.

Merrin wasn't on the beach, around the harbour or anywhere on the high street. Face ashen, Ashton drove the Land Rover back onto the drive at Look Out House. He'd barely spoken as they'd searched, and Jessie had given up trying to talk to him. She watched him hop out of the car after they'd screeched to a halt just before Elsie opened the front door. Jessie had called her grandfather an hour before to fill them in on what had happened, and the older couple had promised to wait for the teenager at the house.

'Darren's here,' Elsie said urgently, encouraging them inside. She was cuddling Peaches to her chest, as if the cockerel were some kind of pacifier. 'He's just arrived. I was going to call, but then I saw you driving up to the gates.'

'Where's Merrin?' Ashton shot back.

'I'm sorry, love, she's not here.' Elsie shook her head.

'Then where's Darren?' Ashton rushed past the older woman, heading for the kitchen just as the teenager appeared in the doorway.

'Merrin's gone,' the boy said roughly, swiping a hand through his messy dark hair. 'She told me to come and find you, and I asked Ella to drive me up.' The teen swallowed, his skin pale. 'We were just walking along the high street with my friends, and this man stopped his car. I thought he was a stranger, but Merrin knew him.' His forehead bunched as he glared at Ashton. 'She said he was your dad.'

'He's been here,' Jessie said. 'What happened, where did she go?' Surely she wouldn't have left? She'd been so happy here.

'Your father told her she had to leave Indigo Cove. I don't know what happened, but it was like she couldn't say no. She didn't even want to come back for her stuff.' He sounded stricken. 'She asked me to ask if you'd take care of the kittens – then she just... went. Will she be okay?' He swallowed. 'Should we call the police?'

'He won't hurt her,' Ashton said, his voice oddly toneless. 'If Merrin wants to leave, we can't stop her.' He shoved his hands into his pockets and flinched when Elsie stroked a palm across his back. Then he shook his head, his shoulders slumping. 'I need to walk,' he said before striding out of the kitchen with all three dogs following behind.

'Give him a minute,' Elsie said, as Jessie started to follow. 'Let him work off some of his feelings, give him time to calm down.'

'Why did Merrin go with him?' Darren asked, as Elsie

poured a hot chocolate for him. The boy's eyes were bright, and Jessie wondered if he was going to cry.

'Perhaps she didn't think she had a choice,' George murmured, wandering into the room to join them. 'I'm a hundred per cent sure the girl wouldn't have wanted to go. Perhaps she was trying to protect her brother.'

'We have to go after her.' Darren gripped his fists to his sides.

'Perhaps we will. Ashton will be able to find them now he knows their new surname and that they're living in Scotland,' Elsie added.

'Then why isn't he here now?' Darren argued. 'Where did he go? Why did he just disappear – doesn't he care about her?'

Elsie shook her head sadly. 'The real problem, Darren, is Ashton cares too much.'

Jessie found Ashton on the beach twenty minutes later. She'd waited until Elsie told her it was okay to go, that he'd had sufficient time to process what had happened. But he needed to talk about Merrin, and Jessie was going to make that easy for him. That's what people who cared for each other did.

She found Ashton pacing by the waves. His jeans were wet and even the dogs looked unsettled. They patrolled around him, like bodyguards on high alert. As Jessie approached, Murphy whined and Phoebe and Bear began to bark, perhaps demanding she do something to fix him.

'Are you okay?' she asked softly, standing beside him and following Ashton's gaze so it was fixed on the horizon too. She pressed a hand to his shoulder, and he recoiled, making everything inside her grow cold.

'I can't do this.' He turned towards her, his eyes emotionless. 'I said I could but... I'd forgotten how it felt to lose someone and

I don't want to do it with you. Christian's right, we both know this'll end sometime – it always does.'

'Will it?' Jessie asked, her voice impassive, even though fear was climbing the inside of her ribs, making her breathless.

Ashton swallowed. 'I'm not going to wait for that. I was happy living in Look Out House with just the dogs.'

'So now you don't want Elsie either?' Jessie snapped.

He shrugged a shoulder, but there was a hitch in his next breath. 'I'm not losing her, but she'll be moving back into her bungalow soon. She's got her own life, needs her own space – and so do I.'

'So you can go back to hiding in your work?' Jessie asked softly.

'Why not?' Ashton's eyes were cold. 'I knew this would happen – I've been waiting for it all to come crashing down.' He shrugged a shoulder. 'It's almost a relief.'

'You're turning your back on Merrin and me too.' Jessie's voice caught and Phoebe rubbed her nose against her thigh.

'I'm being pragmatic. Christian's right. I'm not cut out for this.' He waved a hand between them. 'I knew it, but when I met you again, when Merrin arrived...' He hesitated. 'I let myself believe.' He spread his arms wide, gesturing with his palms as if he were delivering a lecture. His voice was devoid of emotion, his whole body rigid. 'You'll get over this quickly enough.'

Jessie shoved a hand against his side, tried to spin Ashton around so he'd look at her, but he wouldn't meet her eyes. 'You're running again because you're scared.' She swallowed. 'You did the same fourteen years ago, and you promised you wouldn't do it again.' A tear rolled down her cheek and she dried it.

'I'm not running,' he grumbled. 'I'm still here, telling you I don't want this – that it's not for me.'

'And I'm here saying I love you. Is that not for you either?' Her voice cracked.

Jessie watched the rise and fall of Ashton's chest, how he stiffened, bracing himself against her words. 'Jessie...' He shook his head and squeezed his eyes shut. 'You thought you loved Brendon until a few weeks ago.'

She choked. 'You think the way I feel for you is the same?' Jessie wheezed. 'Do you think my feelings are that shallow?' More tears leaked from her eyes and this time she didn't wipe them.

Ashton shoved his hands into the pockets of his jeans. A part of Jessie hoped it was because he wanted to stop himself from reaching for her, but there was a voice whispering at the edges of her mind, telling her perhaps he was right. That a man like Ashton would never love a woman like her. That she'd been kidding herself. And that voice belonged to Maria.

'I'm sorry, but it's not going to work. I don't feel that way about you,' Ashton said roughly.

Jessie's knees went weak and she almost stumbled, nodded as the tears grew heavier and everything inside her turned to ice. Then, for the second time in her life, Jessie's heart broke – but this time, she was the one who ran.

25

Ashton felt light-headed as he approached Look Out House. Even a sprint up the narrow track from the beach hadn't done anything to relieve the acidic burn in his chest. He knew he'd done the right thing, but watching Jessie as she'd run, seeing her tall figure grow smaller until she rounded the corner of the cliff and disappeared had left him aching.

He'd done the right thing. Letting himself get close to her had been madness. It was kinder to let her go now. He'd spent his lifetime avoiding strong feelings and it was time to get back on track.

He blinked moisture from his eyes and blamed it on the run. The dogs had kept up – even Bear had overtaken him on the journey halfway up the hill, his tongue lolling from his jaws, his eyes a picture of excitement as he'd waited at the top for Phoebe and Murphy to catch up.

Ashton grabbed the towel that hung in the downstairs bathroom as he tracked through the house and wiped his face, heading for the kitchen. He needed a glass of water, then he'd get back to work. A few hours on his computer locking down the virtual world would fix this gnawing sense of unease. Give it another week and he'd have forgotten Jessie and Merrin alto-gether. His stomach rolled, but he ignored it as he walked into the kitchen.

'Ella picked Darren up – the boy asked us to call if we got any news about Merrin. Where's Jessie?' Elsie asked, looking behind him as all three dogs started to wind themselves around her legs. 'Did you sort things out with her?' She stopped wiping the counter and stared into his eyes before shaking her head. 'No, Ashton...'

'What?' George drained the last few drops from his mug before picking up some cake. The older man glanced behind Ashton too, looking confused. Then something seemed to pass between the couple and his smile dimmed. 'So you're another birdbrain. I was almost a hundred per cent convinced you weren't. Where's my granddaughter?' He slowly rose from his chair.

'Somewhere on the beach,' Ashton said. He balled his hands into fists and pressed them into his eyes. 'Jessie will be okay, she's better off without me.'

Elsie stared at him as disappointment coloured her face. 'I might have to agree. You pushed her away, didn't you?'

'It's for the best,' Ashton said, going to run the tap and fill up a glass before taking a sip, but even the cool water wouldn't refresh his dry throat.

'Because you won't get hurt?' Elsie's voice was sharp. 'Oh Ashton,' she drew out his name. 'I'd feel sorry for you if I didn't think you were a total nitwit.'

He shoved his hands into his pockets. 'Jessie was never going to stay,' he said softly. 'And Merrin wouldn't either. Sooner or later, she'd have left – everyone does.'

'I didn't,' Elsie said icily. She stared at him, and the moment stretched until he looked away, his cheeks burning.

'No, you didn't,' he agreed. 'I know that, I just...'

'People who stay don't count as much as the ones who

leave?' Ashton heard hurt in Elsie's voice and wished he could push the words back down his throat.

'I didn't say that...' His legs felt hollow, his heart sore – but the feelings would wear off, he'd be okay.

'Tristan Harvey called while you were on the beach,' Elsie said, her voice clipped. 'He wanted you to know everyone in the village is keeping an eye out for Merrin. Ella told me she's told everyone who goes to The Puzzle Club too.' Her eyes flashed. 'So now there are more people who care and are still here, imagine that.' Ashton opened his mouth, but Elsie kept talking. 'Tristan also mentioned my house is ready.' She dried her hands with a tea towel. 'So I think it makes sense for me to move out too. You want to be alone, don't you?'

'I...' Ashton gulped. His eyes swept the kitchen, and he remembered choosing the cabinets with Elsie; chatting with Jessie as she'd made him tea and sharing slices of cake with George and Merrin... How good Look Out House had felt when it was filled with people and noise.

'Do you think I could come and stay with you for a few days?' George asked Elsie. 'Just until Jessie and I work out what we're going to do. We might go back to Oxford early.' Something blocked Ashton's throat and he swallowed.

'Oh, I hope not.' Elsie gave the older man a shy smile, her cheeks reddening. 'You'd be welcome at mine for as long as you like.'

'You can stay here—' Ashton found himself offering.

'I would?' George asked, his attention fixed on Elsie, as if nothing else existed.

She shrugged. 'I've enjoyed the last few weeks.' She took in a deep breath and let it out before wrapping her hands around her waist. 'It helped me to take stock, to realise living alone is...' Her eyes strayed to Ashton before she looked away. 'Not as much fun as when you have company. I see people at The Beach Café most days, but then I go home and...' She shrugged.

'Once you get a taste of companionship again, you remember what you've been missing...' She pulled a face.

George nodded, knitting his fingers together. It was almost like Ashton wasn't in the room. Is this how it would feel when everyone was gone? He leaned back on the counter and watched the couple talk. Even the dogs were ignoring him now.

'It's not easy.' George's voice was rough, and Ashton found himself nodding. 'I think that's why losing my honeymoon album hit me so hard. Because all I had were my memories. I wasn't creating any new ones: I wasn't prepared to take that risk.' He blinked. 'You'd think living seventy odd years and being a professor in maths would make me smarter than that.'

Elsie chuckled and went to press a hand over his. 'I think we're all a little stupid when it comes to life – when it comes to what we need, or the things we're afraid of.' She chose that moment to look back at Ashton and her lips bunched. 'If we pack our things now, would you see your way to driving us to my house, Ashton?' she asked quietly. 'We'll take Peaches, Phoebe and Bear. Let you get back to normal. Unless you want me to take Murphy too?'

'I...' Ashton cleared the emotion from his throat. 'Don't.'

'Don't what?' Elsie asked. He recognised that look on her face: it was the one he'd seen that day she'd caught him stealing food from her kitchen. Half sympathy, half understanding – she knew what he needed, and was going to make sure he understood what he was doing was wrong.

Ashton gulped. 'Don't move out. I know you have to go back to your own house sometime, but... I like having you here.' He looked up. 'You're right, you've always been there for me, you never left. I've always appreciated that.' The tension across his ribs released when Elsie smiled. Then she stepped closer so she could take hold of his hand. She turned it over and linked their fingers.

'You'll never be alone for as long as I'm alive, Ashton.' She cupped his face, then pressed the pad of her finger onto his chin so she could lower it and look him in the eye. 'What about Merrin?'

He sighed. 'I'm going to drive to Scotland and get her back. I'm not going to let Christian take her from me again. If she wants to live in Indigo Cove, I'll tell her she's always got a place with me.' The older woman nodded as if she'd been expecting that all along. 'If she wants to stay in Scotland—'

'She won't,' Elsie said firmly.

'If she does, I'll make sure we keep in touch,' he added, and the older woman nodded again.

'What about Jessie?' George asked sharply.

'I'll talk to her.' He sighed. 'If she'll forgive me, I'll tell her I'm an idiot and... I'm going to ask her to stay.'

Elsie dropped Ashton's hand and pulled him into a hug just as the buzzer by the front gate went off.

'Expecting someone?' George asked, as Ashton turned and then started to run towards the front door. Perhaps Jessie was here, maybe she'd come to give him a piece of her mind – to tell him exactly what she thought? Wasn't that one of the things he loved about her? He found himself running faster and instead of opening the gate from inside the house, he unlocked the door and sprinted down the driveway. But when the gates swung open, instead of Jessie, he found Merrin.

Ashton grabbed his sister's hand and pulled her onto the driveway, closing the gates after checking both ways for the red Audi.

'What happened? Darren told us you went with Christian?' Ashton fired off the questions as relief flooded through him.

Merrin cleared her throat. 'I told Dad I didn't want to live with him anymore.' She blinked, looking surprised. 'I said I wanted to stay here with you. I don't think he knew what to say.'

'He let you go, just like that?' Ashton asked, studying his sister's face. She looked... happy, more confident, almost like she'd matured a few years.

'He told me I'd change my mind. I said I wouldn't – that I was seventeen now, so where I live isn't his choice anymore.' She nibbled her lower lip. 'I'd looked it up – I don't think he expected that. I think he thought I'd just do what he wanted.' She looked embarrassed. 'I always have before.'

'What did he say then?' Ashton asked. He guided Merrin back towards Look Out House and saw George and Elsie were waiting for them.

'He told me he didn't care. He said I was ugly and I eat too much, and he wouldn't miss me,' she said.

'That's not true.' Ashton sighed.

Merrin shrugged. 'I know that now...' she said sarcastically. 'He was just being mean. Some people are–' She shrugged as they reached the doorway and the older couple stood back. 'They don't even need a reason. We have to learn to shut out what they say. To make our own decisions.'

Elsie smiled and patted Merrin's shoulder. 'You're wise for one so young, I think your brother could learn a lot from you.'

Merrin snorted and Ashton nodded. 'You are right. I hope you'll stay, teach me more of those lessons I need to learn...'

'It's okay if I do?' Merrin asked quietly. She started to chew her bottom lip. 'I wasn't sure if you'd want me.'

'Of course I do!' Ashton growled. 'I want you to live here with me. To go to school or college, whatever you like. I missed you.' The words had been hard to get out, but when he saw the smile light up Merrin's face, Ashton knew he'd said the right thing.

'It's only been a few hours.' She giggled, before throwing herself into his arms. 'Can the cats stay too?'

'All of them.' Ashton smiled and hugged her tighter.

'I feel like I'm coming home, does that sound ridiculous?' Merrin asked.

'Nope,' Ashton spoke into her hair, as Elsie joined the hug and George did too. He closed his eyes. This was almost perfect, but there was still something missing – and that something was Jessie.

26

Jessie slumped onto the beach and peered at the horizon through her grandma's camera again but didn't take a shot. She'd been staring through that same lens for the last hour and a half, but no matter how long she looked, she couldn't find the picture she was hoping for. Everything felt off kilter, out of focus, nothing was right.

There was a lead weight in the pit of her stomach after her conversation with Ashton and she had no idea what she wanted to do now. She had to go back to Look Out House sometime, tell her grandad she was going to move out, borrow the Ford Anglia so she could disappear into the sunset. Alone. Was that going to be the story of her life?

'What am I going to do about Ashton, Grandma?' she asked, dropping the camera from her face so she could study the view in all its glory. Light glittered across the waves, and she imagined for a moment Dorothy was here. That they were taking one of their long walks along the shore with the camera.

'You'd tell me to fight,' she realised, letting out a long sigh. 'You'd tell me to stop letting Maria's words get in the way of how I feel about myself – and to tell him I'm worth having.' She breathed in slowly and let it out.

'Everything Maria said was a lie, I know that now. She was an unhappy woman who was deeply insecure, and she wanted to hurt me because somehow that made her feel good.' She shook her head, baffled. 'Ashton's been dealing with the same. His parents couldn't see beyond their own needs – he wasn't important, and, in the end, they deliberately hurt him because they could.' She pressed her fingers against her eyelids and dried the spill of tears.

'I wish he'd understand that what we have is too good for him to walk away from. That he's just afraid of being hurt again. But I don't know if he'll listen, and I don't think I'm strong enough to hang around to find out that he won't.'

She played with the camera lens as her eyes filled with tears once more, adjusting the calibration and shutter speed before staring through it. She still had no idea what she was hoping to find – a happy ending? Would she even know what one looked like if she saw it?

A dog barked somewhere in the distance and Jessie's stomach squeezed, but she kept her attention fixed firmly ahead, lined up the horizon and took the picture.

'I think you'd be proud of me, Grandma,' she said. 'I've taken some photos for The Puzzle Club, and Ella and Arthur love them. I've finished your honeymoon album too. I don't think it's so important to Grandad now, but I'm going to print out all the pictures before I leave Indigo Cove so I can make him a new set of memories.'

'It won't be exactly the same as your album because it won't just have pictures from the past, but some of the future too. Grandad's been so happy here, and I hope he comes back or stays – being in Oxford isn't right for him anymore. I know you'd love Elsie and that you'd be glad he has a new happy ending.'

She swiped a tear as it rolled down her cheek. 'As for me, I've no idea where I'm going next. Perhaps I'll see if I can stay with Rose until I figure things out. I do know I want to be a photographer again – I like the way the world looks through a lens and I'm good at it. It was stupid to let that side of my life go. I thought I could stay and do it here, but...'

She shook her head as she got up and cleaned the sand from her clothes, then lined up a new shot. One final picture, then she'd go, pack her bag before finding somewhere temporary to stay.

'Jessie,' she heard Ashton's voice and spun around. He was just a few metres away from her, flanked by all three dogs. She had no idea how he'd managed to get so close without her noticing.

Jessie folded her arms, even though the heavy weight in the pit of her stomach turned featherlight and began to float away. 'Why are you here?' she asked, her voice toneless.

He ran a hand through his hair, ruffling it. 'Honestly?' he asked, seeming to drink her in. 'Because I've realised your grandad's right and I'm a fool, imbecile, nitwit, take your pick.' He stepped forward. 'I want you to stay,' he said fiercely, but Jessie twisted around so she could study the waves. It hurt to look at Ashton and if she continued, she knew she'd find it harder to turn him down.

'You didn't want me two hours ago, I don't understand what's changed.' She sighed.

'Merrin's back,' he said, moving until they were standing side by side.

'That's good.' Jessie rolled her shoulders, easing out the tension. 'I'm glad, but that has nothing to do with us.' She turned. 'I love you, Ashton, and for the first time in my life, I know I deserve somebody who loves me all the way back.' She blinked. 'I'm done being someone's easy option, the thing they settle for, I want someone who'll fight for me.'

'You're not...' He reached a hand towards her, and she stepped away, shaking her head.

'You walked away so easily.' She pressed a hand to her heart. 'It hurts, but I'll get over it. What I wouldn't get over is staying when your feelings are only lukewarm.' Her breath hitched. 'Because I've been there, I've even done it myself – allowed myself to accept a relationship that wasn't what it should have been because I didn't believe I deserved more. That's why I've realised I have to hold out for everything, no ifs or buts and no running.'

Jessie expected Ashton to turn and leave. He'd said his piece and she knew he wasn't the type of man to fight. Instead, he shoved his hands into his pockets and shut his eyes.

'I've spent my life pushing people away, trying not to care for anyone, making sure I never got hurt. But it happened anyway.' He frowned. 'I once told you that you could rip emotions from me, and I didn't want that.'

Jessie nodded because she knew she'd cry if she spoke.

'But the thing is, I felt them anyway. It didn't matter what I wanted or didn't, or what I decided I wouldn't feel. Elsie's been in my life since I was fifteen and I've loved her from the first night she made me dinner and demanded I tell her all about my homework. How did I not realise that?' Ashton stepped closer. 'I thought I'd closed myself off from people, that I was far too clever to get hurt, but the irony is, I've been letting them in for years. My dogs, Elsie, Jeff, Merrin... I fell for them despite every promise I'd made myself. Then... there's you.' He sighed, clasping his hands together. 'I fell for you fourteen years ago when we kissed that first time on the beach.'

'You ran,' Jessie challenged.

'Well, I didn't acknowledge it then because I'm an idiot and it scared the hell out of me. And I thought leaving would make it easier.'

'Nothing's changed then,' she said sadly.

'Except it has.' Ashton rubbed a hand across his eyes. 'I've realised how awful the idea of living without you is. Because despite everything I've said and done, despite making you think I don't care, I love you and I think I have for a long time.'

Jessie turned to stare at Ashton's face. She knew the bow of his lips, the angular contours of his cheeks, that strong nose and beautiful jawline as if they belonged to her. She loved every inch of him, but it wasn't enough. 'I don't know...' Her voice was hoarse, and she swallowed. 'I don't know what to believe. Words are easy...'

Ashton winced, then his head jerked up and he pointed to Dorothy's camera. 'Look through that. You once told me the camera has a way of narrowing the attention – of blocking everything else out. You said it can show us the truth or misrepresent it entirely. Look at me through Dorothy's camera, Jess, take a photo – tell me what you see.'

Jessie gazed at Ashton for a long moment. 'Will you let me go if I do?' she asked, her insides heavy because despite everything, she couldn't bear the idea.

'If you still want that,' he said, looking unhappy.

She slowly lifted the camera. Spent a few moments adjusting the focus, fiddling with the set-up, ignoring her shaking fingers which were making it difficult to work. Then she allowed herself to examine every curve and line of Ashton's face.

Jessie knew this would be the last time she saw him – she wouldn't be able to face spending time with him after today – so she took her time silently saying goodbye, blinking away the emotions that were making it difficult to see. Then her attention snared on Ashton's eyes. He was staring at her, right into the lens, and there was something she hadn't seen before now...

'Take a photo,' Ashton said. 'Take as many as you like. Then look at them and tell me what you see. Take your time, Jess.' He sounded nervous.

She paused and then snapped three pictures in quick succession. It almost hurt to look at him now, so she dropped the camera and kept her eyes averted.

'Look at them, please,' Ashton repeated. 'Tell me what you see.'

Jessie sighed and began to study the images. 'You look...' Surprised, she peered closer because she wasn't sure if she could trust what she was seeing. The light she'd noticed in Ashton's eyes was the same as the one she'd spotted in her grandfather's when he gazed at Dorothy. The same she'd seen when he looked at Elsie now.

'Can you see the truth, Jess?' Ashton asked almost desperately.

'I... I don't know.' She looked again, checking she was right. 'You love me?' she asked, slowly letting the camera fall to her hip as her insides skipped, and she met Ashton's eyes. 'I think the camera is telling me you love me.'

'That's exactly what it's saying.' Ashton nodded, stepping forward so he could frame her face with his hands. 'I was so afraid you wouldn't see it, that I'd messed it all up. I want you to stay.' He pressed his lips to her forehead and peppered her cheeks with tiny kisses before capturing her mouth. The kiss was warm and tender, and Jessie let herself fall into it. Felt every cell of her body relax.

'I want you to stay,' he murmured, pulling back so he could gaze at her. 'Live in Look Out House with Merrin, Elsie, your grandfather and me.'

'Together?' Jessie laughed. 'That's a lot of people for a man who doesn't like company.'

Ashton shook his head, still drinking her in. 'I was wrong.' He kissed her again.

'You're not running?' Jessie asked, wrapping her arms

around Ashton's neck and pressing her body into his as all three dogs began to bark and chase circles round them.

'I'm not running again, and neither are you, Jess.' Then Ashton pressed his mouth to hers, and this time the kiss was long and deep, and Jessie hoped it would never end.

27

'I'm delighted to announce the winners of The Beach Café's first ever Jigsaw Championship are Elsie Green and George Levine!' Ella boomed, weaving her way between the multitude of customers and spectators so she could present the couple with steaming mugs of hot chocolate decorated with marshmallows and sparkly tinsel cocktail sticks. 'I can't serve alcohol, but you can celebrate with these,' she joked.

'They'll do nicely, plus everyone's invited back to Look Out House for champagne and old fashioneds later,' Elsie declared, winking at Ashton who was standing close by.

Elsie adjusted Peaches who was sitting on her lap and smoothed her candyfloss hair as Jessie nudged into a tiny gap so she could take a photo of the beaming couple. Then she scanned the room and captured Merrin and Darren giggling with a group of their friends who'd come to watch them compete. The teenagers had started visiting the café regularly after Merrin had convinced them puzzles and cake were cool, after all.

'I'd like to present this special prize to our winners,' Ella said, wandering from behind the counter again with a large square parcel wrapped in brown paper. 'It's a collaborative effort from Jessie and Arthur.'

Ella handed the parcel to George, simultaneously elbowing Jessie closer to the table, and waved at Arthur, encouraging him to join them too. He'd been sitting with a group of his artist friends, two of whom were still finishing the puzzle they'd been working on. They didn't have George and Elsie's years of jigsaw experience and were still only halfway through. But they'd become regular visitors to The Beach Café as they'd started to use the space for their meetings, to work or just so they had a warm and inviting place to go, and Ella had been discussing opportunities to sell and display their art.

Elsie and George slowly began to unwrap the parcel and Jessie picked up the camera again. Then she took a quick photo, capturing their expressions as they both realised what they'd won.

'It's a picture.' Elsie gulped, leaning closer to study it.

'In the shape of a heart,' Jessie's grandfather said, sounding surprised. 'Is it made from lots of different jigsaw pieces?'

'Of course. We got puzzles made up from Jessie's photos and then I used some of the pieces in the pictures.' Arthur nodded. 'You need to look closer.'

'I can see Peaches!' Elsie pointed to the picture. 'And I'm in here – oh I like my hair!' She patted a palm on her curls. 'And so are you.' Her voice grew husky as she pointed to George.

'Hang on,' Jessie's grandfather said, peering closer. 'I'm one hundred per cent sure there are a lot of faces I recognise in here.' He swept an arm, encompassing the room. 'There's Ashton, Jessie, Merrin and Darren. Oh, and Lila, Ella and Gryffyn too!' His voice grew louder as he continued to pick out his new friends.

'All of our Puzzle Club members are in the picture,' Ella said, linking hands with Arthur. 'It's a brilliant work.'

'Is that Dorothy?' George asked, tracing a fingertip over the glass.

'Yes.' Jessie had copied her grandfather's photo of them in the gardens at Look Out House. 'It felt like she was part of all this. Without her album, we wouldn't be in Indigo Cove at all...' Jessie said. 'And I wouldn't have taken those photos.'

'So the picture wouldn't exist,' Ella said.

George swallowed and Elsie squeezed his shoulder. 'It's wonderful. Even better than my new album, which I love,' he said. Jessie had presented it to her grandad just before the championships. 'It's funny, but I feel like I've got so much more than my memories back since coming here...' He looked at the picture again. 'But what does this artwork mean?'

'It's... well...' Ella turned to Arthur. 'You'll explain it better than me.' Her cheeks pinked.

The artist kissed her softly on the forehead before nodding. 'It's a visual representation of The Puzzle Club's mission statement. A place to bring people together,' he said grandly.

Darren grinned. 'Or in less complicated words, it's supposed to show us what The Puzzle Club means to everyone who comes here.'

'Is that why it's in the shape of a heart?' Merrin asked.

Jessie nodded. 'It's supposed to show we're a community, that there's love and friendship here if people want it. That's why it includes everyone who comes.'

'Like a puzzle.' Arthur smiled. 'You're all part of this place. Jessie's been sneaking photos of you over the last couple of weeks. I made this picture for the winners, and there are more coming, and Ella will hang them around the café. Some will be for sale, and some won't. We've already had a few orders for puzzle pictures.' He nodded to Jessie. 'We're working together on that.'

'We'll keep adding to ours too,' Ella said, beaming. 'I want everyone who comes to know they've got a permanent spot in our Jigsaw Club if they want it.'

'That's clever...' Merrin said, smiling. 'So now we're all part of one big puzzle.'

'It is clever!' Elsie nodded. 'I've just got one question.' She turned to George. 'Where will we put our prize, in Look Out House or the bungalow?'

Jessie's grandfather smiled, his eyes lighting as he gazed at her. It was a look Jessie recognised because it was the same one Ashton had when he was with her. 'That all depends on when we move into our new home...' he said.

'There's no pressure,' Ashton shouted from across the room. 'You can stay with Jessie, Merrin and me for as long as you like.'

His eyes caught Jessie's and he winked, and she felt her insides tumble like someone had just switched on a washing machine. Her life had transformed since she'd come to Indigo Cove – even more so since Ashton had told her he loved her. Now she was living with him, her grandfather, Elsie and Merrin, taking photos all the time. Next week, she planned to launch a website offering her services as a local photographer – although she had plenty of business already because Lila had been boasting about her cat portraits to everyone who'd listen.

'I've got something to give out too,' Darren piped up, offering postcard-sized pictures to George, Arthur and Gryffyn. 'These are a thank you because the three of you helped me to realise I don't need to give up my art. I showed these to my dad and even he's impressed.'

George nudged his glasses onto his nose and grinned. 'I'm a hundred per cent convinced you might be a genius.'

Arthur turned over his picture and smiled. 'Maths and art: you made them work together. I knew you could.'

The boy flushed. 'It was Merrin's idea.' He gave Ashton's sister a soppy smile. 'She showed me people were making pictures on their computers using a combination of calculations and abstract art. I just downloaded something and tried it. It's called fractural art.' He shrugged as they all examined the intricate, colourful swirls which were quite stunning. 'I've just been messing around, but I enjoyed it. It means I can do art and practise maths at the same time.' He nodded at Arthur.

'Looks like everyone's getting their happy ending,' Ashton suddenly whispered in Jessie's ear, circling her waist and pressing her body into his.

'How did you get across the café so fast?' she asked, as he spun her around and kissed her, pushing the camera to her side so he could tug her even closer.

'I ran,' Ashton murmured, capturing Jessie's mouth again as she encircled his neck and kissed him back. She felt her grandmother's camera being eased from her shoulder, saw a flash in the corner of her eye as someone else took a photo. But she didn't pull away – instead, she leaned into him and deepened the kiss because, for the first time in her life, she knew she was in exactly the right place, and deserved to be there.

A LETTER FROM DONNA

I want to say a big thank you for choosing to read *Summer at the Cornish Beach Café*. If you enjoyed it, and want to keep up to date with all my latest releases, just sign up at the following link. Your email address will never be shared and you can unsubscribe at any time.

www.bookouture.com/donna-ashcroft

Summer at the Cornish Beach Café took me back to glorious Indigo Cove in Cornwall with its windy roads, vibrant sunshine and warm and caring villagers. I hope you enjoyed joining Jessie and her grandfather on their quest to replace his lost honeymoon album. Jessie certainly got a lot more than she bargained for when memories came back not just of George, but for her too, and she had to face up to her past. Especially when it arrived in the shape of brooding hero, Ashton Reynolds, the man who'd broken Jessie's heart fourteen years before...

I hope you enjoyed meeting the regulars at The Beach Café: from the owner Ella, to The Puzzle Club founder Elsie and her cockerel Peaches. I loved writing about these funny, kind-hearted characters and the way they absorbed Jessie, George and Ashton into their eclectic community. Helping with the quest to not only take the lost photos, but also teaching them all how to restart their lives – and ultimately, find their perfect fit.

If you did, it would be wonderful if you could please leave a short review. Not only do I want to know what you thought, it might encourage a new reader to pick up my book for the first time.

I really love hearing from my readers – so please say hi on my Facebook page, through Twitter, TikTok on Instagram or via my beautiful website.

Thanks,

Donna Ashcroft

www.donna-writes.co.uk

facebook.com/DonnaAshcroftAuthor

twitter.com/Donnashc

instagram.com/donnaashcroftauthor

tiktok.com/@donnashc

ACKNOWLEDGEMENTS

I admire people who take the road less travelled. It requires single-mindedness and determination, and my friend Hester has that in spades. This book is dedicated to her in appreciation of that, because she helps me to remember that it's okay – even necessary sometimes – to live your own best life, and that it doesn't have to look like everyone else's.

There are a few special mentions I'd also like to make here: Amanda Baker, friend and physiotherapist, gave me lots of brilliant advice when Jessie was going to be a physio – I changed her to a photographer when that didn't work for the story, but thanks to Amanda, I may include one in a book one day. Phoebe the gorgeous golden retriever in the novel is based on my good friend Julie Anderson's dog. Phoebe is bonkers and beautiful, which is why I wanted to include her. Thanks also to Julie for suggesting George had suffered from a hernia when he was initially recovering from a hip operation. Chris, my Other Half, is a puzzle king and I know one day he'll probably start up his own jigsaw club somewhere. If he does, I will turn up with pink hair and a cockerel or something equally eccentric. Jackie Campbell introduced me to French 75 cocktails and inspired George's old fashioned cocktails which reminded him of his honeymoon. The idea for the jigsaw-making cockerel was inspired by a social media post from my friend Soo Cieszynska. It showed a woman sat on a park bench doing the daily crossword with her cockerel. I loved this partnership – and it sparked the idea for Peaches.

My acknowledgments often mention the same people over and over and I thought momentarily about shaking it up, but then decided that would mean I wouldn't be appreciating those who turn up for me over and over in my daily life. So you might recognise a few names!

Firstly, to Chris, my puzzle making partner: thank you for being there through thick and thin – and to my lovely kids Erren and Charlie who keep life bumpy but interesting! To Jules Wake, my best writing buddy who is there for plot twists, writer's block, the daily word count update and celebrations – I'm so grateful I've got you to keep me going! To The Prosecco Writers – Jules, Elizabeth Finn and Anita Chapman, for our lovely writing breaks away where much of this book was written. To Mel and Rob Harrison of Goodman Fox for looking after my website and for giving me lots of brilliant advice and help with newsletters. To Love & Chocolate – a group of local and wonderfully supportive writers. To my oldest friends Jackie Campbell and Julie Anderson for always being there for me too no matter what.

As always thanks to the fabulous team at Bookouture, including Natasha Harding, Lizzie Brien, Noelle Holten, Kim Nash, Jess Readett, Alexandra Holmes, Sarah Hardy, Peta Nightingale, Richard King and Saidah Graham. Also, to Natasha Hodgson and Catherine Lenderi for their work on this book. Thanks also to the other Bookouture authors for your amazing support and to Carla Kovach for the Motivation Station!

To all the amazing bloggers who support me every time I have a cover reveal, need a review, or publication day support. I can't mention everyone (and apologies if I haven't mentioned you), but I will shout out to those who were part of my last two blog tours including: @iheartbooks1991, @Karen_loves_reading, B for Bookreview, Cal Turner Reviews, Captured on Film, Nat's Bookish Corner, Open Book Posts, Page Turners, Robin

Loves Reading, Sam's Fireside, Shaz's book blog, Splashes into books, staceywh_17, Stardust Book Reviews, This Hannah Reads, and thanks to @Cindy_L_Spear, Writer at Play and Portobello Book Blog for the wonderful features.

Thanks also to wonderful friends, NetGalley users and readers who support me by buying and reading my books, letting me know they've enjoyed them, reviewing, blogging, sharing and cheering me on. In particular to Karen Spicer King, Ian Wilfred, Alison Phillips, Amanda Baker, Katy Walker, Sue Moseley, Danel Munday, Masha Rixon, Lucy Brittain, Elaine Fearnley, Fiona Jenkins, Meg Dean, Sharon Wathall, Kirstie Campbell, Suzanne Peplow, Claire Hornbuckle, Mags Evans, Eva Abraham, Anne Winckworth and Meena Kumari.

Thanks as always to my family: Dad, Mum, John, Peter, Christelle, Lucie, Mathis, Joseph, Lynda, Louis, Auntie Rita, Auntie Gillian, Tanya, James, Rosie, Ava, Philip, Sonia, Stephanie and Muriel.

Finally, to the readers who have been there with me throughout my journey – I wouldn't be here without you. xx

Printed in Great Britain
by Amazon